開企，

是一個開頭，它可以是一句美好的引言、
未完待續的逗點、享受美好後滿足的句點，
新鮮的體驗、大膽的冒險、嶄新的方向，
是一趟有你共同參與的奇妙旅程。

附贈
「中英對話」
強效學習
MP3

Daily Chats

超好聊
英文

一本讓你從聊天到FB、IG、LINE
隨時都能po出超人氣動態的63個潮話題

User's Guide 使用說明

10大生活主題分類 X 63個熱門潮話題，讓你超好聊、PO文不無聊！

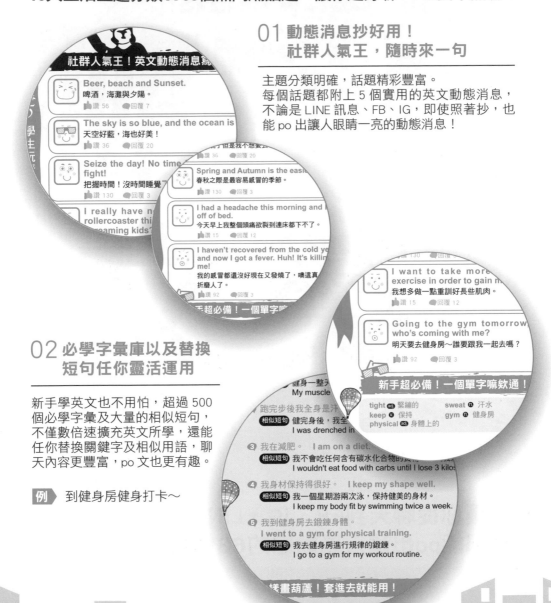

01 動態消息抄好用！
社群人氣王，隨時來一句

主題分類明確，話題精彩豐富。
每個話題都附上 5 個實用的英文動態消息，
不論是 LINE 訊息、FB、IG，即使照著抄，也
能 po 出讓人眼睛一亮的動態消息！

社群人氣王！英文動態消息篇

Beer, beach and Sunset.
啤酒，海灘與夕陽。
讚 56　回覆 7

The sky is so blue, and the ocean is
天空好藍，海也好美！
讚 36　回覆 20

Seize the day! No time
fight!
把握時間！沒時間睡覺

Spring and Autumn is the eas
春秋之際是最容易感冒的季節。
讚 130　回覆 3

I really have n
rollercoaster thi
eaming kids

I had a headache this morning and
off of bed.
今天早上我整個頭痛欲裂到連床都下不了。
讚 15　回覆 12

I haven't recovered from the cold ye
and now I got a fever. Huh! It's killin
me!
我的感冒都還沒好現在又發燒了，噢這真
折磨人了。
讚 92　回覆 3

I want to take more
exercise in order to gain m
我想多做一點重訓好長些肌肉。
讚 15　回覆 12

Going to the gym tomorrow
who's coming with me?
明天要去健身房～誰要跟我一起去嗎？
讚 92　回覆 3

新手超必備！一個單字嘛欸通！

tight adj 緊繃的		sweat n 汗水	
keep v 保持		gym n 健身房	
physical adj 身體上的			

02 必學字彙庫以及替換
短句任你靈活運用

新手學英文也不用怕，超過 500
個必學字彙及大量的相似短句，
不僅數倍速擴充英文所學，還能
任你替換關鍵字及相似用語，聊
天內容更豐富，po 文也更有趣。

例 到健身房健身打卡～

健身一整天
My muscle

跑完步後我全身是汗
相似短句 健完步後，我全
I was drenched in

❸ 我在減肥。 I am on a diet.
相似短句 我不吃任何含有碳水化合物的
I wouldn't eat food with carbs until I lose 3 kilos

❹ 我身材保持得很好。 I keep my shape well.
相似短句 我一個星期游兩次泳，保持健美的身材。
I keep my body fit by swimming twice a week.

❺ 我到健身房去鍛鍊身體。
I went to a gym for physical training.
相似短句 我去健身房進行規律的鍛鍊。
I go to a gym for my workout routine.

樣畫葫蘆！套進去就能用！

03 自己說／寫英文沒把握？讓句型 & 實用會話助你一臂之力

▶ 英文句型就類似數學公式一樣，只要記住用法，將內容填入正確位置，就能舉一反三得出漂亮答案。

▶ 聊天怎麼起頭開話題？超實用會話設計，能聽會說一次搞定！

依樣畫葫蘆！套進去就能用！

句型1 比起以往～
...than before

例句 湯姆跑得比以往快。
Tom runs faster than before.

句型2 例如～
such as...

例句 我喜歡運動，例如棒球、網球和游泳。
I like sports, such as baseball, te

出門超實用！能聽會說一次搞定

Ⓐ Are you going to join summer camp this y
is survival skills in the wild.
Ⓑ I will definitely join the camp this year. Sta
always been my dream.
Ⓐ 你今年要參加暑期營隊嗎？今年暑期營隊主題是如
Ⓑ 我一定會參加今年的營隊。在野外生存一直以來是

Ⓐ You must be crazy. Are you saying that s
campfires, and waking up in the early m
you interest?
Ⓑ Yeah, or what else would you think
It's summer time, and I don't want
定是瘋了。你是說你對於搭帳篷
你對於暑期營隊還

04 短文範例讓你照著用，心情記錄更生動

心情記錄每回都只能短短簡單句，多無趣！？全書每一話題都精心撰寫心情短文範例，不僅可以直接照著寫，更能利用替換關鍵字或相似句，加入更多自己的情緒、心境……用英文記錄生活點滴變得更好玩也更容易！

酸甜苦辣 記下來！

Celebrate in KTV
Friday, September 20
For celebrating my co-worker's birthda
There are not only pop songs to sing but als
We were singing so uncontrollably as to be
voices down. When serving us cold drinks, t
surprised that we were worn out and lying o

到 KTV 去慶祝
9月20日星期五
為了要替我的同事慶生，我們去 KTV 唱歌。那裡不只
可以吃。我們唱瘋到無法把聲音壓下來。當服務生
我們精疲力盡的累癱在沙發上。

MP3 Track 016

次搞定！

summer. Laura asks me to go

e season for swimming. I
than a swimming pool for

05 聽出敏銳英語耳；提升強大英語力！

全書「中英對話」強效學習 MP3，培養你的絕佳聽力、訓練你的準確發音！邊看邊聽效果加倍，更能隨時戴上耳機聽出進步神速的英語力！

Preface 作者序

　　臺灣的英文學習者其實花了很長的時間在背單字、學文法，但是當想要用英文表達事情時，卻常常會卡住。長久下來，學習英文的時間跟效果不成正比，也漸漸的讓許多人打從心底的不喜歡英文。為了徹底解決這些問題，同時想讓大家在愉快的心情下以及不必特別增加多餘的學習時間來學習，因此，我想到了大家每天都會做也喜歡做的事，那就是「記錄」。無論是説話、Line訊息、IG、FB、日記，甚至是小小的一張便利貼，都是許多人每天常用的記錄、抒發管道。我希望以用英文記錄生活的方式，將英文真的落實在我們每一天的生活裡，讓大家都能將每天的遭遇、想法、心情、計畫用英文表達出來，不僅能活用所學、更熟悉生活常見情境的單字、短句之外，同時，在和老外聊天或想用英文互動的時候，都能更自然、順暢。

　　所以，本書以收錄在生活中最常用的話題為主，並以短句開始，讓你練習最簡單的句子，或是你也可以藉由範例的短句直接開口説或照著抄寫，再慢慢地試著將學到的情境單字放進你的各種想法中，天天用、天天寫，自然而然地讓英文融入生活的每個時刻。

　　利用有趣生動的方式來學英文，是我撰寫這本書的目的，期望讀者們能藉著本書清楚、詳細的主題分類以及中英對照強效MP3，日積月累的學習，假以時日一定能練就英語腦，英文聽説讀寫力亦能同時大躍進，完成與世界溝通零距離的目標。

Joseph

Contents 目錄

Part 7 勞工拼經濟

Part 8 小資省錢趣

Part 9 全國瘋節慶

Part 10 人禍比天災更可怕

【特別附錄】
寫英文抄好用～即時速查！

【加碼贈送】
文法充電站！

Unit 01
網路交友

社群人氣王！英文動態消息寫給你看！

I have been writing email with my pen pal for 8 years.
我跟我的筆友保持通信長達八年。

👍 讚 56　💬 回覆 7

Recently I found a website which allows the users to talk to people from all over the world.
我最近發現了一個可以讓我跟來自世界各地的朋友聊天的網站。

👍 讚 36　💬 回覆 20

Sandy said she fell in love with someone who she has only talked to on Facebook.
珊蒂說她愛上了某個她只在臉書上聊過天的人。

👍 讚 130　💬 回覆 3

My parents seem to be very worried about me making friends through the Internet.
我爸媽好像很擔心我在網路上交朋友。

👍 讚 15　💬 回覆 12

I am going to meet a friend I knew from the Internet tomorrow. Is there anything I have to be aware of?
我明天要和一個網友見面，有什麼我應該要注意的事情嗎？

👍 讚 92　💬 回覆 3

新手超必備！一個單字嘛欸通！

e-mail **n.** 電子郵件	online **adj.** 在網路上的	Internet **n.** 網際網路
make friends **phr.** 交朋友	chat room **phr.** 聊天室	chat **v.** 聊天；閒聊
be addicted to... **phr.** 對……成癮		

出門超實用！能聽會說一次搞定！

Ⓐ Candice, I think I am in love. I met a guy on the internet. He's being really sweet and nice to me.

Ⓑ That's why you've spent so much time on your phone recently. But I don't know. Are you sure? Have you two met before?

Ⓐ 凱蒂斯，我想我戀愛了。我在網路上遇到一個男生，他一直對我很體貼。

Ⓑ 原來這就是為什麼你最近在手機上面花了很多時間。但我不確定你真的喜歡他，你們有見過面嗎？

Ⓐ No, never. But we share our photo to each other. You can check his profile on this chat app.

Ⓑ Okay. Let me see. So what's his job? Why can't you meet each other?

Ⓐ 不，我們沒有見過面，但我們有互相分享照片，你可以在這個聊天軟體中看到他的資料。

Ⓑ 讓我看看。所以他是做什麼工作的？為什麼你們不能見面？

Ⓐ He is not in Taiwan and he works as an oversea sales, so he seldom has chance to come back to Taiwan. But he has invited me to go stay with him.

Ⓑ I want to remind you that this might be just a scam. It is highly possible that there is no such person in the world.

Ⓐ 他在國外從事業務性質的工作，所以不在台灣，也很少有機會回來。但他有邀我去跟他一起生活。

Ⓑ 我想提醒你，這可能只是個詐騙，世界上很有可能根本沒有這個人。

Ⓐ Seriously?! I did find it weird when he asked me to send money to his mom because he cannot make transactions oversea.

Ⓑ Okay. Sally, you are fooled. How can you believe people on the internet so easily?

Ⓐ 真的嗎？不過當他無法進行跨國匯款，所以請我匯款給他母親時，我確實覺得有些奇怪。

Ⓑ 好吧。莎莉，你被騙了。你怎麼可以這麼輕易地相信網路上的人？

Unit 01 網路交友

酸甜苦辣 記下來！

A new experience of making friends

Friday, April 19

There are many ways of making friends. Never had I chatted online before. My friend taught me how to chat online. How interesting it was when I began to chat with those strangers online. Only when I went online to talk with people did I realize how fantastic it was to get to know their lifestyles.

交朋友的新體驗

4月19日星期五

交朋友的方式有很多種。我從來沒在網路上聊天過。我朋友今天教我怎麼在網路上聊天。當我開始上網跟陌生人聊天時，我覺得相當有趣。只有在網上聊天時，我才知道能瞭解他們的生活型態是很棒的。

增廣見聞 超簡單！

Thanks to the convenience of the Internet that we can communicate with our friends and other people through the Internet easily, and some people will try to date online first. However, there are several points that people need to be aware of when trying to date online. First, we have to know that there can be deceit, scam, and lies with online communities. Then, do researches and other possible ways to prove the person you have met does exist, for example, start a video chat like a real date online.

感謝網路的發達，讓我們現在可以在網路上跟朋友或是其他人溝通，有些人也會試著在網路上約會。但是，在我們進行網路交友時有幾個重點必須要注意，第一步，我們必須注意到網路上可能存在著許多欺騙跟謊言；再來，我們可以在網路上調查，或找方法驗證這個人是否真的存在，例如可以開啟視訊聊天的功能，來場面對面的真正約會。

來換換口味吧！讓你的表達更豐富！

① 我們透過電子郵件聯絡。　We connect by e-mail.
> **相似短句** 我們透過電子郵件聯絡。　We talked via e-mail.

② 交朋友的方式有很多種。
There are many ways of making friends.
> **相似短句** 線上配對也可以是一種交朋友的方式。
> Internet dating can be one of the ways of making friends.

③ 我從來沒有在網路上聊天過。
Never had I chatted online before.
> **相似短句** 我沒在網路上聊天過。　I've never had an online chat before.

④ 我朋友今天教我如何上網聊天。
My friend taught me how to chat online.
> **相似短句** 我的朋友告訴我如何上網聊天。
> My friend told me how to go to online chat rooms.

⑤ 我妹妹沉迷於網路。　My sister is addicted to the Internet.
> **相似短句** 我妹妹對網路成癮。　My sister's got an addiction to the Internet.

依樣畫葫蘆！套進去就能用！

句型1 我從來沒有～
Never had I...
> **例句** 我從來沒有試過網路交友。
> **Never had I tried Internet dating before.**

句型2 她花時間在～
She spends on...
> **例句** 有空時，她花很多時間在網路聊天上。
> **She spends most of her leisure time on having online chats.**

Unit 02
跟朋友吵架

社群人氣王！英文動態消息寫給你看！

I'm so shocked to find that my ex-best friend says bad things behind my back all the time.

不敢相信我的「前」摯友總是在我背後說我壞話。

👍 讚 56　　💬 回覆 7

Why did she just ignore me? Did I do something wrong?

她為什麼不理我？我做錯了什麼嗎？

👍 讚 36　　💬 回覆 20

Just had a fight with Alex. We hurt each other and ended up in the hospital. So stupid.

剛剛跟愛力克司打了一架。然後我們倆現在都躺在醫院裡。超蠢。

👍 讚 130　　💬 回覆 3

Sally and Emily have been fighting for a month! I'm in between them and I cannot stand it anymore. Why can't they stop being so childish?

莎莉和愛蜜莉已經冷戰一個月了，我再也受不了夾在她們中間了，她們可不可以不要這麼幼稚啊？

👍 讚 15　　💬 回覆 12

I deleted my ex-girlfriend and David on Facebook. I still can't believe how that happened? He was my best friend.

我把我前女友和大衛從臉書上刪掉了。我真不敢相信怎麼會發生這種事？他曾是我最好的朋友耶。

👍 讚 92　　💬 回覆 3

新手超必備！一個單字嘛欸通！

moody adj. 心情不穩的　　**blue** adj. 憂鬱的　　**alone** adj. 獨自的

space n. 空間　　**temper** n. 脾氣　　**apologize** v. 道歉

piss off phr. 發飆　　**get along with** phr. 跟……相處

出門超實用！能聽會說一次搞定！

A Bryan, could you stop criticizing on other people's look? It is really impolite to other people.

B I didn't mean to be rude. I think I am just being funny. Look at Jenny's terrible new hairstyle.

A 布萊恩，你可以停止批評別人的外表嗎？這真的非常不禮貌。

B 我沒有故意要這樣，我只是覺得很有趣。你看看珍妮可怕的新髮型。

A I don't find anything funny at all. And I think Jenny looks great in her new hairstyle. She looks more energetic and bright .

B Okay. Fine. But why are you so pissed? Have I judged on your looks and outfit?

A 我一點也不覺得好笑。而且我覺得珍妮的新髮型很好看，她看起來更亮麗、更有活力了。

B 好吧。但你為什麼要這麼生氣？我有批評你的外表或穿著嗎？

A Yes, you did. Last time I came back from the United States, the first thing you said was "you've become so fat!" Come on, you completely ruined my mood.

B But I was telling the truth! See how much weight you've gained in 10 days. I couldn't even recognize you when I saw you.

A 有，你有。上次我從美國回來時，你說的第一句話是：「你變好胖喔！」拜託！你完全破壞了我的好心情！

B 但我講的是實話啊！你看你在十天內變胖多少，我甚至都認不出你了。

A See, that's not good even if you are telling the truth. Why would it bother you on how much I weigh?

B Alright, I will shut up. I will keep your advice in mind and say sorry to Jenny next time.

A 你看，就算你講的是實話，這樣還是不好。我的體重多少到底關你什麼事？

B 好吧，我閉嘴。我會記住你的建議，然後下次見面時跟珍妮說對不起。

Unit 02 跟朋友吵架

酸甜苦辣 記下來！

Leave me alone!!

Monday, August 26

I was kind of moody today. I just wanted to be alone. Maybe it was because the weather was bad. Whoever spoke to me, I didn't respond to him. It made me impatient that my friend chattered endlessly all the time. When I asked him to shut up, he was so sad and went away. I knew I hurt him so much that I apologized to him.

離我遠一點！

8月26日星期一

今天我有點情緒化，只想要一個人待著。也許是因為天氣很爛的關係，誰來跟我講話我都不理他。當我朋友在我旁邊一直嘮嘮叨叨時，我真的很不耐煩。我叫他閉嘴，他就傷心的離開了。我知道我傷了他，所以還是跟他說抱歉了。

增廣見聞 超簡單！

Have you ever thought about how to end a fight with your friends or parents, or any one that works with you? At first, let the argument simmer down for a while, because sometimes to keep confronting with the one you are argueing with will simply make your relationship worse. Next, consider and reflect on yourself, and then try to understand other people's perspective. Have empathy for other people, and have the same feeling with other people, then the fights and intense situation will ease down.

你有想過當你跟朋友、家人或是任何一起工作的人發生衝突時該怎麼解決嗎？第一，必須先讓爭執緩和下來，因為有時候兩人僵持不下只會讓關係更加惡化。第二，思考並自我反省，試著了解其他人的想法，產生同理心，也就是去設想別人的感受，如此一來衝突跟緊繃的狀況自然會減低許多。

Part 1 市民過生活

來換換口味吧！讓你的表達更豐富！

1 我今天有點情緒化。　I was kind of moody today.
　相似短句 我今天有點憂鬱。　I was a bit blue today.

2 我只想獨處。　I just want to be alone.
　相似短句 我需要一點空間。　I need some space.

3 也許是因為天氣不好的關係。
　Maybe it was because the weather was bad.
　相似短句 可能是因為雨下了一個星期。
　　　　　　Maybe it was because it's been raining for a week.

4 他人不好相處。　He's not easy to get along with.
　相似短句 他不好相處。　He's not a people person.

5 他發脾氣了。　He lost his temper.
　相似短句 他今天發火了。　He was pissed off today.

依樣畫葫蘆！套進去就能用！

句型1 ～讓我很不耐煩。
　It made me impatient that...
　例句 她一直把事情扯到自己，讓我很不耐煩。
　It made me impatient that she made this about her.

句型2 一點也不
　not...at all
　例句 那樣說話一點也不帥。
　Talking like that was not cool at all.

Unit 03
追求

社群人氣王！英文動態消息寫給你看！

Does anyone know who this beauty is?
有人知道這個美麗的女孩是誰嗎？

👍讚 56　💬回覆 7

My brother goes to the library quite often lately, which is really weird because he never does so. And I found out that she is the reason why.
我哥最近很怪常常去圖書館，他之前從來不去。然後我發現她是這一切的原因。

👍讚 36　💬回覆 20

OMG. I found a message written on the coffee cup, which my colleague bought for me, saying: "Good morning, Gorgeous."
天啊，我發現同事為我買的咖啡杯上寫著「早安美女」的訊息。

👍讚 130　💬回覆 3

She asked me to go to a movie with her on Friday!
她邀請我禮拜五跟她一起去看電影！

👍讚 15　💬回覆 12

He is really nice but he is not my type.
他人很好但他不是我的菜。

👍讚 92　💬回覆 3

新手超必備！一個單字嘛欸通！

date **n.** 約會　　love letter **phr.** 情書　　compare **v.** 匹敵
mind **n.** 心裡；心情　　privacy **n.** 隱私　　lover **n.** 愛侶
heart **n.** 心；愛心　　forever **adv.** 永遠地　　kiss **v.** 親吻

出門超實用！能聽會說一次搞定！

A Hi Amy. How are you today? Do you want me to bring dinner for you? I am off from work early today.

B How sweet of you. Thank you, but I am not hungry. I have to hand in a proposal to our client tomorrow morning.

A 哈囉！愛咪，你今天好嗎？你需不需要我帶晚餐給你？我今天提早下班。

B 你真體貼，謝謝，但我現在不餓，我明天早上要把提案交給客戶。

A I am sorry to bother. I hope you won't get too tired from work.

B It's okay. I feel so relaxed when talking with you. I can have short talks during break time.

A 很抱歉我打擾你了，希望你不要工作得太累。

B 沒關係的，我每次跟你講話都覺得好放鬆。我們可以在休息時間小聊一下啊。

A No problem. I will be there in ten minutes and I will bring bagels and coffee for you.

B Tom, you know me so well. Okay, I will wait for you and we can go to the movies after I finish the proposal.

A 沒問題，我十分鐘就到，我會帶貝果跟咖啡給你！

B 湯姆，你真的很懂我。好，那我在這裡等你，等我寫完提案再一起去看電影。

A Absolutely! To be honest, that is why I called you today. I have two movie tickets for free. Shall we have a date?

B Tom, I have never heard expressions of love so straight forward. But yes, we can date starting from today.

A 當然好啊！老實說，這就是我今天打電話給你的原因。我有兩張免費的電影票，我們是不是該約個會？

B 湯姆，我從沒聽過愛表示的這麼直接。但我願意，我們就從今天開始約會吧！

Unit 03 追求

酸甜苦辣 記下來！

The day John and I got together

Tuesday, April 9

There are many ways of showing love to our lovers. I fell in love with John. Therefore, I wrote a love letter to him. In the letter, I told him that no one can compare with him in my mind. At the end of the letter, I drew a heart for expressing my love. After receiving the letter, John was so touched that he said that he would love me forever.

我跟約翰在一起的日子

4月9日星期二

有很多向情人表達愛意的方法，我愛上約翰了，所以我寫了一封情書給他。在信中，我說沒有任何人可以跟他相比，我在信的尾端畫上愛心，以表達我的愛。約翰收到信以後很感動，說他會永遠愛我。

增廣見聞 超簡單！

From getting to know each other, to pursuing, and then to dating, every step is essential to a relationship. When courting a girl, asking her out to have dinner, go to the movies, or simply showing your care about her, are all different methods. That's the case for courting a girl. What about courting a guy? Here is one tip, to live your own life. Let the guy know that you are fully independent, don't be needy, and if he's interested in you, he will take action.

男女從彼此認識到追求、約會，每個步驟都是必要的。當你要追求一位女孩時，可以邀請她一起吃晚餐、一起看電影，或直接表達你對她的關心。這是追女孩的情況，那麼追求男生呢？有一個小秘訣就是活出妳自己，讓對方知道妳是獨立自主的，不需要刻意表現得很需要他，如果他對妳有興趣，自然就會主動追求。

來換換口味吧！讓你的表達更豐富！

① 我試著約瑪麗出去。　I tried to ask Mary out.

相似短句 我試著約瑪麗出去。　I tried to ask Mary on a date.

② 我寫情書給約翰。　I wrote a love letter to John.

相似短句 約翰可以從情書裡知道我有多愛他。
John will know how much I love him as he gets the love letter.

③ 我告訴山姆他在我心中無人能比。
I told Sam that no one can compare with him in my mind.

相似短句 我告訴山姆他是我的唯一。　I told Sam he's the one.

④ 為了有隱密空間，我們去公園。
For enjoying our own privacy, we went to a park.

相似短句 我們去公園約會，享受獨處時光。
We dated in a park to enjoy some private space.

⑤ 我們在公園散步，享受美好的時光。
We walked in the park and enjoyed some quality time.

相似短句 我們去公園散步，享受美好時光。
We took a walk in the park, having the time of our lives.

依樣畫葫蘆！套進去就能用！

句型1 **我碰巧～**
I happened to...

例句 我碰巧和她一起上同一堂化學課。
I happen to be in the same Chemistry class with her.

句型2 **我愛上～**
I fell in love with...

例句 我愛上他了，一見鍾情。
I fell in love with him at first sight.

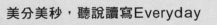

Unit 04
約會

社群人氣王！英文動態消息寫給你看！

It's already half passed ten and where is he? I'm going home.

已經十點半了他人還沒出現！我要回家了！

👍 讚 56　　💬 回覆 7

We went cycling along the coast. This is my darling standing on the shore, looking at the sunset. She is beautiful, isn't she?

我們去海邊騎腳踏車。這張是我親愛的站在海邊看著夕陽的照片。她很正吧。

👍 讚 36　　💬 回覆 20

I went mountain climbing with my boyfriend this morning. It was fun! Look at him! He was so tired when we finally got to the top. lol

今天早上我跟男友一起去爬山，超好玩！看看他，我們爬到山頂的時候他整個累斃了，哈哈。　👍 讚 130　　💬 回覆 3

Can we do something else than watching a movie or dining in a restaurant?

我們可以一起做點看電影或吃飯之外的事嗎？

👍 讚 15　　💬 回覆 12

I have no idea why my girl loves shopping so much. –feeling bored.

我真的不知道為什麼我女朋友這麼喜歡逛街。覺得無聊。

👍 讚 92　　💬 回覆 3

新手超必備！一個單字嘛欸通！

embrace **n.** 擁抱	Valentine **n.** 情人	feast **n.** 大餐
date **n.** 約會	couple **n.** 情侶；一對	hug **v.** 擁抱
together **adj.** 一起的	beloved **adj.** 摯愛的；親愛的	

出門超實用！能聽會說一次搞定！

A Honey. Do you have time this weekend? I think we can plan a small trip to Kaohsiung.

B Sure! We haven't had a proper date for a while since we are all busy at work.

A 親愛的，你這週末有時間嗎？我想我們可以規劃一個去高雄的小旅行。

B 好啊！自從我們都忙於工作之後，就好久沒有來個好好的約會。

A That's what I thought. So are there any specific places you want to visit? I will make the plan this time.

B Thank you, dear. I love you. Can we visit the night market there? That is the place I love most.

A 跟我想的一樣。所以你有沒有特定想去的地方？這次我來計劃。

B 謝謝你，親愛的！我愛你！我們可以去夜市嗎？我最喜歡那裡的夜市了。

A Before we visit the night market, we can go to pier 39 to enjoy the night view, and also I will book the hotel at the 85 sky tower.

B Wow, I have to get prepared for this trip. You are so romantic. Wait! Are you trying to hide anything from me?

A 在我們去夜市之前，我們還可以去 39 號碼頭看夜景。我也會訂東帝士大樓的飯店！

B 哇，我必須要趕緊準備這次的旅行了。你好浪漫！等等，你該不會是想要隱瞞我什麼吧？

A I am serious! You see, we have to try hard to find time to date. Like today, we only have 3 hours.

B I am just kidding. I know what you mean, honey. I can't wait for this weekend!

A 我是認真的！你看，我們得要努力找時間來約會。像今天，我們只有三小時。

B 我只是開玩笑，我懂你的意思～寶貝。我等不及這週末出遊了！

Unit 04 約會

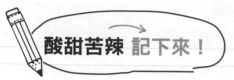

酸甜苦辣 記下來！

My date with Jane

Wednesday, June 12

I wanted a date with Jane. I took Jane to a mountain to watch the night scene. In the mountains were lots of couples watching the night scene. Stars were shining, but the atmosphere was not good enough. Jane and I decided to find a quieter place to get to know each other more. The night scene was so beautiful that we just sat there cuddling with each other to enjoy the serenity of it.

我和珍的約會

6月12日星期三

我想要跟珍約會。我帶她到山上賞夜景，那裡擠滿了很多對看夜景的情侶，星星閃耀但氣氛不夠好。我跟珍決定要到一個比較安靜的地方多瞭解彼此。夜景實在是太美了，我們就這樣坐在那裡依偎在彼此懷裡，享受夜景的寧靜。

增廣見聞 超簡單！

To date with a loved one should be the sweetest thing among all things. However, if you face problems of finding a topic to talk about, or being afraid of running short of words, then please try to be yourself. Don't get too nervous. Being yourself is the highest practice of all thing when dating. Plan a small trip to create memories between you two or simply stay at home, cuddle, cook, and enjoy a lazy Sunday afternoon together are suggestions for some good dates.

跟你所愛的人約會大概是最甜蜜的一件事了！但是如果你遇到了沒有話題聊的困境，就好好的做你自己吧！「不要太緊張，做自己」是在約會時應有的最高指導原則。有時候計畫個小旅行來創造兩人的回憶，或是單純待在家，一起生活、煮飯、享受美好的週日午後，也都是一些約會適用的小建議喔！

來換換口味吧！讓你的表達更豐富！

1 她是我的摯愛。　She is my beloved.
相似短句 她是我此生的摯愛。　She's the love of my life.

2 我們互相擁抱。　We embraced each other.
相似短句 說再見前，他給了我一個擁抱。
He gave me a hug before we said goodbye.

3 約翰請我吃情人節大餐。
John invited me to have a Valentine's feast.
相似短句 我們今天去吃情人節晚餐。
We had a Valentine's dinner today.

4 我和他今晚要約會。　I have a date with him tonight.
相似短句 我們今晚要約會。　We are going on a date tonight.

5 我們在一起五年了。　We've been together for five years.
相似短句 我們在一起五年了。
We've been seeing each other for five years.

依樣畫葫蘆！套進去就能用！

句型1 決定要～
decided to...
例句 我們決定要去看電影，因為展覽並不有趣。
We decided to go to the movies because the exhibition wasn't interesting.

句型2 邀請我
invited me to...
例句 傑森邀請我參加他的私人派對。
Jason invited me to his private party.

Unit 05
跟情人吵架

社群人氣王！英文動態消息寫給你看！

I don't know why she doesn't want to have dinner with my family.

我不知道她為什麼不想跟我的家人一起吃個飯。

👍 讚 56　💬 回覆 7

Why he keeps talking about that girl? What's so interesting about her?

他幹嘛一直講那個女孩子的事情？她有那麼有趣嗎？

👍 讚 36　💬 回覆 20

Ehhh!!! Why he keeps calling me? I can't answer the phone is because I am busy, okay?

吼！他幹嘛一直打電話給我？我不能接電話就是因為我在忙，好嗎？

👍 讚 130　💬 回覆 3

What's wrong with her? She's so grumpy today! I only missed one call from her because I was in the toilet and she got angry right away.

她到底怎麼回事？她今天超爆躁的。我不過漏接了一通電話，只因為我在廁所，她就發飆了。

👍 讚 15　💬 回覆 12

I don't understand why he always spends so much time with his buddies, instead of staying with me. Am I not important to him?

我真不懂他為什麼總是花那麼多時間跟他的朋友混在一起，而不是多陪陪我？我對他來說難道一點都不重要嗎？

👍 讚 92　💬 回覆 3

新手超必備！一個單字嘛欸通！

quarrel n. 爭吵　　　　**suspicious** adj. 可疑的　　　**cheat** v. 欺騙

hardly adv. 幾乎不⋯⋯　**jealous** adj. 忌妒的　　　**relationship** n. 感情

shout v. 吼叫　　　　　**communicate** v. 溝通

出門超實用！能聽會說一次搞定！

A Joanna, please hurry up. We are going to be late! Do you have any idea that we need to catch a flight, and the flight doesn't wait for people!

B Almost done! I need 10 more minutes. We can change the flight, so please stop being that mad.

A 喬安娜，請你快一點，我們要遲到了。你知不知道我們今天要趕的是飛機，而飛機是不會等人的！

B 快好了！我需要再十分鐘，我們可以改班機時間阿，所以拜託不要這麼生氣。

A How can you say that? Do you understand how much it costs to change a flight, just because you can't understand the idea of being 'on time'?

B Hey, stop yelling at me. I told you that I would go out only when I am well prepared. I haven't put on the makeup yet.

A 你怎麼可以這麼說呢？你知道更改班機需要多少錢，就因為你根本不了解「守時」的意思？

B 嘿！不要對著我吼。我告訴過你，我只會在準備好之後才出門，而我現在都還沒上妝呢！

A Why do you need to spend over 50 minutes before you go out? Putting makeup on, and dressing up are just a waste of time.

B I don't think it's a waste of time. Rather, I think when you play online game is a waste of time.

A 你到底為什麼每次出門前都要花超過 50 分鐘的時間？上妝打扮根本就是浪費時間！

B 我不覺得那是浪費時間，我反而認為你玩線上遊戲也是在浪費時間。

A Alright, stop. I will go first, and see when you will come, and which flight you will take.

B Fine. Whatever you say. I suggest we should just cancel the flight. I don't want go out with you now.

A 好，停。我先走，然後你再看什麼時候要來，要搭哪一班飛機。

B 好，隨便你怎麼說。我覺得我們可以直接取消這班飛機，我現在不想跟你出門了。

美分美秒，聽說讀寫Everyday

Unit 05 跟情人吵架

酸甜苦辣 記下來！

A call from his company

Tuesday, October 15

I have quarrels with my boyfriend all the time. I don't know whether he loves me or not. What drives me crazy is that he cancels our dates very often. He canceled our date again due to a phone call from his company in the afternoon. I was so angry because I felt he didn't pay much attention to me. I am not supposed to talk to him for three days.

一通他公司打來的電話

10月15日星期二

我總是在跟我男朋友吵架，我不知道他是否來愛我，而且令我抓狂的是他總是取消我們的約會。他下午又因為一通他公司打來的電話，就直接取消掉我們的約會，我真的超生氣的，他根本就就沒有在關心我啊，我決定我要三天不跟他講話了。

增廣見聞 超簡單！

Sometimes, we see news on TV showing cases of abusive relationships that cause harm to the other one. How do you determine whether you are in an abusive relationship or not? Most important of all, you should be aware of any violent behavior, no matter it is verbally or emotionally. For example, if your partner can never take responsibility on their own, and you are the one who is being blamed, then you might be in an emotionally abusive relationship.

有時候我們會在新聞上面看到因為恐怖情人而另一方被傷害的新聞。那我們要如何檢視自己是否正處於一段恐怖關係中呢？最重要的一點，可能是要注意到你是否疑似受虐，不管是言語還是精神上。舉例來說，如果你的伴侶從來不為自己負責，而你總是成為被責罵的那位，那你可能已經在一段精神虐待的關係中。

來換換口味吧！讓你的表達更豐富！

❶ 我老是跟我男友吵架。
I have quarrels with my boyfriend all the time.
（相似短句）我和男朋友老是吵架。
All my boyfrieng and I do is argue.

❷ 我男友總是臨時取消我們的約會。
My boyfriend cancels our dates abruptly very often.
（相似短句）我男友常常取消我們的約會。
My boyfriend calls off our date very often.

❸ 我的男友很可疑。　**My boyfriend is suspicious.**
（相似短句）我覺得我男朋友有了別的女人。
I have a feeling that my boyfriend is cheating on me.

❹ 我很容易嫉妒。　**I get jealous easily.**
（相似短句）我就是個善妒的人。　I am just a jealous person.

❺ 我男朋友根本不在乎我。
My boyfriend doesn't even care about me.
（相似短句）我男朋友根本不花時間陪我。
My boyfriend hardly spends time with me.

依樣畫葫蘆！套進去就能用！

（句型1）他們好像
They seemed to...

（例句）他們好像吵架了。我好幾天沒看見他們交談了。
They seemed to have had a fight. I hadn't seen them talking for days.

（句型2）令我抓狂的是
What drove me crazy was that...

（例句）令我抓狂的是他說這是我的錯。
What drove me crazy was that he said that it was my fault.

美分美秒，聽說讀寫Everyday

Unit 06
學習做菜

社群人氣王！英文動態消息寫給你看！

I baked cookies by myself today!

我今天自己考了餅乾！

👍 讚 56　💬 回覆 7

I learned how to make beautiful macarons today!

我今天學會了怎麼做出漂亮的馬卡紅！

👍 讚 36　💬 回覆 20

Cooking is not that hard. There are many easy ways to make delicious food.

作菜一點都不難。有很多簡單的方式就可以做出美味的料理。

👍 讚 130　💬 回覆 3

This is the first time for me being in charge of making a nice dinner for my family.

這是我第一次為全家人煮一頓豐盛的晚餐。

👍 讚 15　💬 回覆 12

Lacking of experience made me feel busy and the kitchen was a mess. Thankfully the food tasted so right.

缺乏經驗讓我手忙腳亂而且把廚房弄得一團亂。幸好最後做出好吃的料理了。

👍 讚 92　💬 回覆 3

新手超必備！一個單字嘛欸通！

bake ⓥ 烤；烘焙　　**broil** ⓥ 煎烤　　**practice** ⓥ 練習
grill ⓥ 用（烤架）烤　　**cook** ⓥ 烹飪　　**supermarket** ⓝ 超市
recipe ⓝ 食譜

出門超實用！能聽會說一次搞定！

Ⓐ Mom, can you show me how to cook? I don't think it's healthy to eat out all the time.

Ⓑ Finally! I would love to. Which dishes do you want to learn first? Scrambled egg, soup, or fried rice?

Ⓐ 媽，你可以教我怎麼做菜嗎？我覺得一直吃外面不是很健康。

Ⓑ 終於，我很樂意！你想先學哪一道菜？炒蛋，湯，還是要學炒飯？

Ⓐ Mom, those are not challenging enough. Can we try pasta? I want to know how to prepare that kind of dishes.

Ⓑ Okay. Let's start with preparing the ingredients. Onions, green peppers, pasta, chopped chicken and the most important one, the sauce is necessary when you want to make pasta.

Ⓐ 媽，那些也太沒挑戰性了，我們可以學煮義大利麵嗎？我想知道該怎麼準備這道菜。

Ⓑ 好，我們先從準備材料開始。洋蔥，青椒，雞肉，和最重要的醬都是做義大利麵的必要素材。

Ⓐ I can help you chop the onions and green peppers. You will find that I actually got talent on cooking.

Ⓑ Wow, you do got talent. Next, please help me put pasta in the water before it boils. And I will stir-fry the onion with pepper.

Ⓐ 我可以幫你切洋蔥跟青椒！你會發現，我其實在煮飯上面是很有天份的。

Ⓑ 哇，你真的有天份欸！下一步，幫我在水滾之前放入義大利麵，然後我會一起炒洋蔥跟青椒。

Ⓐ I can make the tomato sauce. Mom, actually, I want to make the dish for my boyfriend. Tomorrow is his birthday.

Ⓑ It's fine, honey. But I hope you would like to cook for me next time.

Ⓐ 我可以做番茄醬汁。媽，其實我是想做這道菜給我男友。明天是他生日。

Ⓑ 沒關係，寶貝。但希望下次你也會樂意為我煮飯喔。

Unit 06 學習做菜

酸甜苦辣 記下來！

There's still a long way to go
Sunday, February 23
I love eating and cooking. I practiced cooking a lot so I can be a good cook. I went to a bookstore to buy lots of recipes to cook better. Before getting home, I went to a supermarket to buy cooking ingredients. I know it is difficult to become a good cook. And there's still a long way for me to go to get qualifications of a cook. Mom spent much time teaching me how to cook today. I hope I can cook well enough to hold a feast someday.

我還有段路要走呢！

2月23日星期日

我很喜歡吃和烹飪。為了要成為一個厲害的廚師，我常常練習煮菜。我去書店買了很多食譜，為了要增進我的廚藝。回家之前我去超市買了一些材料，我知道要成為一個很好的廚師很難，要得到廚師的資格還有一條很長的路要走。媽媽今天教我怎麼煮菜。我希望我的烹飪能力可以好到辦一桌筵席。

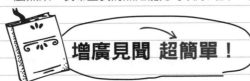

增廣見聞 超簡單！

There are many ways to collect recipes. You may follow instructions on recipes from different chefs, like one of the celebrity chefs, Jamie Oliver. He delivered a speech on TED promoting his biggest hope is to have food education in every school. Due to his own experience in coping with dieting, he became an activist on fighting against obesity and incorrect knowledge about food. Not to eat out may not be his primary demand, but to eat healthy definitely is.

現在有很多方法可以收集到食譜，也可以跟隨著不同廚師的食譜來下廚，例如有名的傑米奧利佛。他曾在 TED 大會上發表演說來推動他最大的心願，就是希望把食物教育落實在每一所學校裡。由於他自身對抗肥胖的經驗，讓他成為了一位推廣正確飲食的社會運動者。不要外食或許不是他的主要訴求，但是「吃得健康」絕對是。

來換換口味吧！讓你的表達更豐富！

1 我烘焙餅乾。　**I baked cookies.**
　相似短句　我替小侄子烤了生日蛋糕。
　　　　　I baked a birthday cake for my nephew.

2 我煎魚。　**I broiled fish.**
　相似短句　我在派對上烤豬排。　**I grilled a pork chop at the party.**

3 我練習煮菜。　**I practice cooking a lot.**
　相似短句　我最近常常煮菜。　**I cook a lot lately.**

4 我到超市買烹飪要用的材料。
　I went to the supermarket to buy cooking ingredients.
　相似短句　我去超市買晚餐要用的材料。
　　　　　I did some shopping for dinner in the supermarket.

5 要成為一個好廚師很不容易。
　It is difficult to become a good cook.
　相似短句　要成為一個出色的廚師沒有捷徑。
　　　　　There's no shortcut to become an outstanding cook.

依樣畫葫蘆！套進去就能用！

句型1　我知道～很難。
　I know it is difficult to...
　例句　我知道要把胡蘿蔔切丁很難。
　I know it is difficult to dice carrots.

句型2　難怪
　no wonder...
　例句　難怪他每次煮這道湯時都會哭。這是洋蔥湯啊。
　No wonder he cries every time he makes this soup.
　It is onion soup.

Unit 07
中醫

社群人氣王！英文動態消息寫給你看！

This Chinese medicine is so bitter.

這中藥好苦。

👍 讚 56　💬 回覆 7

The medicine smells so strong that everyone is staring at me when I was about to drink it.

中藥的味道重到我正要喝的時候所有的人都轉過來看我。

👍 讚 36　💬 回覆 20

The doctor knew all my problems as soon as she touched my wrist. That was amazing.

醫生一搭我的脈搏就知道我所有的問題，超神奇。

👍 讚 130　💬 回覆 3

It's a little bit weird but I like the smell of the traditional medicine shop.

我知道這有點怪，但我很喜歡中藥材舖的味道。

👍 讚 15　💬 回覆 12

Acupuncture looks scary but it really works.

針灸看起來很恐怖但是真的有效。

👍 讚 92　💬 回覆 3

新手超必備！一個單字嘛欸通！

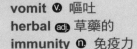

vomit ❤ 嘔吐	**nauseous** adj 噁心的	**herb** ⓝ 藥草
herbal adj 草藥的	**consult a doctor** ❤ 看病	**odor** ⓝ 氣味
immunity ⓝ 免疫力	**medication** ⓝ 治療	

出門超實用！能聽會說一次搞定！

ⒶMike, can you recommend doctors who can cure my shoulder? I have got pain in my shoulder for over a week.

ⒷI know one or two famous doctors, but I don't know if you would accept traditional Chinese method.

Ⓐ麥可，你可以幫我推薦哪位醫生，來治療我的肩膀嗎？它已經痛了一個多星期了。

Ⓑ我知道一兩個有名的醫生，但我不確定你能不能接受傳統中醫療法。

ⒶI don't mind, as long as they would cure my shoulder. By the way, I tried acupuncture before.

ⒷGreat. I asked my doctor, and he said 'Guasha' treatment might work for you. It can relieve the pain on the shoulder and head.

Ⓐ我不介意，只要他們可以治好我的肩膀，況且我以前還試過針灸。

Ⓑ很好。我剛問我的醫師，他說「刮痧」療法或許對你有效。它可以消除肩膀和頭的不適。

ⒶWhat is Guasha? I haven't heard it before.

ⒷGuasha is an action that the doctor scraps your back and results in small bruises on your shoulder. It is believed that through scraping, some bad element will be released.

Ⓐ什麼是刮痧？我從來沒聽過這個。

Ⓑ刮痧是一種醫生在你背上刮的動作，它會導致肩膀上出現小淤青。人們認為透過刮痧，不好的東西會被釋放掉。

ⒶBruises? Sounds scary! But whatever, as long as it works. I can't stand it anymore.

ⒷI will book the appointment for you. You may google it if you want. There are pictures you can check.

Ⓐ淤青？聽起來很可怕！但隨便了，只要它有效。不然我實在無法再忍痛了。

Ⓑ我幫你預約時間，你可以上網搜尋一下，上面有很多照片你可以看。

Unit 07 中醫

酸甜苦辣 記下來！

Old people believed...

Wednesday, December 18
Old people believe in Chinese medication. They say medicine in the hospital are usually too strong for them. I am afraid of taking herbal medicine. Chinese herbal medicine has an awful odor. I had never been sick before, but I went to a Chinese herbal doctor today because of the flu. The doctor said that I was so weak that I must take some herbs to nourish my body for a while, or I would have weak immunity against viruses.

老人都相信

12月18日星期三
老人都很相信中醫。他們說醫院裡的藥通常對他們來說太強烈了。我很怕吃中藥，中藥有一種可怕的味道。我從來沒有生病過，但今天我因為流行感冒去看中醫。醫生說我身體很虛，必須以中藥調養一段時間，否則我對病毒的免疫力會很差。

增廣見聞 超簡單！

Traditional Chinese medicine and treatments are practices and concepts developed 2000 years ago. For example, Chinese herbal medicine, acupuncture, tuina, and qigong are probably things that amaze the Westerners. It's been a long discussion between the effect of Chinese medicine and western medicine. It's better to say that Chinese medicine and Western medicine are complimentary of each other, since they all seek to cure the patient, but in a completely different way.

傳統中醫療法是一套在兩千年前就開始發展的方法跟理念，像是中藥、珍灸、推拿，氣功大概也是會讓西方人覺得新奇的事。對於中醫跟西醫之間的療效一直被廣泛的討論，目前最適合的解釋是中西醫互補，因為他們可以用完全不同的方法達到治癒病人的目的。

1 我想要吐。　**I feel like vomiting.**
　（相似短句）我吃東西後很想吐。　I got nauseous after eating.

2 媽媽帶我去看中醫。
　Mom took me to see a Chinese herb doctor.
　（相似短句）我去看中醫。　I went to consult a Chinese herb doctor.

3 我很怕吃中藥。　**I am afraid of taking herbal medicine.**
　（相似短句）我很怕吃中藥。
　　　　　　I'm scared to take Chinese herbal medicine.

4 中藥有可怕的氣味。
　Chinese herbal medicine has an awful odor.
　（相似短句）中藥聞起來很可怕。
　　　　　　Chinese herbal medicine smells terrible.

5 我的免疫系統很差。　**I have weak immunity against viruses.**
　（相似短句）我能怎麼增強免疫力呢？
　　　　　　How can I boost my low immune system?

（句型1）我不被允許
　　　I am not allowed to...

（例句）因為在進行治療，我不被允許吃冰的、辣的和油的東西。
　　　I am not allowed to eat anything iced, spicy, and greasy for the medical treatment.

（句型2）深信
　　　believe in...

（例句）我深信中藥的醫療效果。
　　　I believe in the medicinal effects of Chinese herbal medicine.

Unit 08
網咖

社群人氣王！英文動態消息寫給你看！

I love the days when I was in high school. I used to go to Internet cafe and play computer games with Chris and Scott.

我懷念我高中的那段日子。我總是跟克利斯和史考特去網咖玩電腦。

👍讚 56　💬回覆 7

I thought the Internet speed will be faster so I came to an Internet cafe to finish my report, but now I found it too noisy here.

我本來想說網路速度比較快所以到網咖來寫報告，結果這裡超級吵。

👍讚 36　💬回覆 20

He has stayed in the Internet cafe for 2 days playing computer games.

他已經在網咖裡面打了兩天的電玩了。

👍讚 130　💬回覆 3

The internet cafe I used to go with my sister had been closed since last month.

我跟姊姊常常去的那間網咖上個月結束營業了。

👍讚 15　💬回覆 12

The internet cafe is getting cheaper nowadays.

網咖收費越來越便宜了。

👍讚 92　💬回覆 3

新手超必備！一個單字嘛欸通！

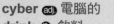

cyber adj. 電腦的	**cafe** n. 咖啡廳	**access** v. 進入
drink n. 飲料	**convenient** adj. 便利的	**Internet** n. 網際網路
online game n. 線上遊戲		

出門超實用！能聽會說一次搞定！

A Do you have any plans after class? I will be at the internet café after school. See you there. Don't stand me up this time.

B I am sorry, James. I am not able to meet you there because I am grounded for a month.

A 你下課後有什麼計劃嗎？我會去網咖喔！我們在那裡見，別再放我鴿子了。

B 抱歉，詹姆士。我今天不能跟你在那裡見面，因為我被禁足一個月。

A Why did you get grounded by your mom? Did you skip class again? Carl, I told you!

B No. I didn't skip class. It's just my English test score is terribly low, so my mom decided to hire a tutor for me.

A 為什麼你會被你媽禁足？你該不會又翹課了吧？卡爾，我提醒過你了！

B 不，我沒有翹課。只是我的英文成績低得可怕，所以我媽決定幫我找一個家教。

A Okay. That's not called "grounded". You are more like being in jail. When can you be free?

B I will say after mid-term exam. By the way, the speed of the internet connection in my house increased a lot.

A 好，所以這不應該叫「禁足」，你比較像是去坐牢了。你什麼時候才可自由啊？

B 我想應該是期中考後吧，對了！我家的網路連線速度變快很多。

A That's cool. Mine hasn't upgrade yet. But my dad said he will consider to reinstall the internet in our house, so that I don't need to go to the internet café to play internet games.

B How thoughtful of your mom and dad! But I agree, after all that's not a good place for us. I cannot stand the smell of smoke there.

A 好酷喔，我們家的還沒升級。但我爸說他會考慮幫我們家重新申請網路，這樣我就不用一直跑網咖玩線上遊戲。

B 你爸媽也太貼心了！但我同意，畢竟網咖不是一個好地方，我已經受夠那裡的煙味了。

Unit 08 網咖

酸甜苦辣 記下來！

Go to the cyber café

Thursday, January 16

There are more and more cyber cafes in Taiwan. I accessed the Internet in a cyber café today. It's very convenient for many people to go to cyber café. There are lots of people enjoying playing online games in the cyber café. The cyber café offers free drinks in order for people to not have to leave when they are thirsty.

去網咖

1月16日星期四

台灣有越來越多的網咖。我今天也去了網咖上網。對很多人來說,去網咖很方便。那裡有很多人都在玩線上遊戲。網咖還提供了免費的飲料,以便大家口渴時不用離開。

增廣見聞 超簡單！

Internet café had once become extremely popular among teenagers in Taiwan. Almost 60% of teenagers admit that they have been to Internet café. But what for? Most of them stayed at Internet café for playing online games. Others, like students living in remote residential areas with no Internet connection, will need a place like the Internet café to finish their work. There's an interesting fact that, Internet café or cyber café is originated from western country for business people to use.

網咖曾一度在台灣青少年中造成旋風,超過百分之六十的青少年承認自己曾到過網咖,但他們去做什麼呢?多數人待在網咖是為了玩線上遊戲,而其他少數住在偏遠地區的孩子,如果家裡沒有網路,就需要去網咖完成需要上網找資料的作業。有趣的是,網咖其實源自於西方,且一開始是專供商務人士使用的。

1 台灣有越來越多的網咖。
There are more and more cyber cafés in Taiwan.
相似短句 台灣有很多網咖。　Cyber cafés are everywhere in Taiwan.

2 我到網咖上網。　**I accessed the Internet in a cyber café.**
相似短句 我去網咖上網。
I went to a cyber café and surfed the Internet.

3 到網咖上網很方便。　**It's convenient to go to the cyber café.**
相似短句 網咖真的相當方便。　Internet café is really convenient.

4 我朋友花很多時間在上網玩遊戲。
My friend spends lots of time playing online games.
相似短句 我朋友有點沉迷於線上遊戲。
My friend was slightly addicted to online games.

5 網咖提供了免費的飲料。　**The cyber café offers free drinks.**
相似短句 網咖裡會販賣食物和飲料。
They sell food and drinks at the Internet café.

依樣畫葫蘆！套進去就能用！

句型1 **究竟～**
What on earth...
例句 線上遊戲究竟有什麼好玩的？
What on earth is fun about online games?

句型2 **很多人都～**
There are lots of people...
例句 很多人都在網咖吃東西。
There are lots of people that have meals at the cyber café.

Unit 09
健身房

社群人氣王！英文動態消息寫給你看！

Working out everyday keeps the doctor away!
每天健身遠離醫生！

👍 讚 56　💬 回覆 7

I tend to go to the gym instead of jogging in the park. It's much comfortable especially in the summer time.
比起在公園慢跑，我更習慣去健身房。那裡比較舒服，尤其是夏天的時候。

👍 讚 36　💬 回覆 20

I went swimming this morning and did weight exercise this afternoon. What a sporty Saturday!
我早上去游泳下午去重訓，超運動的週六。

👍 讚 130　💬 回覆 3

I want to take more weight exercise in order to gain muscle.
我想多做一點重訓好長些肌肉。

👍 讚 15　💬 回覆 12

Going to the gym tomorrow, who's coming with me?
明天要去健身房～誰要跟我一起去嗎？

👍 讚 92　💬 回覆 3

新手超必備！一個單字嘛欸通！

tight adj. 緊繃的	**sweat** n. 汗水	**kilo** n. 公斤
keep v. 保持	**gym** n. 健身房	**training** n. 訓練
physical adj. 身體上的		

Part 2 週末享娛樂

出門超實用！能聽會說一次搞定！

A Check out this leaflet! If you join the Workout club now, you can have 30% off on annual fee of the first year and enjoy 90% off on monthly fees for two years.

B Sounds great! Are you considering joining that club? That's a great bargain if you take it at this moment.

A 看看這個傳單！現在參加健身俱樂部就可以享第一年年費七折，還有兩年月費一折優惠！

B 聽起來不錯呢！你們考慮要參加俱樂部嗎？如果你現在報名的話，這倒是不錯的優惠。

A Yes. I would love to. As you can see, I gained quite a lot of weight after I got married. Besides, I want to go to the gym with friends, for example, like you.

B No problem! You are welcome to join us this weekend! But there are several things that I would like to remind you first.

A 是的，我想啊。你看看，我自從結婚後增加不少體重。除此之外，我很想跟朋友們一起去運動；例如跟你。

B 沒問題！歡迎你這周加入我們的行列！但是有一些事情我必須要先提醒你！

A Okay, sounds weird. What should I be aware of if I go to the gym? Isn't it just jogging on treadmill or doing weight trainings?

B Yes, you are right, partially. But, some bad habits in gym clubs are really annoying; such as some people not wiping out their sweat on the treadmill after workout.

A 嗯，聽起來有點怪異。有什麼事情是我去健身房需要注意的？不就是去跑步機上慢跑或重訓？

B 是的，你說對了某些部份。但是有些壞習慣在健身房裡面真的很令人困擾；例如有些人運動完不會擦掉在跑步機上的汗水。

A Oh my god! That's disgusting. And what else? Don't shout or scream while working out?!

B Exactly! I know it's a bit difficult for people, because we need an outlet so that we can push up the utilities. Anyway, just keep in mind of those trivial things.

A 我的天啊，這超噁的。所以還有別的嗎？不要在做重訓的時候大叫嗎？

B 沒錯！我知道這對有些人來說有點難，因為我們在做重訓時難免需要一點宣洩。總之，這些小事要注意一下！

Unit 09 健身房

酸甜苦辣 記下來！

Saving my body shape

Friday, November 29

My body shape was changing. I went to a gym for physical training. In addition to shaping my body, losing weight was another advantage. I don't want to get fatter and fatter in my early twenties. Keeping a good shape costs time and efforts.

拯救身材大作戰

11月29日星期五

我的身材慢慢地走樣，我到健身房去健身，除了要雕塑我的身材曲線之外，另一個好處是可以減輕我的體重。我不希望我在二十歲就開始變得越來越胖，保持身材是很需要時間跟精力的。

增廣見聞 超簡單！

Except terrible habits in gym, there are other suggestions that you might want to take: first, get to know the machine and how to use them in a proper way. By doing it in a correct way can effectively achieve the goal. Also, dress up comfortably to the gym is important as well. You need clothes that fit you well, and a pair of right shoes. Last, don't forget to pack up a bag for the gym and put some towels in it, in case you would like to take a shower after working out.

除了在健身房可怕的壞習慣之外，你可能還有其他的健身建議需要注意：第一，了解運動器材正確的使用方法，正確使用可以幫助你有效達成運動目標。第二，以合適的穿著上健身房也很重要，例如合身的衣服還有正確的運動鞋。最後，別忘記準備一個去健身房使用的包包，裡面裝幾條毛巾，以防你運動完後會想要沖個澡。

來換換口味吧！讓你的表達更豐富！

1 我全身都好痛。 **My body ached all over.**
(相似短句) 健身一整天後，我的肌肉好緊繃。
My muscle felt tight after working out all day.

2 跑完步後我全身是汗。 **I sweated after running.**
(相似短句) 健完身後，我全身濕透。
I was drenched in sweat after working out.

3 我在減肥。 **I am on a diet.**
(相似短句) 我不會吃任何含有碳水化合物的食物，直到我減了3公斤。
I wouldn't eat food with carbs until I lose 3 kilos.

4 我身材保持得很好。 **I keep my shape well.**
(相似短句) 我一個星期游兩次泳，保持健美的身材。
I keep my body fit by swimming twice a week.

5 我到健身房去鍛鍊身體。
I went to a gym for physical training.
(相似短句) 我去健身房進行規律的鍛鍊。
I go to a gym for my workout routine.

依樣畫葫蘆！套進去就能用！

(句型1) **受～的歡迎很久**
have been popular with...
(例句) 塑身腳踏車受女性的歡迎很久了。
These fitness bikes have been popular with ladies.

(句型2) **除了～之外**
In addition to...
(例句) 除了健身之外，安迪去健身房也認識朋友。
In addition to working out, Andy went to the gym to meet people.

Unit 10
夜市

社群人氣王！英文動態消息寫給你看！

 Shilin Night Market is the best place to go when visiting Taiwan.
來臺灣旅遊的時候絕對不能錯過士林夜市。

 讚 56　　回覆 7

 The food in the night market is so delicious and cheap! Can't stop eating! They are getting me fat!
夜市的小吃好好吃又好便宜，我根本無法停下來，要變胖了！

 讚 36　　回覆 20

 I found so many traditional snacks in the night market.
我在夜市裡發現好多傳統的小點心。

 讚 130　　回覆 3

 When I was a kid my grandpa used to take me to the night market to play games and have late night snacks.
我還小的時候我祖父常常帶我去夜市玩遊戲、吃宵夜。

 讚 15　　回覆 12

 You can nearly find everything in the night market.
你幾乎可以在夜市裡找到所有的東西。

 讚 92　　回覆 3

新手超必備！一個單字嘛欸通！

night market ⓝ 夜市　**crowded** adj. 擠滿人的　　**noisy** adj. 吵鬧的
meatball ⓝ 貢丸　　**oyster omelet** ⓝ 蚵仔煎
snack ⓝ 小吃　　**stinky tofu** ⓝ 臭豆腐　**grilled sausage** ⓝ 烤香腸

出門超實用！能聽會說一次搞定！

A My friend, George, who comes from Italy, wants to visit our famous night market in Taiwan. I will take him to the most famous night market in Tainan. Can you be the tour guide for George?

B No problem at all! I would love to see their astonished faces when they see the food there.

A 我的義大利朋友喬治想要逛逛我們台灣有名的夜市！我會帶他去台南最有名的夜市看看。你願意來當喬治的導遊嗎？

B 沒問題。我想看看他們看到食物時臉上驚訝的表情！

A Hi Sara, this is George. So can we start from this end? I want to introduce him the pearl milk tea.

B Sure. And I know there are stinky tofu, oyster omelets and other incredible food for an Italian.

A 哈囉～莎拉，這位是喬治！所以我們可以從這一端開始逛嗎？我想介紹他喝珍珠奶茶。

B 好啊！我知道還有臭豆腐，蚵仔煎，和其他極美味的食物可以推薦給義大利人。

A Take your time. We have time to visit those stands row by row. I remember the most famous stinky tofu is right at this end of the row.

B Really? I will go queuing first. We have to spend at least 15 minutes on queue and it's all for stinky tofu.

A 慢慢來，我們有的是時間一條一條的逛。我記得最有名的臭豆腐就在這道路的盡頭。

B 真的嗎，那我先去排隊。我們至少要為了臭豆腐花15分鐘排隊。

C I cannot believe that Taiwanese have the patience and have time to be in the queue for famous food stand.

B I am used to it now. It's part of the culture, so I guess we need to be used to it. You will feel worth the 15 minutes wait when you taste the food.

C 我不敢相信，台灣人有這種耐心跟時間在這裡為食物排隊。

B 我已經習慣了，這是文化的一部分，所以我猜我們都得去習慣它！等你嚐到那些食物以後心情將會好一點，因為發現那15分鐘的確值得。

酸甜苦辣 記下來！

Go go night market!

Wednesday, October 2

I really love shopping at the night market. Products in the night market are cheaper. I love the genuine human warmth in the night market, too. I ate grilled sausages and stinky tofu in the evening. I always net goldfishes and play darts whenever strolling about the night market. I make a resolution to eat up all the snacks in night markets. Night markets in Taiwan have two characters. One is being crowded, and the other is having lots of snacks.

走走走！去夜市！

10月2日星期三

我真的很喜歡逛夜市，在夜市裡賣的東西都比較便宜，而且我也喜歡夜市裡溫暖的人情味。我晚上吃烤香腸跟臭豆腐。我在夜市閒逛時總是會玩撈金魚和射飛鏢，我決定要吃遍夜市裡所有的小吃！台灣的夜市有兩個特色，一個就是很擠，另一個就是充滿了許多小吃。

增廣見聞 超簡單！

Night markets in Taiwan are probably places that surprised foreigners most. Since there is no such culture in Western countries, they feel very curious about the night market culture. In most of western countries, clothes shop and shopping malls close early at 8pm. Bar and restaurants are places they can go for relaxing after work. Apart from culture aspects, food in night market, such as pearl milk tea, fried chicken, stinky tofu, is also the point that attracts foreigners.

台灣的夜市大概是讓外國人最驚訝的地方，因為西方國家並沒有這種文化，所以會特別感到好奇。在多數西方國家，服裝店或購物中心都在晚上八點左右就關門，酒吧跟餐廳才是他們下班後去放鬆的地方。而除了文化層面之外，珍珠奶茶、炸雞、臭豆腐等夜市美食也是吸引外國人的重點之一。

來換換口味吧！讓你的表達更豐富！

❶ 我家附近有一個夜市。
There is a night market near my home.
相似短句 我家附近有個夜市。
There is a night market in my neighborhood.

❷ 那裡總是很擠又很吵。　**It's always crowded and noisy.**
相似短句 那裡總是很多人又很吵。
It's always full of people and noisy there.

❸ 我真的很喜歡逛夜市。
I really love shopping at the night market.
相似短句 我超級喜歡逛夜市的。　I am a big fan of night markets.

❹ 那衣服很吸引人。　**The clothes were attractive.**
相似短句 那衣服很值得購買。　The clothes are really worth buying.

❺ 它真的超便宜的。　**It's a steal.**
相似短句 它便宜得不可置信。　It's unbelievably cheap.

依樣畫葫蘆！套進去就能用！

句型1 **我決定要～**
I made a resolution to...
例句 我決定要瘦五公斤。
I made a resolution to loose five kilos.

句型2 **～真好吃。**
How yummy...
例句 港式點心真好吃！
How yummy the dim sum was!

Unit 11
KTV

社群人氣王！英文動態消息寫給你看！

He can sing every song by that singer.
只要是那個歌手的歌他都會唱。

👍讚 56　💬回覆 7

The last time I went to KTV was 5 years ago.
我上次去 KTV 已經是五年前的事了。

👍讚 36　💬回覆 20

She is always eating every time she comes with us to KTV. She never sings. She says she can't sing but she loves to listen to us singing.
她每次跟我們來 KTV 都在吃東西，從來不唱歌。她說她不會唱歌，但很喜歡聽我們唱。

👍讚 130　💬回覆 3

I know a cheaper place to go. Who's coming tonight?
我知道有個地方比較便宜。今晚誰要一起來？

👍讚 15　💬回覆 12

Amy always talks loudly, but when she sings, she becomes so tender and graceful.
艾咪講話總是很大聲，不過一旦她開始唱歌，就會變得溫柔又優雅。

👍讚 92　💬回覆 3

新手超必備！一個單字嘛欸通！

b-day ⓝ 生日	**sing** ⓥ 唱歌	**enjoy** ⓥ 享受
karaoke ⓝ 卡拉 OK	**crazily** adv 瘋狂地	**dance** ⓥ 跳舞
sofa ⓝ 沙發	**be worn out** phr 精疲力盡	

出門超實用！能聽會說一次搞定！

A It's Andrew's birthday on Sunday! Shall we go to Karaoke to celebrate his birthday?

B I will ask for other people to join. I cannot wait. I can't remember when was the last time I've been there.

A 這周日是安德魯的生日耶！我們可以一起去卡拉 ok 慶生嗎？

B 我會找其他人一起參加。我等不及了，都想不起來上次去唱歌是什麼時候了。

A You sound old. But I have to admit that I really look forward to our party at Karaoke this time.

B Does that remind you of the old times? I remember Andrew was always the one who held the microphone for all night.

A 你聽起來落伍囉！但我承認我也很期待這次卡拉 ok 派對。

B 這喚醒了你的往日回憶嗎？我記得安德魯總是整晚麥克風不離手的其中一人。

A Yes! No one can get the microphone from him! Jimmy even had a fight with him.

B Oh my. That was hilarious. I don't know what song I would request on that day.

A 是啊！沒有人可以從他手中拿走麥克風，吉米還因此跟他吵架呢！

B 我的天啊，這太好笑了。這樣我都不知道我那天可以點什麼歌。

A The key is that the songs we request might reveal our age! Last time I went to Karaoke with my colleagues, I got teased all the time.

B Poor you. Just rock the party this time in karaoke! I am glad Andrew is the same age as we are.

A 關鍵是，我們點的歌會洩漏我們的年紀，上次我跟同事去唱，我一整場都被笑。

B 真可憐！我們這次就在卡拉 ok 辦派對玩個夠！我覺得很慶幸安德魯跟我們同年。

Unit 11 KTV

酸甜苦辣 記下來！

Celebrate in KTV

Friday, September 20

For celebrating my co-worker's birthday, we went to KTV. There are not only pop songs to sing but also food to eat in KTV. We were singing so uncontrollably as to be unable to hold our voices down. When serving us cold drinks, the KTV waiter was surprised that we were worn out and lying on the sofa.

到 KTV 去慶祝

9月20日星期五

為了要替我的同事慶生，我們去 KTV 唱歌。那裡不只有流行歌曲可以唱，還有東西可以吃。我們唱瘋到無法把聲音壓下來。當服務生拿飲料來的時候，很驚訝地發現我們精疲力盡的累癱在沙發上。

增廣見聞 超簡單！

Karaoke, is an activity and a place for people to hang around to have party or simply to meet up with friends. There's no time restriction to this kind of activity. College students will even stay at karaoke for whole nights till the morning, having fun and singing. Karaoke can be seen in western countries, but unlike karaoke in Asia countries, karaoke equipments are set up in a bar or restaurant.

KTV 是一種活動也是一種地方讓人們可以跟朋友一起聚會開派對，而且這活動沒有時間的限制，大學生甚至會待在 KTV 一整晚純粹就開心玩樂還有唱歌。KTV 在西方國家也可見，但不像 KTV 在亞洲國家的形式，它就只是一台卡拉 ok 機器被放置在酒吧或是餐廳。

來換換口味吧！讓你的表達更豐富！

❶ 我們到 KTV 幫同事慶生。
For celebrating my co-worker's birthday, we went to KTV.
(相似短句) 我們到卡拉 OK 慶祝同事生日。
We celebrated my colleague's b-day at a karaoke.

❷ 我喜歡唱歌。 **I like to sing.**
(相似短句) 我喜歡唱歌。 I enjoy singing.

❸ 我喜歡到 KTV 唱歌。 **I enjoy singing at KTV.**
(相似短句) 我喜歡去卡拉 OK。 I love going to karaoke.

❹ 我們瘋狂地跳舞。 **We danced crazily.**
(相似短句) 我們那天晚上跳舞跳瘋了。
We danced like crazy that night.

❺ 我們最後都累攤在沙發上。
We were worn out and lying on the sofa in the end.
(相似短句) 最後我們太累了，都在沙發上睡著了。
We all ended up so tired and crashed out on the sofa.

依樣畫葫蘆！套進去就能用！

句型1 不僅～還有～
not only... but also...
(例句) 那間卡拉 OK 不僅乾淨，還有很多歌。
The karaoke was not only clean but also had so many songs.

句型2 我最好～
I had better...
(例句) 我最好搭計程車回家，因為我醉了。
I had better take a taxi home because I am drunk.

Unit 12
調酒

社群人氣王！英文動態消息寫給你看！

I want to be a bartender.
我想成為一名調酒師。

👍 讚 56　　💬 回覆 7

Gin tonic is the easiest cocktail to make.
琴通寧是最容易調製的調酒。

👍 讚 36　　💬 回覆 20

You can find lots of recipes on the internet for making all kinds of cocktails. It's not necessary to buy a book.
你可以從網路上找到各種雞尾酒的食譜，不需要特地去買一本書。

👍 讚 130　　💬 回覆 3

My favorite cocktail is Tequila Sunrise. It's colorful and sweet. I always have one when I am depressed.
我最喜歡的雞尾酒是龍舌蘭日出，顏色很漂亮又很甜，心情不好的時候我總是會喝一杯。

👍 讚 15　　💬 回覆 12

Cocktail can get you drunk easily because they are sweet like juice.
雞尾酒很容易醉，因為喝起來甜甜的像果汁。

👍 讚 92　　💬 回覆 3

新手超必備！一個單字嘛欸通！

cocktail ⓝ 雞尾酒	mix ⓥ 混合	drink ⓝ 飲料
wine ⓝ 酒	wine mixer ⓟʰʳ 調酒師	taste ⓥ 品嚐
glass ⓝ 一杯（酒）	mint wine ⓟʰʳ 薄荷酒	soda ⓝ 蘇打水

出門超實用！能聽會說一次搞定！

A Do you want to visit the new lounge bar this Friday? I heard the cocktail and food there taste great.

B Sure! To be honest, I seldom visit lounge bars. I am afraid that I don't know how to order the drinks there.

A 你這周五想不想去新的酒吧看看？我聽說那裏的雞尾酒跟食物味道都不錯。

B 好！但老實說，我很久沒去酒吧了。我擔心我連怎麼點酒都不會了。

A No worries. I can introduce some of the cocktails to you now. Don't forget I worked as a bartender before.

B How can I forget that. The first time I got drunk was all because of you. You let me had at least three tequila shots.

A 別擔心，我現在就可以介紹幾款調酒給你！別忘記我之前當過調酒師。

B 我怎麼可能忘記。我第一次喝醉就是因為你一直讓我連續喝了三杯龍舌蘭。

A Come on. That's not a big deal. I will introduce some other cocktails to you, like Long Island Ice Tea.

B What is Long Island Ice Tea? Just please; don't get me drunk this time. I don't want to go to work with a hangover the next morning.

A 還好吧，這不是什麼大事啊！我會介紹其他款調酒給你，例如長島冰茶。

B 什麼是長島冰茶？反正就是拜託，這次別讓我喝醉，我不想帶著宿醉去上班。

A No, I can promise you that I will order drinks that are suitable for you. Long Island Ice Tea is the most seen cocktail in clubs; it's the mix of Gin, vodka, and lime.

B Well, sounds like it will have a strong effect. Although, comparing to tequila shots, Long Island Ice Tea sounds much better.

A 不會，我可以承諾你，我會幫你點適合你的酒。長島冰茶是酒吧中最常見的酒，它是由琴酒，伏特加跟萊姆汁調成的。

B 它聽起來還是會有很大的副作用，雖然跟龍舌蘭比起來好多了。

Unit 12 調酒

酸甜苦辣 記下來！

Show time! Green Explosion!

Friday, May 17

I'm learning wine tasting. To make impressive mixed drinks one needs creativity. I found it interesting when I put something new in wine. Creating mixed drinks full of imagination makes me happy. I mixed a whole new cold drink named "Green Explosion" today. It was mainly mixed up with mint wine and ice cream soda.

綠色爆炸登場！

5月17日 星期五

我正在學習品酒，要做出令人難忘的調酒需要創意。我發現當我放新的東西到酒裡時，我會覺得很有趣。創造出充滿想像的調酒讓我心情很愉快。我今天調了一種全新的清涼飲料，名叫「綠色爆炸」。主要是由薄荷酒與冰淇淋汽水製成。

增廣見聞 超簡單！

Cocktail refers to alcoholic drink that mixes two or more ingredients in it, for example, Long Island Ice Tea, Cosmopolitan, and Margarita. The most common seen liquors are vodka, Gin, and lime that are used as based liquor in cocktail. Also, sometimes we will see news broadcasting about the competition of bartenders, and we will see bartenders showing different high technical skills for both entertainment and professions. And that is the International Flair Bartender Competition.

雞尾酒，也就是「調酒」，指的是由多種配方調製而成的酒精飲料，像是長島冰茶、柯夢波丹和瑪格麗特。最常見的調酒是用伏特加、琴酒和萊姆酒作為基底調製而成。另外，我們有時在電視上看到的調酒師比賽，會看見他們展現出各種高超技巧，兼具娛樂與專業，那就是「國際花式調酒大賽」。

來換換口味吧！讓你的表達更豐富！

❶ 我從舅舅的身上學到很多調酒知識。
I learned a lot about wine mixing from my uncle.
相似短句 我從舅舅的身上學到很多調酒的知識。
I get to know so much about mixing cocktails from my uncle.

❷ 調得酒苦到難以入口。 **The mixed drink is too bitter to taste.**
相似短句 你調的調酒太苦了。
The cocktail you mixed is way too bitter.

❸ 我在學習品酒。 **I'm learning wine tasting.**
相似短句 品酒的世界博大精深。
There's still so much to know about wine tasting.

❹ 要調出令人難忘的調酒需要創意。
To make impressive mixed drinks one needs creativity.
相似短句 要調出令人難忘的調酒需要創意。
One needs creativity to make an unforgettable cocktail.

❺ 我發現在酒中加入新東西很有趣。
I found it interesting when I put something new in wine.
相似短句 在酒裡加了新東西後，喝起來不僅不一樣，還很不錯。
Wine can taste different but nice when something new is added.

依樣畫葫蘆！套進去就能用！

句型1 老師要求我們～
The teacher asked us to...
例句 老師要求我們在調雞尾酒時要用量杯。
The teacher asked us to use measuring glass to mix cocktail.

句型1 我發現～很有趣。
I found it interesting...
例句 我發現任何東西加了點檸檬汁之後都會變清爽，很有趣。
I found it interesting that everything tasted lighter with a bit of lemonade.

美分美秒，聽說讀寫Everyday

Unit 13
放寒假

Part 3 全民樂逍遙

社群人氣王！英文動態消息寫給你看！

Taking the kids to visit the National Palace Museum today!
今天帶孩子們去故宮參觀！

👍讚 56　💬回覆 7

Made the kids do their winter vacation homework this afternoon. –feeling tired.
今天下午教小朋友寫他們的寒假作業。覺得累。

👍讚 36　💬回覆 20

We still have classes because we are 12th grade students. What a NICE winter vacation!
我們還是要去上課因為我們是高三生。好個寒假呀！

👍讚 130　💬回覆 3

It's winter vacation but we cannot go anywhere for it's cold and rainy all the time.
因為太冷又一直下雨，難得寒假卻哪裡都去不了。

👍讚 15　💬回覆 12

I watched 8 movies and read 5 novels during the winter vacation.
寒假中我看了八部電影又讀了五本小說。

👍讚 92　💬回覆 3

新手超必備！一個單字嘛欸通！

dormitory ⓝ 宿舍　　**essay** ⓝ 論文　　**hand in** 🔤 繳交
upcoming 🔤 即將到來的　　**take a break** 🔤 休息　　**enjoy** ⓥ 享受
winter vacation 🔤 寒假

出門超實用！能聽會說一次搞定！

Ⓐ Winter break is about to start. We have six weeks of holiday this year.

Ⓑ Do you have any plans? I am not allowed to have my own plans, so I can only hear from you guys on your plans.

Ⓐ 寒假已經快要到了。今年我們有六周的假期。

Ⓑ 你有什麼計畫嗎？我不能有自己的計畫，所以只能聽你分享。

Ⓐ Why? I don't have any plan at all. If you want to, we can hangout together whenever we have time.

Ⓑ Sorry, Annie. I have to help my mom manage her stores during winter break, so I can go out only at night after the store is closed.

Ⓐ 為什麼？我並沒有任何計畫。如果你願意，我們只要有時間都可以一起出去。

Ⓑ 安妮對不起。寒假的時候我必須幫我媽顧店，所以我只能在打烊後的晚上出去。

Ⓐ That's fine. We can hang out on weekends. Besides, it's warmer to go out during the day.

Ⓑ True. It's freezing at night. Usually, I stay in bed watching movies, and that's it.

Ⓐ 沒關係。我們可以週末出去。而且在白天出門比較暖和。

Ⓑ 沒錯。晚上超級冷。我通常會窩在被子裡看電影。

Ⓐ Sounds like you have build up your winter break night routine. Mine is pretty much the same as yours, but I go out skiing sometimes.

Ⓑ Seriously, I couldn't imagine people go out and ski during the night.

Ⓐ 聽起來你已經規劃好你寒假晚上的行程了。我跟你的非常像，只是我有時會出去滑雪。

Ⓑ 說真的，我無法想像有人會在夜晚出去滑雪。

Unit 13 放寒假

酸甜苦辣 記下來！

Good suggestion from my sister!

Monday, January 27

I want to study English harder. But if it wasn't my sister's suggestion, I wouldn't know how to. My sister suggested that I should keep an English dairy. It was a good suggestion for me to do so. Keeping a dairy in English improves not only my writing skills but also my English ability in general. It seems that my English will get better and better if I maintain the habit of keeping a dairy in English.

我姐給的好建議

1月27日星期一

我打算更努力學英文，但如果不是我姐姐建議的話，我不知道該怎麼做。她建議我用英文寫日記，這對我來說真的是個好主意。用英文寫日記不只讓我的寫作能力進步，也增進我的英文能力。看起來我的英文將會變得更好，如果我持之以恆的寫英文日記。

增廣見聞 超簡單！

Instead of staying at home all the time, applying for some part-time work may be a choice for college students. It could be a part-time work as a waiter / waiterss, or a sales person during a year-end clearance sale. In this, one can not only earn money, but also earn valuable social experiences. As for parents, it will be better if parents could encourage your child to either go work or simply help you out on housework.

與其待在家，找一份兼執的工作對大學生來說也許不錯。當一個餐廳服務生或是年終特賣會的兼執工讀生不僅可以存錢，還可以學到寶貴的社會經驗。所以對於家長來說，鼓勵小孩找份打工，或是單純的分擔家務都是不錯的選擇。

來換換口味吧！讓你的表達更豐富！

① 下星期就要放寒假了。
Winter vacation will begin next week.
(相似短句) 寒假快到了。　Winter vacation is just around the corner.

② 我得待在宿舍裡寫論文。
I have to stay in the dormitory and write my essay.
(相似短句) 我得去圖書館寫論文。
I have to go to the library to work on my essay.

③ 我最好儘快趕工。
I had better finish my work as soon as possible.
(相似短句) 我最好再加把勁。　I'd better work harder.

④ 我好期待即將到來的假期。
I am looking forward to the upcoming vacation.
(相似短句) 我等不及享受即將來到的假期了。
I can't wait for the coming vacation.

⑤ 我交出我的論文了！　**I handed in my essay.**
(相似短句) 我終於完成論文了。　I finally finished my essay.

依樣畫葫蘆！套進去就能用！

(句型1) ～是個好建議。
It was a good suggestion to...
(例句) 去滑雪場打工是個好建議。
It was a good suggestion to do part-time job at a ski resort.

(句型2) 儘快～
...as soon as possible
(例句) 我們都希望儘快擺脫學校。
We all wanted to get rid of school as soon as possible.

Unit 14
放暑假

社群人氣王！英文動態消息寫給你看！

College students are the ones who really can enjoy the summer vacation.
大學生才是真正能享受暑假的人們。

👍讚 56　💬回覆 7

I applied for some summer course in the US.
我申請了美國的夏季課程。

👍讚 36　💬回覆 20

Now is the best time to visit Penghu.
現在最適合去澎湖玩。

👍讚 130　💬回覆 3

I feel lonely in summer vacation because my birthday is in July.
暑假總是讓我覺得很寂寞，因為我的生日在七月。

👍讚 15　💬回覆 12

I used to miss my classmates during summer vacation when I was in elementary school.
國小的暑假我總是會很想念我的同學。

👍讚 92　💬回覆 3

新手超必備！一個單字嘛欸通！

apply ⓥ 申請	**survival skills** phr. 求生技巧	**tent** ⓝ 帳篷
overnight ⓐ 通宵	**heat** ⓝ 暑熱；高溫	
particular ⓐ 特別的	**summer vacation** phr. 暑假	

出門超實用！能聽會說一次搞定！

Ⓐ Are you going to join summer camp this year? The camp goal is survival skills in the wild.

Ⓑ I will definitely join the camp this year. Staying in the wild has always been my dream.

Ⓐ 你今年要參加暑期營隊嗎？今年暑期營隊主題是如何在野外生存。

Ⓑ 我一定會參加今年的營隊。在野外生存一直以來是我的夢想。

Ⓐ You must be crazy. Are you saying that setting up tents and campfires, and waking up in the early morning is you interest?

Ⓑ Yeah, or what else would you think about summer camps? It's summer time, and I don't want to skip the chance.

Ⓐ 你一定是說你瘋了。你是說你對於搭帳篷、升營火和早起有興趣？

Ⓑ 對阿，不然你對於暑期營隊還有其他想法嗎？現在是夏季，而我不想要錯過這次機會。

Ⓐ Alright, other then the camping part, I am attracted to the part where we can go teach English in remote areas afterwards.

Ⓑ That sounds good as well. So we will experience living in the wild first, and then head to schools to teach children.

Ⓐ 好吧，除了營隊部分，我對另外一個之後在偏遠地區教英文的計畫感興趣。

Ⓑ 那聽起來也非常不賴。所以我們會先體驗野外生活，然後再去學校教小朋友。

Ⓐ Exactly. Okay, I will join the camp, but can you be on the same team with me? Otherwise, I have zero knowledge about wild life.

Ⓑ Sure. I will take you into my team, and teach you some skills and knowledge about it.

Ⓐ 沒有錯。恩，我會參加營隊，但是你可以跟我同一隊嗎？不然我對於野外生活的認識是零。

Ⓑ 當然好。我會帶你進入我的隊伍，然後教你一些相關的技能和知識。

Unit 14 放暑假

酸甜苦辣 記下來！

SUMMER VACATION!!

Wednesday, July 31
This summer is hotter than before. I am very afraid of the heat. It is burning hot through the whole summer. Whenever it becomes hot, I sweat all the time. As a result, I like to go swimming on summer vacations. It's so comfortable to swim in a swimming pool in the summer.

暑假！！

7月31日星期三
今年的暑假比往年來的熱，而我很怕熱。這整個夏天都熱炸了，只要一變熱，我就全身是汗。所以，我很喜歡暑假的時候去游泳。在夏天去泳池游泳真的很舒服耶！

增廣見聞 超簡單！

There are varieties of summer camps that are held during summer vacation. Especially in the United States, there are all kinds of camps that are categorized by either duration or the theme. For example, there are traditional overnight camps from 1 week to 5 weeks; and there are single focus specialty camps, such as sports camps, technology camps, art camps, and Military camps. Also, if your child needs special camps, you can join camps that are mainly for Aspergers, Learning Disabilities, and so on.

有各式各樣的夏令營會在暑假時舉辦，特別是在美國，夏令營有很多種類，可以依據時間長度跟主題來分類。例如：傳統的宿營，時間長度從一周到五周都有，也有單一主題式的夏令營，像是運動、科學、藝術或是軍事的營隊。另外，如果您的小孩需要特別照護，那麼就可以選擇專門提供給亞斯伯格症或是學習障礙等的孩子所參加的夏令營。

來換換口味吧！讓你的表達更豐富！

① 我覺得很寂寞。　**I feel lonely.**

（相似短句）我覺得很孤單。　I feel alone.

② 在野外生存一直以來是我的夢想。
Staying in the wild has always been my dream.

（相似短句）我一直夢想著能在野外生活。
I've always dream about staying in the wild.

③ 你一定是瘋了。　**You must be crazy.**

（相似短句）你瘋了嗎？　Are you nuts?

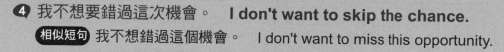

④ 我不想要錯過這次機會。　**I don't want to skip the chance.**

（相似短句）我不想錯過這個機會。　I don't want to miss this opportunity.

⑤ 特別是在美國……　**Especially in the United States, ...**

（相似短句）特別是在美國……　In particular in the United States, ...

依樣畫葫蘆！套進去就能用！

句型1 比起以往～
...than before

（例句）湯姆跑得比以往快。
Tom runs faster than before.

句型2 例如～
such as...

（例句）我喜歡運動，例如棒球、網球和游泳。
I like sports, such as baseball, tennis and swimming.

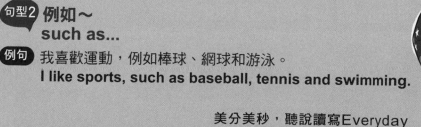

Unit 15
春天郊遊

社群人氣王！英文動態消息寫給你看！

The pink and white cherry blossoms are so beautiful!
粉色和白色的櫻花好美麗！

👍 讚 56　💬 回覆 7

I went picnic with my friends this afternoon.
今天下午我和朋友們一起去野餐。

👍 讚 36　💬 回覆 20

It's nice to walk the dog in the park in Spring because the weather is getting warmer.
春天的時候很適合去公園遛狗，因為天氣漸漸變得暖和了。

👍 讚 130　💬 回覆 3

I forgot to bring an umbrella with me when I went out. So I entered a cafe when the rain suddenly came.
出門的時候忘了帶傘，於是只好在下起雨的時候躲進咖啡館。

👍 讚 15　💬 回覆 12

My boyfriend took me to a beautiful garden on Yangmingshan.
男友帶我去了陽明山上一座很漂亮的花園。

 👍 讚 92　💬 回覆 3

新手超必備！一個單字嘛欸通！

blossom ⓝ 開花（期）　　spring ⓝ 春天　　picnic ⓝ 野餐
breeze ⓝ 微風　　comfortable ⓐⓓⓙ 舒服的　　peach ⓝ 桃子
gentle ⓐⓓⓙ 和煦的　　chirp ⓥ （小鳥）發啁啾聲

出門超實用！能聽會說一次搞定！

Ⓐ Hey Carl, do you know which flower is in season? Finally, it's spring now.

Ⓑ Okay. Let me see. There's a flower festival held this weekend. Daffodil, Tulip, and Primrose can all be seen in the festival.

Ⓐ 嘿！卡爾，你知道這個季節有什麼花嗎？終於，現在是春天了。

Ⓑ 恩，讓我看看。這個周末有舉辦一個花卉慶典。水仙花、鬱金香和報春花都可以在這慶典看到。

Ⓐ We can plan a spring outing! Let's welcome the wonders of life after winter.

Ⓑ I will prepare a picnic basket, picnic blanket and tons of beer. Sounds wonderful, huh?

Ⓐ 我們可以計畫一個春天郊遊！讓我們歡迎寒冬後的生命奇觀。

Ⓑ 我會準備一個野餐籃、野餐墊和大量的啤酒。聽起來棒極了，嗯？

Ⓐ I will prepare the food like sandwiches, cakes, scones, and coke to put in the basket.

Ⓑ Terrific. I will ask my wife to prepare some food as well. Also, we can rent bikes there!

Ⓐ 我會準備籃子裡的食物，像是三明治、蛋糕、烤餅和可樂。

Ⓑ 太棒了。我也會請我老婆準備些食物。我們還可以在那裡租腳踏車！

Ⓐ Imagine that we are riding on the bicycle path along the fields of flower! I love spring.

Ⓑ Sounds great. Just be careful, don't fall off from the bike like last time we were in the green tunnel.

Ⓐ 想像一下我們騎在周圍環繞著花海的腳踏車道！我愛春天。

Ⓑ 聽起來棒極了。只是小心點，別再從腳踏車上摔下來，像上次我們在綠色隧道時一樣。

Unit 15 春天郊遊

酸甜苦辣 記下來！

Go Picnicking!

Tuesday, March 5

Spring is a comfortable season. It's warm. My family went picnicking in Mt. Yang-Ming. We had a good time. There are many birds chirping around in spring. It's really enjoyable to lie on the grass and appreciate the beauty of nature.

去郊遊！

3月5日星期二

春天真是個舒服的季節，天氣很溫暖，我們家去陽明山郊遊，我們玩得很開心。春天鶯聲燕語，躺在草坪上享受大自然的美，真是享受阿！

增廣見聞 超簡單！

In Taiwan, only college students could have the privilege of enjoying spring break for around 4-6 days. Normally, spring break happens before or after tomb sweeping festival. If you are not a college student, you can still plan your own spring break trip, like mentioned in the conversation. From January to April, there are series of flower festival in Yangming Mountain, such as sakura, and Calla Lily. These Festivals attract thousands of tourists every year.

在台灣，只有大學生能夠享有四到六天的春假。一般來說，春假期間通常在清明節的前後，如果你不是大學生，其實也還是可以計畫你的春季旅遊，像是對話中提到的；從一月到四月，陽明山就有一系列的花季，例如賞櫻跟賞海芋，每年都會吸引上千名遊客參觀。

Part 3 全民樂逍遙

來換換口味吧！讓你的表達更豐富！

❶ 我們去陽明山郊遊。　**We went picnicking in Mt. Yang-Ming.**
　(相似短句) 我們昨天去野餐。　We went on a picnic yesterday.

❷ 春天鶯聲燕語。
There are many birds chirping around in spring.
　(相似短句) 森林裡迴盪著鳥叫聲。
　　The woods resounded with the chirping of birds.

❸ 那是令人驚嘆的風景。　**The scenery was breathtaking.**
　(相似短句) 那個景色太令人驚嘆了。　The scenery was fantastic.

❹ 樹木正在開花。　**The trees are in blossom.**
　(相似短句) 桃子樹在四月盛開。　The peach trees blossom out in April.

❺ 有陣舒服的微風。　**There was a nice breeze.**
　(相似短句) 那裡只有來自南海溫柔的風。
　　There were only gentle sea breeze from the south.

依樣畫葫蘆！套進去就能用！

(句型1) **～真的很享受。**
It's really enjoyable to...
(例句) 在冬天泡溫泉真的很享受。
It's really enjoyable to go to a hot spring in winter.

(句型2) **這樣的天氣很適合～**
The weather was good for us to...
(例句) 這樣的天氣很適合去野餐。
The weather was good for us to go on a picnic.

Unit 16
夏天游泳

社群人氣王！英文動態消息寫給你看！

I applied for the swimming course next month.
我報名了下個月的游泳課程。

👍 讚 56　💬 回覆 7

I am planning to take the test for being a lifeguard.
我打算要去考救生員執照。

👍 讚 36　💬 回覆 20

I really want to go to the beach and swim in the sea. –feeling so hot.
我真的好想去海邊游泳啊！覺得好熱！

👍 讚 130　💬 回覆 3

She went surfing in Hawaii! I can only surf the Internet at home…
她去夏威夷衝浪了！而我只能在家上網……

👍 讚 15　💬 回覆 12

I really want to try rafting. Is there anyone also interested in this?
我很想去泛舟，有誰對泛舟也有興趣的嗎？

👍 讚 92　💬 回覆 3

新手超必備！一個單字嘛欸通！

burning adj. 發熱的	**scorching** adj. 灼熱的	**summer** n. 夏天
swimming n. 游泳	**pool** n. 泳池	**float** v. 漂浮
relaxing adj. 放鬆的	**sweat** v. 流汗	

出門超實用！能聽會說一次搞定！

A I need to get a swimsuit for this summer. Laura asks me to go swimming with her.

B Yeah. You reminded me that it's the season for swimming. I can recommend some places other than a swimming pool for you.

A 我需要為這個夏天買件泳衣。蘿菈要我跟她去游泳。

B 對耶。你提醒我現在是游泳的季節。我可以推薦你一些除了游泳池的地方。

A Cool! Where are the places I can go? Sometimes the swimming pool is crowded in summer time.

B I often go swimming in whitewater, which is located in the deep forest in New Taipei city.

A 酷！還有哪些地方我可以去？有時候夏天的游泳池充滿了人潮。

B 我常常去新北市森林裡的急流游泳。

A Wouldn't it be dangerous? I just saw the news last week reporting a group of teenagers being saved from drowning.

B There's no lifeguard around whitewater. However, the depth of the water isn't deep.

A 那樣不會很危險嗎？我上禮拜才看到新聞報導，說有群少年溺水被救起來。

B 急流附近沒有救生員，但是水的深度並沒有很深。

A That's the thing. You probably didn't notice the vortex underneath the water, and that is the most dangerous part.

B Alright. I just wanted to recommend you another place to go for swimming. Thanks for reminding me of the danger of whitewater.

A 這就是重點。你可能沒有注意到水下暗藏的漩渦，而這也是最危險的地方。

B 好吧。我只是想推薦你另一個可以去的地方。謝謝你提醒我急流的危險。

Unit 16 夏天遊泳

酸甜苦辣 記下來！

Chocolate bars!!

Saturday, August 3

I went swimming with my younger brother today. There were many people taking a sunbath on the meadow. My brother and I chased about and splashed water on each other along the river. We were so excited that we played more than three hours. Not applying sun block to our bodies, our skin began to peel. Ha-ha. Both of us now look like chocolate bars.

巧克力棒！

8月3日星期六

我跟弟弟今天去游泳，大家都在草地上做日光浴。我和弟弟沿著河裡追逐與互相潑水，我們興奮的玩了超過三個小時。因為我們沒有擦防曬乳，我們兩人的皮膚開始脫皮。哈哈～我們兩個現在看起來像巧克力棒一樣！！

增廣見聞 超簡單！

Where can you go swimming in the summer except going to swimming pools? Wild swimming can be exciting but it's not fun at all to go swimming in a place that is not qualified as a safe place. You could meet the vortex that is hidden under deep water, or you are not able to estimate when the river will be in spate. Thus, it is possible for you to get drowned. Then where else? Water theme park is also a good choice. You could have loads of fun with all sorts of amusement facilities and without being concerned of safety issue.

夏天游泳除了泳池還有哪些好去處？在野外游泳可能是一件刺激的事，但如果你去的地方是沒有獲得安全認證的，那可就不好玩了。因為你有可能會遇到隱藏在水下的漩渦，或是遇到無預警的溪水暴漲，就有可能有溺水的危險。那還有哪些地方適合游泳呢？水上樂園也是一個不錯的選擇，你可以使用多種的娛樂設施玩樂，不用擔心安全問題。

❶ 整個夏天都熱炸了。
It is burning hot through the whole summer.
相似短句 整個夏天都悶熱不已。　The whole summer is scorching hot.

❷ 我每個週末都會去游泳。　**I went swimming each weekend.**
相似短句 我都在早上游泳，以避開人潮。
I went swimming every morning to avoid the crowd.

❸ 我相信游泳是最好的運動。
I believe swimming is the best exercise.
相似短句 我喜歡游泳，因為游泳既安全又溫和。
I love swimming because it's safe and mild.

❹ 泳池裡都是小朋友。
The swimming pool is crowded with children.
相似短句 泳池裡到處都是小朋友。
Kids are everywhere in the swimming pool.

❺ 游在泳池中真的很舒服。
It's so comfortable to swim in a swimming pool.
相似短句 游泳很好，泡在水裡也很令人放鬆。
Swimming is nice, and floating in the water is also relaxing.

依樣畫葫蘆！套進去就能用！

句型1 **只要～，我就會～**
Whenever..., I...

例句 只要我的侄女來，我就會帶她去游泳池。
Whenever my niece came over, I took her to the swimming pool.

句型2 **看起來～**
look like...

例句 看起來游泳池沒開門。
It looks like the pool is closed.

Unit 17
秋天遠足

社群人氣王！英文動態消息寫給你看！

Autumn is very cozy for taking a walk along the river bank.
秋天是很適合在河邊散步的季節。

👍 讚 56　　💬 回覆 7

We went hiking in the mountain today, and the autumn leaves are so spectacular.
我們今天去爬山，山裡的紅葉真壯觀。

👍 讚 36　　💬 回覆 20

We baked some chestnut for snack. It was really good.
我們烤了栗子當點心，很好吃。

👍 讚 130　　💬 回覆 3

I will go to harvest kakis with my brother next weekend.
下週末我要跟我哥哥去採柿子。

👍 讚 15　　💬 回覆 12

The wind is getting chilly that I have to put on my scarf.
風越來越冷了，我已經需要戴圍巾了。

👍 讚 92　　💬 回覆 3

新手超必備！一個單字嘛欸通！

nature n 自然	**leaves** n 葉子	**fall** n 秋天（美）
autumn n 秋天（英）	**hiking** n 健行	**cool** adj 涼爽的
blow v 吹拂	**turn** v 轉變	

出門超實用！能聽會說一次搞定！

Ⓐ Could you recommend some other things to do in autumn? I don't want to loose any chance to go out before winter comes.

Ⓑ Tramping might be a choice for you. Tramping is a walking trip, which is similar to hiking activity.

Ⓐ 你可以推薦我一些秋天可以做的事情嗎？在冬天來之前我不想失去出門的機會。

Ⓑ 遠足對你來說或許是個好選擇。遠足跟健行很像，是一種徒步旅行。

Ⓐ Thanks for your explanation, but I am not interested in hiking for no reason.

Ⓑ You must have misunderstood the idea of tramping. You don't actually climb a mountain; instead, the road for tramping is easier and smoother.

Ⓐ 謝謝你的解釋，但是我對於健行沒有興趣，沒有任何理由。

Ⓑ 你一定是誤解遠足的概念了。遠足所走的路是比較平順的，而不是叫你真的去爬一座山。

Ⓐ Great. I am interested in it now. So when can we plan the first tramping trip?

Ⓑ I will be off for three days at the end of October, and I think it's the best time to go on a tramping trip.

Ⓐ 讚。我現在有興趣了。所以我們什麼時候可以計畫第一次遠足？

Ⓑ 十月的最後三天我放假，我想那會是去遠足最好的時間。

Ⓐ Where to go? Another thing is that I cannot find that much information about tramping on the Internet.

Ⓑ We can go to Yilan. Trust me; you are going to fall in love with it, because the weather and the scenery are perfect for each other.

Ⓐ 去哪呢？還有件事，是我無法在網路上找到太多跟遠足有關的資訊。

Ⓑ 我們可以去宜蘭。相信我，你會愛上這玩意兒，因為那裡的天氣和景色會完美地交融。

酸甜苦辣 記下來！

Go hiking with grandpa

Sunday, October 27

I went hiking with my aged grandpa. Going hiking is very good to his health. Although it was fall, the sunshine was burning hot. We all enjoyed ourselves, but we were tired to death. In order to keep a good shape, I will still go hiking with my grandpa next time. My legs got muscular pains after getting home and so did grandpa's. I really wanted a body massage.

跟阿公去爬山

10月27日星期日

我跟我年邁的阿公去爬山，爬山對他的健康十分有益。雖然已經是秋天了，但是陽光還是很灼熱，我們都玩得很開心，但是也累壞了。為了要維持我的身材，我下次還是會跟阿公去爬山。到家以後我的腳好痠，而且阿公的腳也是，害我好想要來個全身按摩。

增廣見聞 超簡單！

In New Zealand, a long and vigorous walk is called tramping. In England, they call it "walk". Due to the limitation of topography, this kind of activity isn't common in Taiwan. However, in Europe or Australia, the "walking / tramping tour" is popular in summer and autumn. You can go walk from coast to coast, or walk along the lovely old county inn or cottages. For people in Taiwan, although it is hard to find an appropriate tramping route, autumn is still the best season to go travel.

在紐西蘭，花時間走一段費力的路被稱做「健行」，在英國，健行也被稱做「walk」。因為地形的限制，這種活動在台灣並不普遍，然而在歐洲、澳洲，健行是一種在夏秋季常被從事的活動。你可以從一個海岸走到下一個海岸，或是沿著美麗的鄉村小路走。在台灣雖然很難找到一條合適的健行道路，但秋天也還是一個棒的旅遊季節。

來換換口味吧！讓你的表達更豐富！

❶ 我們在長途的旅行後感到勞累。
We were fatigued after the long journey.
（相似短句）我們在長途旅行後累翻了。
We got worn out after a long journey.

❷ 我感到與大自然更貼近。 **I felt closer to nature.**
（相似短句）我喜歡自然。 I'm a nature lover.

❸ 樹葉轉紅。 **The leaves turned red.**
（相似短句）秋天時，樹葉變成金黃色。
The leaves turned yellow in fall.

❹ 秋天健行很不錯。 **It's good to go hiking in fall.**
（相似短句）秋天是健行的最佳時節。
Autumn is the best season for hiking.

❺ 秋天微風徐徐感覺很涼。
It is pretty cool with the breeze blowing around in fall.
（相似短句）我很享受秋天的微風。 I enjoy the easy breeze in fall.

依樣畫葫蘆！套進去就能用！

（句型1）～是個不錯的景致。
It's quite a view to see...
（例句）從山頂看這座城市的風景真不錯。
It's quite a view to see the city from the hill top.

（句型2）～對～十分有益。
be very good to...
（例句）今天的天氣很適合在公園裡踢足球。
Today's weather is very good to play soccer in the park.

Unit 18
冬天泡溫泉

社群人氣王！英文動態消息寫給你看！

I went to a hot spring trip with my family last weekend.
上週末和家人去了一趟溫泉之旅。

 讚 56　　回覆 7

I consider the hot spring in Japan to be the best in the world.
我覺得日本的溫泉是全世界最棒的。

讚 36　　回覆 20

Kids love hot spring eggs for it is tasty and fun.
小孩子很喜歡溫泉蛋，因為好吃又好玩。

讚 130　　回覆 3

It's weird to me wearing a swimming suit in the hot spring, while most of the Taiwanese people are very used to it.
我覺得穿泳衣泡溫泉很奇怪，但是大部分的臺灣人很習慣這樣。

讚 15　　回覆 12

After entering the hot spring, I feel comfortable and my body gets warmer.
洗完溫泉後，我覺得很舒服而且身體變暖了。

 讚 92　　回覆 3

新手超必備！一個單字嘛欸通！

freezing adj. 極冷的	**warm up** phr. 使暖和	**hot spring** n. 溫泉
bath n. 沐浴	**sulfur** n. 硫磺	**skin** n. 皮膚
cold adj. 冷的		

Ⓐ Did you check the news? An old man passed out when taking a hot spring bath.

Ⓑ I feel sorry for him and his family. Did the news specify the reason that caused the man's death?

Ⓐ 你注意到新聞了嗎？一個老男人在泡溫泉的時候過世了。

Ⓑ 我為他及他的家人感到遺憾。新聞有提到造成他死亡的原因嗎？

Ⓐ Yes. He has a record of heart disease, and he stayed in the hot spring for over 15 minutes.

Ⓑ Okay. That is the lesson for people. We have to be careful when reading those notifications while we enjoy the hot spring.

Ⓐ 有，他得過心臟病，而且他在溫泉裡待超過 15 分鐘。

Ⓑ 恩，這給人們上了一課。我們在享受溫泉的同時必須非常仔細地閱讀那些告示。

Ⓐ Alright, Sam, cheer up! I plan to go to Beitou for hot springs this weekend with my girlfriend. Do you want to join us?

Ⓑ What a coincidence! Kelly and I are going to Beitou as well. We love hot springs in Beitou so much.

Ⓐ 好了，山姆，提起精神！我計畫這周末要帶我女朋友去北投泡溫泉。你要加入我們嗎？

Ⓑ 多麼巧啊！凱莉和我也要去北投。我們超愛在北投泡溫泉。

Ⓐ Me too. I love the surroundings and the scenery around. Sometimes, I will imagine that I am in Japan.

Ⓑ Have you book the room yet? If not, we can help you with it. I have a VIP card from Season Spring hotel.

Ⓐ 我也是。我喜歡周圍的環境和景色。有時候我會幻想自己在日本。

Ⓑ 你們訂房間了嗎？如果還沒，我們可以幫你訂，我有季節溫泉飯店的 VIP。

Unit 18 冬天泡溫泉

酸甜苦辣 記下來！

Free but disgusting
Sunday, January 26
Spring baths are getting is more and more popular in Taiwan. Taking a hot spring bath does the skin good. I took a hot spring for free in Pei-Tou today. After long work hours in the office, soaking my body in a hot spring was a wonderful experience. But I saw somebody with skin disease soaking in the water, too. It was so gross that I got out of the pool immediately. Besides, the temperature of the hot spring was too hot to bear.

免費但是很噁心
1月26日星期日
溫泉在台灣越來越流行了，泡溫泉對皮膚很好。我今天到北投去泡免費的溫泉。在辦公室長時間的工作之後，泡在溫泉裡真的是很棒的經驗。但是我看到有皮膚病的人也下去泡，我覺得實在是太噁心了，我馬上就從池子裡跑出來。而且，那個溫泉的溫度也太熱讓人無法忍受。

增廣見聞 超簡單！

Taiwan is lucky to be located in between the plates, which results in having unique environments that can produce hot springs. The most special one might be springs in Green island. The spring there is an undersea spa that exists in only Italy, Japan and Taiwan. Taking hot springs can boost blood circulation, reduce stress and promote sleep. However, people should also be aware that it is better not to stay over 30 minutes in a hot spring, and drink water afterwards.

台灣地處板塊交界是很幸運的一件事，因為如此，我們有獨特的環境可以產出溫泉。在台灣溫泉中，最特別的當屬綠島的溫泉，那裏的溫泉是海底泉，全世界只有義大利、日本跟台灣擁有。泡溫泉可以促進血液循環，減少壓力、促進睡眠，但是人們還是得注意，最好不要在溫泉裡面泡超過 30 分鐘，而且泡完之後要記得補充水份。

來換換口味吧！讓你的表達更豐富！

❶ 天氣真是冷斃了。　**It's damn cold today.**

(相似短句) 今天冷翻了。　It's freaking freezing today.

❷ 我去泡溫泉讓身體變溫暖。

I went to the hot spring to warm up my body.

(相似短句) 泡玩溫泉後，我的體溫變高了。
My core body temperature increased after the hot spring.

❸ 我以前從來沒泡過溫泉。

I've never been to a spring bath before.

(相似短句) 我以前從沒試過溫泉。　I haven't tried hot spring before.

❹ 泡溫泉對皮膚很好。

Taking a hot spring bath does the skin good.

(相似短句) 硫磺溫泉對皮膚很好。
Sulfur spring is excellent for your skin.

❺ 在這種冷天泡溫泉真的很舒服。

It's very comfortable to take a hot spring bath in such a cold day.

(相似短句) 在冷天裡泡溫泉真是太棒了。
Taking a hot spring bath in the cold weather feels so great.

依樣畫葫蘆！套進去就能用！

(句型1) 從～離開。
get away from...

(例句) 終於能從那座陰鬱的城市離開，我真是太高興了。
I was so happy that I could finally get away from the cloudy city.

(句型2) ～太噁心了！
It was so gross that...

(例句) 因為很噁心，所以小孩在溫泉裡尿尿。
It was so gross when I saw that the kid pced in the hot spring.

Unit 19
出國旅遊

社群人氣王！英文動態消息寫給你看！

Why does everyone post the photo of the aircraft wing when they go on a trip?

為什麼大家出國旅遊的時候都在傳機翼的照片？

👍讚 56　💬回覆 7

I lost my passport and mobile phone in Paris. What should I do now?

我在巴黎弄丟了我的護照和手機，我現在該怎麼辦？

👍讚 36　💬回覆 20

We went skiing this morning and it was fun!

今天早上我們去滑雪，好好玩。

👍讚 130　💬回覆 3

The cuisine in Italy is so delicious and cheap comparing to other countries in Europe.

義大利的美食比歐洲的其他國家還好吃又便宜。

👍讚 15　💬回覆 12

I bought some souvenir for my family and friends.

我買了一些紀念品給家人和朋友。

👍讚 92　💬回覆 3

新手超必備！一個單字嘛欸通！

travel ⓥ 旅遊	**abroad** adv 國外的	**foreign** adj 外國的
trip ⓝ 旅程	**plane** ⓝ 飛機	**delay** ⓥ 延遲
flight ⓝ 航班	**airsick** adj 暈機的	**turbulence** ⓝ 亂流

出門超實用！能聽會說一次搞定！

Ⓐ I booked a flight ticket and the hostel at the travel tourism exhibition. Anyone wants to join?

Ⓑ Ben, you haven't even told us when it is and where the destination is.

Ⓐ 我在旅遊展訂了飛機票和青年旅館。有人要加入嗎？

Ⓑ 班，你都還沒有告訴我們時間及地點。

Ⓐ Sorry. I'm just too excited about it. I plan to go next summer around July, and the destination will be Sri Lanka.

Ⓑ Cool, man. Please count me in. I have been wanting to visit that place for a long time, just that I couldn't find a travel mate.

Ⓐ 抱歉。我只是對於這個太興奮了。我計畫明年夏天大概七月的時候去斯里蘭卡。

Ⓑ 酷。請算我一份吧。我想去這地方想很久了，只是我遲遲無法找到一個旅伴。

Ⓐ Okay. There is only one spot left now. I've searched some information on the Internet, and looks like ten days are the best length of time to travel in Sri Lanka.

Ⓑ Do we need to apply visa for that? And how much is the visa? Why did you choose to go in July?

Ⓐ 好。現在只剩一個缺了。我已經透過網路查了些資訊，看起來去斯里蘭卡玩十天是最佳的旅遊長度。

Ⓑ 我們需要申請簽證嗎？簽證多少錢啊？還有為什麼選在七月呢？

Ⓐ Yes, we need to apply visa, but I am not sure how much it costs. We can avoid rain season if we travel in July.

Ⓑ I see. I will check how much the visa is, and also I will ask my friend if they want to join us.

Ⓐ 是的，我們需要申請簽證，但我不太確定多少錢。我們七月去可以避開雨季。

Ⓑ 了解。我會去確認簽證需要多少錢，我也會去問有意願加入我們的朋友。

Unit 19 出國旅遊

Part 3 全民樂逍遙

酸甜苦辣 記下來！

Being stupid in Paris

Monday, January 6

I dreamed about travelling abroad. I was sick of work. Therefore, I went travelling. I strolled in Paris and went to Versailles Palace. While taking a picture, I stumbled and nearly fell on my face. How embarrassed I was! I really wished I had paid attention to the pit in the ground.

在巴黎耍蠢

1月6日星期一

我一直都很想要出國旅遊。我好厭倦我的工作，所以我去旅行。我在巴黎街頭閒逛，也去凡爾賽皇宮看看。當我要拍照的時候，不小心絆了一下，差一點就要跌個狗吃屎。真的超尷尬的！我真希望我有注意到地上那個坑洞。

增廣見聞 超簡單！

Searching on the Internet or with books might be the best way to find a good deal on flight tickets, or finding hotel rooms for individual travelers. Besides, you can sometimes get good deal from travel and tourism exhibition which is held once every season. Traveling abroad with a Taiwan passport is really convenient now. There are over a hundred countries that offer Taiwanese a visa waiver, including countries in the European Union and the United States.

在網路或書上搜尋低價機票跟住宿，對自助旅行者來說是最省錢的方式，除此之外，在每一季的旅展中偶爾也可以找到划算的價格。現在，用台灣的護照出國可說是非常方便的，目前已有超過 100 個國家給予台灣免簽證的服務，其中也包括歐盟國家和美國。

① 我花很多錢出國旅遊。 **I spent a lot of money traveling.**

(相似短句) 出國旅遊花了我很多錢。
It cost me a lot of money to travel abroad.

② 我在國外旅遊。 **I traveled abroad.**

(相似短句) 我曾在幾個國家旅行過。
I have traveled in some foreign countries.

③ 我幾個星期以前決定要去旅行。
I decided to go on a trip a few weeks ago.

(相似短句) 這個旅行算是臨時起意的。
This traveling trip is kind of a last-minute thing.

④ 飛機在兩個小時的誤點後起飛。
The plane took off after a delay of two hours.

(相似短句) 這班飛機誤點了兩個小時。
The flight was delayed by two ours.

⑤ 飛機一起飛我就暈機了。
I got airsick when the airplane took off.

(相似短句) 亂流讓我暈機。 The turbulence made me airsick.

(句型1) **注意～**
paid attention to...

(例句) 我搭公車時注意我的包包，因為我的錢包在裡頭。
I paid attention to my purse when taking the bus because my wallet was in it.

(句型2) **更慘的是～**
It was even more miserable that...

(例句) 更慘的是，我發現我的護照不見了。
It was even more miserable that I found my passport missing.

Unit 20
奧林匹克運動會

社群人氣王！英文動態消息寫給你看！

Everyone is looking forward to the opening ceremony of the Olympic Games.
大家都很期待奧運會的開幕式。

👍讚 56　💬回覆 7

When it comes to the Olympics, swimming is the must-see sport to me.
一提到奧運，對我來說游泳是一定要看的項目。

👍讚 36　💬回覆 20

I saw the Olympic archery on TV. It was so cool that I decided to learn archery.
我在電視轉播上看到奧運的射箭比賽。因為實在太帥氣了我決定要學射箭。

👍讚 130　💬回覆 3

Taekwondo is the most popular sport among Taiwanese audiences.
跆拳道是最受臺灣觀眾矚目的項目。

👍讚 15　💬回覆 12

I hope one day we no longer have to use the name of "Chinese Taipei", but "Taiwan" to attend the Olympics.
希望有一天我們不再需要使用「中華台北」的名義參加奧運，而是用「臺灣」。

👍讚 92　💬回覆 3

新手超必備！一個單字嘛欸通！

stadium ⋒ 體育場	**race** ⋓⋒ 賽跑	**ticket** ⋒ 票卷
upcoming ⓐ 即將到來的	**afford** ⋓ 負擔	**capture** ⋓ 捕捉
appreciate ⋒ 欣賞；表示感激		**painting** ⋒ 畫作

出門超實用！能聽會說一次搞定！

A I went to Athens this summer, where the Olympic games originated. I just couldn't believe that I was at the ancient stadium and listening to an audio guide.

B I envy you. But just when you were in Athens, the Olympics started! I spent nearly two weeks following games that I was interested in.

A 我今年暑假去了奧運的起源地——雅典。我當時簡直無法相信我在古代的體育場聽語音導覽。

B 我羨慕死你了。不過當你在雅典時，奧運比賽正好開始！我花了快兩個周末的時間追蹤我感興趣的比賽。

A Which game are you interested in? I love watching Michael Phelps swim.

B I know him! People call him "The Baltimore Bullet"! I love watching Usian Bolt in race matches.

A 哪種比賽你感興趣？我喜歡看麥克‧菲爾普斯游泳。

B 我知道他！人們稱他為「巴爾的摩子彈」！我喜歡看尤塞恩‧博爾特的賽跑。

A I did make the plan to go to London for the Olympic Games, but the room rates and prices for tickets were crazy. I couldn't afford it.

B Then I will suggest you start saving money for the 2016 Summer Olympics in Brazil.

A 我曾計畫過去倫敦看奧運比賽，但住房價格和票價實在是太誇張。我負擔不起。

B 那我會建議你開始為 2016 年在巴西的夏季奧運存錢。

A Thanks. I prefer to visit Russia for the winter Olympic games this year. I can afford it.

B That's great! I did't know you love watching winter Olympic games as well. Let's go skiing next time.

A 謝啦。但我比較想去今年冬天在俄羅斯的奧運。我可以負擔得起。

B 太棒了！我不知道你也喜歡看冬季奧運。我們下次去滑雪吧。

Unit 20 奧林匹克運動會

酸甜苦辣 記下來！

Volunteer

Thursday, June 19

Dad promised me that we could go to Brazil in 2016, after I finish the exam. I searched online for information about the Olympics in Rio. Surprisingly, I saw that they are searching for 2,000 IT volunteers to take the Game to the world. I then applied for the job secretly without telling anyone. I started to dream that I would be chosen to be one of the volunteers working on scoreboards and providing IT support, which is my major. I can be so close to the game right there in Rio! Hope my dream can come true. Sadly, all I can do is wait for the result to be published.

志工

6月19日星期四

爸爸答應我，等我考完試之後他會在 2016 年帶我去巴西。我上網找了里約奧林匹克的資料，令人驚訝的是，我看到他們正在招募兩千名資訊志工，幫忙傳播奧運的訊息到全世界；於是，我就偷偷的申請，沒有告訴任何人。我開始夢想自己會被選為志工，可以處理得分板，我主修的資訊領域專長也可以派上用場。另外，我還可以真的很貼近比賽現場！希望我的夢想可以成真，但令人傷心的是，我現在能做的只有等候結果了。

增廣見聞 超簡單！

The upcoming Olympic games in 2016 will be in Rio de Janeiro, Brazil. The following Olympic games will be in Tokyo, Japan. According to news reports, high school students in Japan are working very hard on studying and learning English, in order to welcome medias, athletes of all countries. Recently, there are high school students offering free tour guides especially for foreigners for practicing their English. From this news, we can tell the importance of English when holding such International Events.

即將到來的 2016 年奧運將會在巴西的里約熱內盧舉辦，而接著，2020 年的奧運將會在東京舉辦。根據報導，日本高中生已經在努力加強英文，以便隨時歡迎屆時來到東京的各國媒體與運動員，最近，更已經有高中生特別針對外國人提供免費導覽，藉此來練習他們的英文能力。由此，我們也可以知道英文對於舉辦國際活動的重要性。

❶ 我上網找了關於里約奧林匹克的資料。
I searched online for information about the Olympics in Rio.
(相似短句) 我上網找了關於里約奧林匹克的資料。
I searched the Rio Olympics information online.

❷ 令人驚訝的是，我看到他們正在招募兩千名資訊志工。
Surprisingly, I saw that they are searching for 2,000 IT volunteers.
(相似短句) 意外的是我發現他們正在招募兩千名資訊志工。
Accidentally, I found them looking for 2000 IT volunteers.

❸ 希望我的夢想可以成真。　**Hope my dream can come true.**
(相似短句) 希望我可以實現夢想。　Hope I can realize my dream.

❹ 傷心的是我現在能做的只有等候結果了。
Sadly, all I can do is wait for the result to be published.
(相似短句) 在他們公佈結果之前，我只能等待。
I can only wait before they publish the result.

❺ 我還可以很貼近里約的比賽現場！
I can be so close to the game right there in Rio!
(相似短句) 我還可以在里約的比賽現場！
I can be on the spot of the game in Rio.

依樣畫葫蘆！套進去就能用！

(句型1) **找尋什麼……**
Searched for...
(例句) 我在線上找工作。
I searched for the jobs online.

(句型2) **我所能做的……**
All I can do is....
(例句) 我所能做的就是找出正確答案。
All I can do is to find out the correct information.

Unit 21
世界盃足球賽

社群人氣王！英文動態消息寫給你看！

Bars are crowded with people wearing soccer uniforms at 3 am.
凌晨三點的酒吧裡塞滿了穿著足球球衣的足球迷們。

👍讚 56　💬回覆 7

My neighbors are so noisy. I know the World Cup is exciting but it's 2:30 in the morning! I need to sleep!
我的鄰居好吵。我知道世界盃很精彩，但是現在是凌晨兩點半欸！我需要睡覺啊！

👍讚 36　💬回覆 20

My boyfriend flew to Brazil to see the World Cup. Man, he is so crazy about it!
男友飛去巴西看世界盃了。天啊，他真的不是普通的熱衷啊。

👍讚 130　💬回覆 3

They say girls hate the World Cup because boys are so crazy about it.
他們說女生都討厭世足賽，因為男生們都太熱衷了。

👍讚 15　💬回覆 12

I stayed up late watching the World Cup with my friends last night. It was a really good game.
我昨天晚上跟朋友一起熬夜看世足賽，那真的是一場很棒的比賽。

👍讚 92　💬回覆 3

新手超必備！一個單字嘛欸通！

movement ⓝ 動作，移動	**goal keeper** ⓝ 守門員	**loose** ⓥ 失去
speed ⓝ 速度	**acceleration** ⓝ 加速	**training** ⓝ 訓練
championship ⓝ 冠軍	**adjust** ⓥ 調整	

出門超實用！能聽會說一次搞定！

A Kin, are you okay? Stop yawning. It looks like you didn't get enough sleep recently.

B I got only four hours to sleep last night. I think it was worth it, because France won the game against England.

A 金，你還好嗎？不要再打哈欠了。看起來你最近並沒有足夠的睡眠。

B 我昨晚只有睡四小時。我認為非常值得，因為法國贏得了和英格蘭的比賽。

A Wait, you were watching the game last night? To be honest, I watched world cup every night.

B Oh my! Are you trying to hide the truth that you also did not get enough sleep?

A 等等，你昨晚看了比賽？老實說，我每天晚上都在看世界盃。

B 喔我的天啊！你是想試著隱藏你也沒足夠睡眠的事實嗎？

A I'm not cheating. Anyway, the game last night could be called the "classic" filled with excitement.

B Literally speaking, it's the goalkeeper who saved France. Otherwise, we probably lost the game.

A 我沒有要隱瞞。總而言之，昨晚的比賽可以稱之為「經典」且充滿了刺激。

B 不誇張，是那守門員救了法國。不然我們很有可能輸了比賽。

A You are right. There's a video clip showing every movement when he stopped the ball, which is impressive.

B France's next game with Brazil is on Sunday! I hope France can win this time as well.

A 你說的對。短片秀出了他接下球的每一瞬間，令人驚艷。

B 法國和巴西的下場比賽在週日！希望法國也能贏得這次比賽。

酸甜苦辣 記下來！

My favorite football players!!!

Tuesday, July 8

The News broadcast is all about the accident of Neymar during the game with Coloumbia. His backbone was injured in the game. He is one of my favorite football players. Thus, I just can't help feeling the cruelty that athletes might go through. What if it is a serious accident, then his career may just stop. Luckily, the condition of his injury was no big deal. The news also indicates that there are fewer injuries in this year's World Cup, comparing to the injury numbers with previous World Cups. The performance of the team is highly associated to the number of injuries, which is probably why German won.

我心中最喜愛的足球員

7月8日星期二

新聞一直在轉播內馬爾在跟哥倫比亞比賽中受傷的消息，他的脊椎骨頭裂掉了。他一直是我心中最喜歡的足球員，因為這則新聞，我會一直想到運動員需要承受的風險，如果今天是很重大的意外，那麼他很可能將被迫中止職業生涯。但幸運的是，他的傷勢最後確定沒有大礙，且新聞也有報導，這次比賽的受傷人數比往年都低；而團隊合作能力跟受傷數量也呈高度相關，這大概就是為什麼德國最後會贏得冠軍。

增廣見聞 超簡單！

The game mentioned in the conversation is the FIFA world cup. FIFA world cup in 2014 was held in Brazil. German won the championship of 2014 FIFA world cup. Before the game, reports revealed the high technology that is used for training in Germany. They use a system to measure the speed, distance, acceleration, and heart rate of every football player. Thus, the training can be adjusted according to the data.

在對話中提到是世界盃指的是「足球世界盃」。2014 足球世界盃今年在巴西舉辦，德國是這一次的冠軍隊伍。在比賽前，已有報導指出德國將高科技用於訓練過程中，他們使用了一套可以幫每一位球員測量速度、距離、加速度、心跳頻率的系統，因此訓練方式可以隨時依數據調整。

來換換口味吧！讓你的表達更豐富！

❶ 如果是個嚴重的意外，他的職業生涯可能就此停止了。

What if it is a serious accident, then his career may just stop.

(相似短句) 嚴重的意外會毀了他的職業生涯。

A serious accident could ruin his career.

❷ 他在比賽中摔斷了脊椎骨。

His backbone was injured in the game.

(相似短句) 他在比賽中摔斷了脊椎骨。

He broke his backbone in the game.

❸ 我不得不一直想到運動員所需要承受的殘酷。

I just can't help feeling the cruelty that athletes might go through.

(相似短句) 我一直想到運動員所需要承受的殘酷。

I keep thinking about the cruelty that athletes should suffer.

❹ 幸運的，傷勢無嚴重大礙。

Luckily, the condition of the injury was no big deal.

(相似短句) 幸運的，傷勢並無大礙。

Fortunately, the injury does not cause a great matter.

❺ 而團隊表現能力則是跟受傷人數是有高度相關的。

The performance of the team is highly associated to the number of injuries.

(相似短句) 而團隊表現能力會影響受傷人數。

The performance of the team can affect the number of injuries.

依樣畫葫蘆！套進去就能用！

(句型1) 我不得不～

I can't help but...

(例句) 我不得不大聲尖叫當我知道德國隊得冠軍時。

I can't help but shout out loud when I knew Germany won the championship.

(句型2) 跟……高度相關

is highly associated with...

(例句) 造成受傷得原因跟哥倫比亞隊高度相關。

The cause of the injury is highly associated with the national team of Colombia.

Unit 22
亞洲運動會

社群人氣王！英文動態消息寫給你看！

I didn't know that the flag of North Korea is forbidden in the Game.

我不知道朝鮮國旗在仁川亞運當中是被禁止的。

👍 讚 56　💬 回覆 7

I was traveling in South Korea when the 2014 Asian Games were held.

仁川亞運的時候我剛好在韓國旅行。

👍 讚 36　💬 回覆 20

China is so strong that she won 100 or more medals than South Korea.

中國好強，比韓國多贏了一百多面獎牌。

👍 讚 130　💬 回覆 3

I consider table tennis the most fierce and exciting sport.

我認為桌球是最刺激又激烈的項目。

👍 讚 15　💬 回覆 12

When it comes to the Asian Game, baseball might be the most popular one.

提到亞運，最受矚目的項目大概就是棒球了吧。

👍 讚 92　💬 回覆 3

新手超必備！一個單字嘛欸通！

participate Ⓥ 參與	**boycott** Ⓥⓝ 杯葛（抵制）	**dispute** Ⓥⓝ 爭議
medal ⓝ 獎牌	**recruit** Ⓥ 招募	**qualification** ⓝ 資格
rank Ⓥⓝ 排名	**athlete** ⓝ 運動員	

出門超實用！能聽會說一次搞定！

A The 17th Asian Games will take place for 16 days in Incheon, South Korea, from September 19th to October 4th, 2014.

B Yeah, I know. I will go visit Incheon with our National team and send the first-hand news back to Taiwan.

A 第 17 屆亞運從 2014 年 9 月 19 號到 10 月 4 號共 16 天，將會在韓國仁川舉行。

B 恩，我知道。我會跟國家代表隊一起去仁川，把第一手資訊送回台灣

A What a fantastic job! I will definitely stand by the television to see those athletes' performances.

B You bet! You know what; even North Korea will participate in the Asian Games.

A 多麼棒的工作啊！我鐵定會守在電視機旁，看那些運動員的表現。

B 最好是！你知道嗎？連北韓也會參加這次的亞運。

A I thought they were boycotted because of the disputes with South Korea, but it's good to see them anyway.

B I am looking forward to the performance of Taiwan this time. Last time, we earned nearly 40 medals! I wish we could get more this year.

A 我以為他們因為和南韓的糾紛而不能參賽，不過能看到他們倒也不錯。

B 我非常期待台灣這次的表現。上一次我們贏了將近 40 面獎牌！希望今年能贏更多。

A We will! Our baseball team will definitely win the champion this year. I can't accept that we keep losing games to South Korea.

B Well. This year we recruited two oversea baseball players to join our national team, so it's possible we can win the championship.

A 我們會的。我們棒球隊今年必定會奪冠。我無法接受我們一直輸給南韓。

B 恩。今年我們延攬了兩位海外球員加入國家代表隊，所以我們很有可能奪得這次冠軍的頭銜！

Unit 22 亞洲運動會

酸甜苦辣 記下來！

Gold medal plate competition

Sunday, September 28

Gold medal plate competition between Taiwan and Korea will be held at 5pm this afternoon. I can't wait for the game to begin! Jimmy and I are going to Taipei city council to watch the game. I enjoy watching the game with other supporters. Also, I can enjoy watching it on a large screen displaying the live game. I will prepare a cheer megaphone and a cheer headband for watching the game. Jimmy will prepare some snacks and drinks, and a red cloth with the word "TAIWAN IS THE CHAMPION!" on it. Other then all that, I look forward to hearing something new of what the anchor might say.

金牌爭奪戰

9月28日星期天

台韓金牌戰將會在今天下午五點舉行。我等不及比賽開始了！吉米跟我會去市政府看比賽。我很喜歡跟一大群支持者一起用大螢幕看比賽播出，我準備了加油棒跟加油頭帶可以在現場用。吉米則會準備零食、飲料跟紅布條，上面會寫上「台灣是冠軍！」，除了這些，我還很期待這次播報員會用什麼新奇的方式報導。

增廣見聞 超簡單！

Asian game is held every four years for athletes around Asia. This game is recognized by the Olympics, and the record in Asia games will effect the qualifications of joining the Olympic games. This year, the game was held in Incheon, Korea. Taiwan earned 51 medals in total and is ranked no.9 among all Asian countries based on the numbers of medal. The following next Asian games will be held in Jakarta, Indonesia in 2018.

亞運是為亞洲選手舉辦的四年一次運動會，它為奧運官方所認可，所以在亞運中的比賽成績也同時是決定能否參加奧運的關鍵。今年亞運在韓國仁川舉行，台灣總共獲得了 51 面獎牌，在亞洲國家中排名第九；而下一屆的亞運則會在 2018 年於印尼雅加達舉行。

❶ 我等不及比賽開始了！ **I can't wait for the game to begin.**

相似短句 我好緊張即將開始的比賽！ I feel so excited for the upcoming game.

❷ 我很喜歡跟一大群支持者一起看比賽。
I enjoy watching the game with other supporters

相似短句 我喜歡跟著大群的支持者一起看比賽。

I love being with other supporters to root for the team.

❸ 除了這些，我還很期待這次主播會說什麼新的東西！
Other than all that, I look forward to hearing something new of what the anchor might say.

相似短句 除了比賽，我還很期待這次主播會說什麼新的東西！

Other than the game itself, I expect what something new the anchor will be saying this time.

❹ 吉米跟我會去臺北市政府看比賽。
Jimmy and I are going to Taipei city council to watch the game.

相似短句 吉米跟我選擇去臺北市政府看比賽。

Jimmy and I chose to go to Taipei city council to enjoy the game.

❺ 台韓金牌戰在今天下午五點舉行。
Gold medal plate competition between Taiwan and Korea will be held at 5pm this afternoon.

相似短句 台韓將在今天下午五點爭奪金牌。

Taiwan and Korea is going to compete for the gold medal plate at 5pm this afternoon.

依樣畫葫蘆！套進去就能用！

句型1 為……準備……
Prepare...for...

例句 我替主播準備水。
I prepared water for the anchor.

句型2 除此之外
Other than that,

例句 除此之外我還會到機場歡迎我們隊回來。
Other than that, I will also go to the airport to welcome our team back.

Unit 23
世界大學運動會

社群人氣王！英文動態消息寫給你看！

Taiwan is going to host the Universiade in 2017.
臺灣即將要主辦 2017 年的世大運。

👍 讚 56　　💬 回覆 7

I am working hard in order to have a chance to attend the Universiade.
我很努力的訓練，希望可以有機會參加世大運。

👍 讚 36　　💬 回覆 20

Hosting the Univeriade is a good opportunity for people from other countries to know Taiwan.
主辦世大運是個讓外國人認識臺灣的好機會。

👍 讚 130　　💬 回覆 3

Besides baseball and basketball, sports are not that popular in Taiwan.
除了棒球和籃球之外，臺灣其他運動不怎麼受到歡迎。

👍 讚 15　　💬 回覆 12

The Universiade might be a good chance to know how many terrific and potential athletes we have.
世大運或許是個讓我們瞭解我們有多少優秀又有潛力的運動員的好契機。

👍 讚 92　　💬 回覆 3

新手超必備！一個單字嘛欸通！

organize ♥ 組織　　university ⁿ 大學　　Universiade ⁿ 世界大學運動會
attend ♥ 參與　　demonstrate ♥ 展現　　athletes village ⁿ 選手村
construction ⁿ 建設　　talent ⁿ 才華

出門超實用！能聽會說一次搞定！

Ⓐ There's a thousand days left to welcome the World University Games in Taipei.

Ⓑ My mom participated in organizing the event from 2012, and she said that the contructions has been delayed. Hopefully, it will be done by then.

Ⓐ 現在離台北的世界大學運動會開始只剩下幾千天的時間了。

Ⓑ 我媽從 2012 年開始參與籌辦這場盛事。她說工程有延誤，希望能如期完成。

Ⓐ But before 2017, we can join the Universiade in 2015 in Gwangju, Korea. World University Games is held every two years.

Ⓑ The winter Universiade will be held at the same year at a different place. Those athletes are going to Spain in 2015!

Ⓐ 但是 2017 年前，我們可以參加 2015 年在韓國光州廣域市舉辦的世大運。世大運每兩年辦一次。

Ⓑ 冬季世大運會在同年不同地點舉辦。那些運動員在 2015 年會去西班牙。

Ⓐ Taiwan has never attended the Universiade until 1987. But the results of the game soar up afterward.

Ⓑ Wish we could get more medals in South Korea and Taiwan games!

Ⓐ 台灣直至 1987 年前都沒有參加過世大運，不過我們的比賽表現還是有急起直追。

Ⓑ 希望我們可以在南韓和台灣贏得更多獎牌。

Ⓐ Universiade offers great chances for young athletes to demonstrate their talent.

Ⓑ I agree. I especially like the idea of promoting "exercise" into our daily life as well.

Ⓐ 世大運提供年輕選手一個很好的機會來展現他們的才能。

Ⓑ 我同意。我還特別喜歡推廣每天運動這想法。

Part 4 全台瘋運動

酸甜苦辣 記下來！

National Delegates
Friday, October 3
My coach tolde me that I have a chance to be a national delegate for weight lifting. I was so happy to hear that and I truly wish I could attend Universiade in 2017 as a national delegate. I am currently a freshman in college doing my second semester, so that means I have two more years to prepare for the game. Mommy and daddy feel happy when they heard the news but they also reminded me that I should not ignore my study in college. I am grateful because my family did not stop me from my interest, in weight lifting. Thus, I will not make them feel disappointed with me.

國家代表
10月3日星期五
教練跟我說我有可能被選為舉重的國家代表，我聽到這個消息真的很開心，也非常希望我可以以國家代表的身份參加 2017 年的世界大學運動會。我是正在讀大一第二學期的新生，這表示我還有兩年可以為比賽做準備，爸爸媽媽聽到這個消息也都替我開心，同時也提醒我不要忽略了課業。我很感激我的家人沒有扼殺我對於舉重的興趣，所以我不會讓他們對我失望的。

增廣見聞 超簡單！

Comparing to Sport meets we used to attend in school, the Universiad is an international sports event. Universiads in English is called "World University Games" for university athletes. The sport event is held every two years in different cities in different countries. The next Universiad will take place at Gwangju, South Korea. And the following Universiad in 2017 will be in Taipei, Taiwan. Currently, there are several constructions undergoing, such as the Taipei Arena, and the Athlete's village in Linko city.

世界大學運動會（世大會），相較於我們一般參加過的學校運動會來說是個國際級運動競賽。世大會一詞在英語用字中還有另一種更直白的說法為「World University Game」，是專為大學運動員所舉辦。此一運動競賽每兩年會在不同的國家、城市舉辦，下一次是在南韓光州，而再下一場則是會於 2017 年在台北舉辦，現在已經有數個建設正在進行，例如台北大巨蛋以及位於林口的選手村。

來換換口味吧！讓你的表達更豐富！

1 教練跟我說我有機會被選為舉重國家代表。
My coach told me that I will have a chance to be a national delegate as the weight lifter.

(相似短句) 教練跟我說我有機會被選為舉重國家代表。
My coach says it is possible for me to be chosen as a national delegate for weight lifting.

2 我現在是正在讀第二學期的大一新生。
I am currently a freshman in college doing my second semester.

(相似短句) 我現在是正在讀第二學期的大一新生。
This is my first year in college and I am doing my second semester.

3 我不會讓他們對我失望的。
I will not make them feel disappointed with me.

(相似短句) 我不會讓他們對我失望的。 I will not let my parents lose hope in me.

4 我很感激我的家人沒有阻擋我的舉重的興趣。
I am grateful because my family did not stop me from my interest.

(相似短句) 我很感激我的家人沒有反對我成為一名舉重選手。
I am grateful that my family did not oppose my will to be a weight lifter.

5 我不要忽略了課業。 **I should not ignore my study in college.**

(相似短句) 我應該要專注於課業。 I should stay focused on my study in college.

依樣畫葫蘆！套進去就能用！

(句型1) **阻擋……去……**
Stop...from...

(例句) 爸爸並沒有阻擋我追求夢想。
Dad did not stop me from pursuing my dream.

(句型2) **有機會做～**
to have the chance to do sth...

(例句) 我很開心我有機會加入這團隊。
I am lucky to have the chance to join the team.

美分美秒，聽說讀寫Everyday

Unit 24
聞名國際的台灣選手

社群人氣王！英文動態消息寫給你看！

Thanks to the news, everyone in Taiwan knows Jeremy Lin.
託新聞的福，幾乎所有的臺灣人都知道林書豪。

👍 讚 56　　💬 回覆 7

There was a time when Jeremy Lin was so popular in Taiwan that kids all wanted to play basketball and be like him.
曾經有段時間林書豪在臺灣紅到孩子們都想打籃球，想變得跟他一樣。

👍 讚 36　　💬 回覆 20

I am a fan of Lu Yen-hsun, and he is the reason why I started playing tennis.
我是盧彥勳的球迷，並且他是我開始打網球的原因。

👍 讚 130　　💬 回覆 3

Yani Tseng is the most famous golfer in Taiwan.
曾雅妮是臺灣最有名的高爾夫選手。

👍 讚 15　　💬 回覆 12

I can see Yani Tseng's commercial advertisement everywhere.
不管在哪裡都看得到曾雅妮的廣告。

👍 讚 92　　💬 回覆 3

新手超必備！一個單字嘛欸通！

persistence ⓝ 堅持	**attitude** ⓝ 態度	**career** ⓝ 職業
professional ⓐⓓⓙ 專業的	**apply** ⓥ 申請	**estimate** ⓥ 估計
Linsanity ⓝ 林來瘋	**earn** ⓥ 爭取	

出門超實用！能聽會說一次搞定！

A My friend Diva, who is from the United States, has been asking me things about Jeremy Lin all the time, ever since she knew that I am from Taiwan.

B I have the same issue as yours. Betty, who attends Chinese class in Taiwan, has invited me to go to Taoyuan to watch a Golf game because Ya-ni Tseng will be in the game.

A 當我美國的朋友蒂娃知道我來自台灣時，就不斷地向我詢問關於林書豪的消息。

B 我跟你有相同的問題。來台灣上中文課的貝蒂也因為曾雅妮會出場的關係，邀請我去桃園看高爾夫球比賽。

A Both our friends are crazy! But I do feel happy to see Jeremy Lin and Ya-Ni Tseng become so popular around the world, and they are from Taiwan.

B I agree! Don't forget another famous tennis player, Rendy Lu. I became one of his fans on his Facebook fan page.

A 我們的兩位朋友都瘋了！但是看到台灣出身的選手們這麼受歡迎我非常開心。

B 我同意。也別忘了另外一位知名的網球手，盧彥勳。我是他臉書粉絲專頁的其中一員。

A Me too. I love his attitude of being polite and persistence on his career as a professional tennis player.

B Also, I collected all the reports and magazines that is about Jeremy Lin, the Linsanity!

A 我也是。我喜歡他的謙和有禮，以及在專業網球選手職涯上堅持的態度。

B 我也收集了關於林書豪；也就是「林來瘋」全部的報導及雜誌。

A Wow. He is coming back from the United States this summer because Nike invited him to teach basketball in a summer camp.

B Are you serious? I will definitely apply for that summer camp! Thanks for the news, buddy.

A 哇。Nike 邀請他在台灣的暑期營隊指導籃球，所以今年夏天他會從美國回來。

B 你是認真的嗎？我一定會申請今年的暑期營隊！多謝提供資訊，兄弟。

美分美秒，聽說讀寫Everyday

酸甜苦辣 記下來！

Good News!!
Sunday, July 20
The deal is set! Lakers traded Jeremy Lin from Rockets this summer. I became one of his fans when Linsanity were at rage in 2012. I am happy to see the news, although I am also quite concerned about the cooperation between Jeremy and Kobe Bryant. Except the news about Jeremy Lin, there are also good news about Yani Tseng. She hit the wall after 2012. She hasn't been ranked as no.1 in world Golf rankings after 2012. However, the good news is that she is back! Currently, she is ranked no.20 and trying so hard to pass the obstacles and break other's doubt on her.

好消息！
7月20日星期天
交易確定了！林書豪今年夏天會換到湖人隊，我在 2012 年林來瘋訊瘋時就成為了他的粉絲，所以我很高興看到這個消息，但也對於柯比（Kobe）跟他之間的合作有點擔心。除了林書豪的新聞之外，還有一個關於曾雅妮的好消息，她自從在 2012 年遇到撞牆期之後就沒有再登上世界第一，而好消息就是：她要回歸了！目前，她在世界的排名已經到了 20 名，她很努力的要克服障礙並瓦解大家對她的懷疑。

增廣見聞 超簡單！

You can never under estimate the power of Taiwanese athletes. "Linsanity" is the word invented with the fame around Jeremy Lin in 2012. He is the character who not only broke people's image of an typical Asian guy, but also earned the respect from people because of his attitude. Same goes to Ya-ni Tseng and Rendy Lu. Ya-ni Tseng is the youngest player to win five championships and ranked as number 1 in Women's World Golf rankings from 2011-2013. Rendy Lu reached quarterfinals of the 2010 Wimbleson Championship.

大家絕對不要低估台灣運動員的實力。林來瘋這個名詞是在 2012 年，因林書豪所引發的旋風而出現。林書豪不僅打破了人們對於亞洲男性的刻板印象，他謙虛的態度同時也贏得了大家的尊敬。同樣的，曾雅妮跟盧彥勳也是；曾雅妮是史上同時擁有五座高爾夫冠軍盃最年輕的選手，並且她也創下 2011 到 2013 年在高球榜蟬聯第一的紀錄。而盧彥勳，則是在 2010 溫布頓網球賽中打進了前八強，一夕成名。

來換換口味吧！讓你的表達更豐富！

① 林書豪今年夏天要被交易到湖人隊。
Lakers traded for Jeremy Lin this summer.
相似短句 林書豪將被火箭隊交易到湖人隊。
Jeremy Lin joins the Lakers in trade with the Rockets.

② 但也對於柯比跟他之間的合作有點疑慮。
I am quite concerned about the cooperation between Jeremy and Kobe Bryant.
相似短句 我擔心科比跟他之間的合作。
I am worried about the cooperation between Jeremy and Kobe Bryant.

③ 我在2012年林來瘋旋風時成為他的粉絲。
I became one of his fans when Linsanity were at rage in 2012.
相似短句 我在2012年林來瘋旋風時成為他的粉絲。
I became one of his fans when Jeremy Lin became so popular in 2012.

④ 她在2012年後遇到撞牆期。　**She hit the wall after 2012.**
相似短句 她面臨阻擋她前進的障礙物。
She faced obstacles that stoped her progress.

⑤ 好消息是她回來了！　**The good news is that she is back!**
相似短句 我們很開心看到雅妮回來了！
We are glad to see Yani Tseng back on track.

依樣畫葫蘆！套進去就能用！

句型1 對～感到疑慮。
be concern about...
例句 我對他的膝傷可能影響他的表現感到疑慮。
I am quite concerned about the knee injury which may affect his performance.

句型2 克服……
get over...
例句 她需要克服心中的恐懼。
She has to get over the fear inside her.

Unit 25
上語言課

社群人氣王！英文動態消息寫給你看！

I decided to take Spanish as my second language.
我決定要修西班牙語做為第二外語。
👍 讚 56　💬 回覆 7

French is so difficult. It's killing me...
法文好難，我快死了⋯⋯
👍 讚 36　💬 回覆 20

**My English teacher is so funny.
I never get bored with his class.**
我的英文老師好有趣，上課從來不覺得無聊。
👍 讚 130　💬 回覆 3

Our German teacher recommended us some German music. I found them very nice and this will definitely help improve my listening skill.
德文老師推薦了德語歌給我們。我發現德語歌很好聽，而且這一定可以幫助我練習聽力。
👍 讚 15　💬 回覆 12

I am going to make a presentation about the culture differences between Japan and Taiwan in Japanese during class tomorrow.
我明天上課要用日文報告臺灣與日本的文化差異。
👍 讚 92　💬 回覆 3

新手超必備！一個單字嘛欸通！

English ⓝ 英文	**Japanese** ⓝ 日文	**score** ⓝ 分數
homework ⓝ 功課	**oral** adj 口頭的	**practice** ⓥ 練習
fluently adv 流利地	**doze off** phr 打瞌睡	

114

出門超實用！能聽會說一次搞定！

Ⓐ Jenny, could you help us read this paragraph? You are so quiet today.

Ⓑ Teacher, Jenny has a cold. She is unable to speak now. I can read the paragraph for her.

Ⓐ 珍妮，妳可以幫我們念這段嗎？妳今天好安靜。

Ⓑ 老師，珍妮感冒了，她今天不能說話，我可以幫她念這段。

Ⓐ Okay. Never mind. Let's check the vocabularies in this paragraph. First, "herbal" is the collection of plants that are made for medicine use.

Ⓑ I know. My mom always forces me to drink up Chinese medicine, which is so disgusting.

Ⓐ 好，沒關係。我們來看這段的單字。第一個，「藥草」就是可以作為醫療用途的植物。

Ⓑ 我知道！我媽每次都逼我喝完很噁心的中藥。

Ⓐ It's for your own good. Next, "declare" is the verb that means to make a statement publicly.

Ⓑ What about "claim"? What's the difference between "declare" and "claim"?

Ⓐ 那都是為了你好。第二個，「宣稱」是一個表示在大眾面前做出聲明的動詞。

Ⓑ 那聲稱呢？聲稱跟宣稱兩個之間有什麼不同？

Ⓐ Good question. "Claim" is used in our daily life, but "declare" is a verb that is more serious, for example, "declare" war.

Ⓑ Thank you. I finally understand the difference between them. Otherwise, it's hard to tell the difference by reading the Chinese translation.

Ⓐ 好問題。聲稱是我們一般在日常生活中使用的，但宣稱這動詞更加嚴肅，例如「宣」戰。

Ⓑ 謝謝。我終於了解這兩者的不同。不然光看中文解釋很難分辨。

酸甜苦辣 記下來！

I fell asleep in English class

Monday, September 9

I went to English class tonight. It was embarrassing that I dozed off during class. The teacher called my name suddenly, and I woke up from my sweet dream. He said that it was alright to sleep in class, but never snore loudly and grind your teeth when sleeping. I will not burn the midnight oil ever again. I swear I will study English harder.

我竟然在英文課睡著了

9月9日星期一

我今天晚上去上英文課，但是很糗的是我在課堂上打瞌睡了。老師突然叫我的名字，然後我就從我的美夢驚醒。他說上課其實是可以睡覺的，但是不要大聲打呼又磨牙。我絕對不會再熬夜了，我發誓我會更努力念英文。

增廣見聞 超簡單！

Usually, for second language learners, it is easy the translations in their first language will confuse the learner. Like mentioned in the conversation, the same Chinese meaning could explain different English vocabularies, but actually the usage isn't the same as we recognize it. Therefore, students will sometimes misuse the vocabulary when writing or speaking. Thus, students should carefully understand the usage of vocabularies when memorizing them.

通常來說，學習第二語言的人很容易被自己母語的翻譯搞混。就像對話中提到的，同一個中譯可以用來解釋不同的英文單字，但事實上卻不應該是這樣，導致學生在寫文章或說英文時常會誤用單字。正確的做法應該是，學生應該要在背單字的同時，認真了解單字在句子中的用法。

1 我今天晚上去上英文課。　**I went to English class tonight.**
　相似短句 我今晚有英文課。　I had English class tonight.

2 我得到了好成績。　**I got a good score.**
　相似短句 我的成績還不錯。　My score was not bad.

3 我沒完成我的回家作業。　**I didn't finish my homework.**
　相似短句 我沒能完成回家作業。　I couldn't finish my homework.

4 我上課時打瞌睡。　**I dozed off in class.**
　相似短句 我在化學課打瞌睡。　I fell asleep in Chemistry class.

5 我以後絕不會再熬夜了。
　I will not burn the midnight oil ever again.
　相似短句 我絕對不會再熬夜了。　I'm not staying up late anymore.

句型1 **經過一次又一次的練習～**
By practicing again and again...
　例句 經過一次又一次的練習，我終於能說流利的西班牙語。
By practicing again and again, I could finally speak fluently in Spanish.

句型2 **很糗的是～**
It was embarrassing that...
　例句 很糗的是，我念錯老師的姓氏。
It was embarrassing that I pronounced the teacher's last name wrong.

美分美秒，聽說讀寫Everyday

Unit 26
考試

社群人氣王！英文動態消息寫給你看！

I finally finished all my midterm exams today! And the final exams start from tomorrow...

我今天終於考完了所有的期中考了！然後明天開始考期末考……

👍讚 56　　💬回覆 7

I have to sing a song in French for my pronunciation test tomorrow. Is there any recommending song for me to sing?

我明天的發音考試要唱一首法文歌，有人有推薦的曲子嗎？

👍讚 36　　💬回覆 20

I feel so frustrated with my mathematic test today.

今天的數學小考讓我覺得好挫折。

👍讚 130　　💬回覆 3

I dare not to sleep. I can't finish reviewing the whole textbook.

我不敢睡，我根本複習不完整本課本。

👍讚 15　　💬回覆 12

These coffees and red bulls are going to help me stay up late in order to pass the final exam tomorrow.

為了明天的期末考，我將依賴這些咖啡和提神飲料熬一整夜。

👍讚 92　　💬回覆 3

新手超必備！一個單字嘛欸通！

nervous adj. 緊張的	**test** n. 考試	**pass** v. 通過
fail v. 失敗於……	**rank** v. 排名	**study** v. 讀書
study plan phr. 讀書計畫	**mid-term exam** phr. 期中考	

出門超實用！能聽會說一次搞定！

Ⓐ Hi Sara, how are you? Could I borrow your Biochemistry lecture notes from last week?

Ⓑ No way. I plan to study that session this weekend. Didn't you come to class last week?

Ⓐ 哈囉，莎拉，你好嗎？我可以跟你借上週的生物科學上課筆記嗎？

Ⓑ 不要！我打算這週末要複習上週的課程。你上週沒有來嗎？

Ⓐ No. I didn't feel quite well last week, so I had to skip that class. However, Jimmy told me that we are going to have a quiz about last week's session. Now you see why I need the notes.

Ⓑ Well, Arthur. This is not the first time that you did not feel well for biochemistry class.

Ⓐ 沒有。我上週身體不舒服，所以必須請假。但吉米說我們下次小考要考上周的課程內容，現在你知道我為什麼需要筆記了吧！

Ⓑ 嗯，亞瑟，這已經不是第一次我聽到你生物科學課時身體不舒服。

Ⓐ Sara, please, you know the quiz is 10% of our grade. I need your help.

Ⓑ Alright. Let's go to the print shop and copy the notes because I have to go back to New York this weekend, so I can't leave the notes to you.

Ⓐ 莎拉，拜託。你知道這小考佔學期成績百分之十，我需要你的幫忙。

Ⓑ 好吧。我們一起去影印店複印筆記，因為我這周要回紐約，不能直接將筆記借給你。

Ⓐ No problem! There's a bookstore just around the corner. They offer print service for college students.

Ⓑ Okay. Let's go. But Arthur, this is the last time I will lend my notes to you. Hope you will remember when the final is; otherwise, you will have a miserable winter vacation.

Ⓐ 沒問題！就在轉角那邊有間書局，他們有提供影印服務給大學生。

Ⓑ 好，我們走吧！但亞瑟，這是最後一次我借筆記給你。希望你會記得期末考是什麼時候，不然你寒假應該會過得很悲慘。

酸甜苦辣 記下來！

The answers didn't show up in my dream

Wednesday, June 19

Today I woke up late. And I hurried to the exam room by taxi. The examination questions were quite familiar, and it seemed that they had showed up in my dream last night. But the saddest thing was that I didn't dream of the answers in my dream. I'm afraid of not passing the exam. I don't want to spend another year studying those boring textbooks..

答案都沒出現在我夢裡
6月19日星期三

我今天起得比較晚，所以我直接搭計程車趕到考場。考試題目看起來好熟悉，好像在昨晚的夢裡有出現過。但是最傷心的點是我根本就沒有夢到答案阿。我真的很害怕我沒有通過考試，我不想再花一年讀那些無聊透了的教科書。

增廣見聞 超簡單！

The design of academic year schedule in Taiwan is similar to universities in the United States. The only difference might be the time difference, because the schedule is planned along with New Year vacation. Our final examination time is held before New Year time. What about the universities in the United Kingdom? There are three terms in each academic year: autumn, spring, and summer terms. Interestingly, there's no class in the summer term. Instead of preparing for final exam, they are busy with preparing essays for the class.

台灣的學期制度大部份與美國相似，唯一不同的大概是開學時間，因為台灣的開學日是跟著新年假期來做規劃。但若是英國的大學呢？英國大學的學制分為三期：分別是秋季、春季跟夏季班，有趣的是，在夏季班的時間，學生不用上課也不用準備期末考，而是忙碌於準備課堂交付的小論文。

來換換口味吧！讓你的表達更豐富！

1 期中考到了。　**The mid-term exam is coming.**
> 相似短句 期中考幾天內就要到了。
> The midterms are coming up in a week.

2 我今晚很緊張所以睡不著。
I am too nervous to sleep tonight.
> 相似短句 我好緊張，睡不著。　I'm so nervous that I couldn't sleep.

3 我明天有考試。　**I have a test tomorrow.**
> 相似短句 明天就要考試了。　The test is tomorrow.

4 我沒通過考試。　**I didn't pass the exam.**
> 相似短句 我期中考沒過。　I failed the midterm.

5 我排名第三。　**I ranked third.**
> 相似短句 我得到第三名。　I got third place.

依樣畫葫蘆！套進去就能用！

句型1 太～以至於無法～
too... to...
> 例句 我病得太重以至於無法參加考試。
> **I was too sick to take the exam.**

句型2 最傷心的是～
The saddest thing was that...
> 例句 最傷心的是，我這麼努力卻只得到第三名。
> **The saddest thing was that I worked so hard but still ended up with third place.**

Unit 27
社團活動

Part 5　學生玩青春

社群人氣王！英文動態消息寫給你看！

Which club should I join in? Basketball club or Baseball club?

我應該參加哪個社團呢？籃球社還是棒球社？

👍讚 56　💬回覆 7

The fee for the coffee researching club is too expensive.

咖啡研究社的社費太貴了。

👍讚 36　💬回覆 20

The students who go to the study club are so nerdy. Club activities are meant to be letting students to do something else but studying.

那些參加讀書會的同學太無趣了。社團活動就應該要做些讀書以外的事情啊。

👍讚 130　💬回覆 3

I think I spent too much time on the activities and had no time for studying.

我覺得我花太多時間在社團上了，都沒有時間念書。

👍讚 15　💬回覆 12

The friends I met in the voluntary service club are so nice and kind, and we are like a big family.

我在服務性社團裡遇到的朋友都很好很親切，我們就像一個大家庭一樣。

👍讚 92　💬回覆 3

新手超必備！一個單字嘛欸通！

social club phr 社團活動	college n 大學	student n 學生
friend n 朋友	name tag phr 名牌	number n 號碼
address n 地址	horsemanship n 馬術	join v 加入

出門超實用！能聽會說一次搞定！

Ⓐ I got plenty of leaflet from different clubs, such as soccer, basketball, photography, cricket, and rowing! It's hard to decide which one I should go.

Ⓑ True. I don't think we have to make decisions at this moment. We can try out different clubs. It's free to enter during the first and second week.

Ⓐ 我拿到好多不同社團的傳單，例如足球，籃球，攝影，板球，和划船隊。好難決定要去哪一個啊！

Ⓑ 真的。我覺得我們不需要現在做決定。我們可以先去參加看看不同的社團。第一跟第二周是免費加入的。

Ⓐ That's great news. Last year, I joined the movie club, and we held a summer night movie festival. That was really fun! I suggest you can try movie club first, and see what activities they plan to hold this semester.

Ⓑ Thank you. So why don't you keep staying in the movie club? Though it surprises me that you love movie that much.

Ⓐ 那真是好消息。話說去年我參加電影社，還一起舉辦了夏日夜電影節。非常有趣呢！我建議你可以先試試看電影社，看他們這學期要舉辦哪些活動。

Ⓑ 謝謝！但你怎麼不繼續待在電影社呢？雖然我是有點驚訝你這麼熱愛電影。

Ⓐ This time, I prefer to change to sports club because I've gained a lot of weight in the movie club. Trust me, never eat chips while you are watching movie, because it's hard to stop.

Ⓑ I see. Then I need to consider if I want to join the movie club. Anyway, I would like to try rowing club first.

Ⓐ 我這次決定要換到運動類社團，因為我在電影社時增加不少體重。相信我，千萬不要邊吃洋芋片邊看電影，真的很難停下來。

Ⓑ 了解。這樣我要考慮要不要參加電影社了。總之，我想先試試看划船社。

Ⓐ Do we have girls rowing team in the university? If yes, then I think you are going to fall in love with it.

Ⓑ Yes, we have both boys and girls rowing team. But to tell the truth, I wish I could be in the boys' team so that I can meet some hot guys.

Ⓐ 我們學校有女生划船隊嗎？如果有的話，我相信你會愛上它。

Ⓑ 有的，我們有男生女生划船隊。但老實說，我希望我可以進男生划船隊去遇見些帥哥！

Unit 27 社團活動

酸甜苦辣 記下來！

Making friends in a social club

Monday, March 18

Social clubs are important to a college student. I joined a social club to make friends. I was excited when I went to a social club. People there were friendly and talkative, and I had a good time. There was a name tag on everyone's clothes for knowing each other. We left our telephone numbers and addresses so that we could contact each other after club.

社團課認識新朋友

3月18日星期一

社團活動對一個大學生來說很重要，我加入一個社團來認識朋友。當我到了那裡我好興奮，大家都很親切又健談，我有個很愉快的時光。大家的衣服上都有名牌以方便認識彼此，我們留下了彼此的電話號碼和地址，這樣社團課後我們就能聯絡了。

增廣見聞 超簡單！

There are varieties clubs and societies in universities worldwide. The most renowned or famous club we heard might be Fraternity and Sorority. Like the movie 'American Pie', people must be introduced to join a Fraternity. After that, several activities needs to get "passed". Otherwise, you are not being considered to be a part of them. However, it's hard to describe what kinds of activities it is because different fraternities have their own rules. The simplest rule might be how many girls you take to the party.

全世界大學應該都有著多元的社團俱樂部活動。我們聽過最有名的大概是美國的「兄弟會」和「姐妹會」。就像電影《美國派》演出的，一定要經由「介紹」才能入會。之後，學生必須有各式各樣的活動參與，否則就不能算是他們的一份子。然而，很難去清楚描述到底有哪些活動跟規定，因為每個兄弟會的規定都不盡相同，我聽過最簡單的，大概是取決於你必須帶多少漂亮女孩子去參加派對吧！

來換換口味吧！讓你的表達更豐富！

❶ 我碰巧認識她。　**I happened to know her.**
> 相似短句　我們早就認識了。　We already knew each other.

❷ 他打斷我們的對話。　**He cut in our talk.**
> 相似短句　他打斷我們的對話。　He interrupted our conversation.

❸ 社團對一個大學生來說很重要。
Social clubs are important to a college student.
> 相似短句　大學生很在意社團。
> College students care a lot about social clubs.

❹ 我參加社團來認識朋友。
I joined a social club to make friends.
> 相似短句　我參加社團好認識新朋友。
> I joined a social club so I can meet people.

❺ 每個人衣服上都有名牌。
There was a name tag on everyone's clothes.
> 相似短句　每個人衣服上都有名牌。
> Everyone's got a name tag on their clothes.

依樣畫葫蘆！套進去就能用！

句型1 我邀請誰去～
I invited... to...
> 例句　我邀請請室友去社團辦的派對。
> **I invited my roommate to the party held by the club.**

句型2 當～時，我很興奮。
I was excited when...
> 例句　當看到他們在台上表演吉他時，我很興奮。
> **I was excited when I saw them playing guitar on stage.**

Unit 28
運動會

社群人氣王！英文動態消息寫給你看！

I fell over and made my team lose the relay race. I'm sorry. Gosh...it hurts so bad.
接力賽的時後跌倒了，害我的組輸了比賽。我很抱歉。噢……而且傷口超痛。

👍讚 56　💬回覆 7

We did lots of training in order to win the race.
為了贏得比賽我們做了很多訓練。

👍讚 36　💬回覆 20

The training is exhausting...
特訓超累……

👍讚 130　💬回覆 3

Thanks to my classmate taking this nice picture of me when I scored during the game.
感謝我的同學在我得分的時候幫我拍了這張照片。

👍讚 15　💬回覆 12

We won the champion!!!
我們贏得冠軍了！

👍讚 92　💬回覆 3

新手超必備！一個單字嘛欸通！

championship ⓝ 冠軍	**feet** ⓝ 腳（**foot** 的複數）	**game** ⓝ 比賽
warm up phr 暖身	**leap** ⓥ 跳躍	**run** ⓥ 跑步
athlete ⓝ 運動員	**track-and-field race** phr 田徑賽	

出門超實用！能聽會說一次搞定！

Ⓐ Kevin is really good at sports! You can see him at racing, basketball, volleyball, and even tug-of-war competitions.

Ⓑ Yes, but I heard that he broke his arm just an hour ago during basketball game! He won't be able to attend other competitions in this sports meet anymore.

Ⓐ 凱文真的是一名運動好手。你可以在賽跑，籃球，排球，甚至是拔河比賽場看到他。

Ⓑ 是啊，但我聽說他在一個小時前的籃球比賽中摔斷了手。之後運動會的比賽項目都無法參加了。

Ⓐ Really?! What a pity. I admit that I am one of his admirers. I am sure other admirers feel the same as me.

Ⓑ Do you want to send him greeting cards to wish him to get better soon? Also, we can go visit him in the hospital.

Ⓐ 真的？那真是太可惜了。我承認我是他的粉絲之一，相信其他崇拜者也會跟我一樣感同身受。

Ⓑ 你們要不要寫張慰問卡片祝他早日康復？而且我們也可以去醫院探望他。

Ⓐ I love this idea. I believe he must feel really disappointed that he cannot join the sports meet.

Ⓑ Wait! If Kevin drops out of the game, who is going to take his place? I am taking his baton in relay race later.

Ⓐ 我喜歡這點子。我相信他一定因為不能參加運動會而非常失望。

Ⓑ 等等！如果凱文沒參加比賽，那誰要來頂替他的位置？我等等在接力賽中要接下他的棒子呢！

Ⓐ I guess Larry will volunteer to take up his position in all games, because they are best friends.

Ⓑ Being best friends does not prove that Larry is a sportsman. We all know Larry is slow at running...

Ⓐ 我猜賴瑞會自願頂替他在所有比賽中的位置，因為他們是彼此最好的朋友。

Ⓑ 是好朋友也不能夠代表賴瑞是個運動員，我們都知道賴瑞跑很慢……

酸甜苦辣 記下來！

The sprint starts tomorrow!

Tuesday, April 16

I am going to join the one-hundred-meter sprint. I had planned to enroll in the pole vault. I feel my improvement and I really like this kind of feeling. I hope my dream will come true one day.

明天就要比短跑了！

4月16日星期二

我將要參加一百公尺的短跑。本來我是想要參加撐竿跳的。我感覺到我的進步，而且我真得很喜歡這種感覺，希望有一天我的夢想可以成真。

增廣見聞 超簡單！

In Taiwan, schools hold sports meet events every year. Normally, sports meet is combined with the school's anniversary celebration event. Race game, long jump, board jump, volleyball, tug-of-war, and other sports activity all can be seen in sports meet event. Other than sports meet in school, other well-known events such as Olympics and Asia games are categorized as sports meets event as well. To promote spirit of sports and to understand substance of sports, holding a sports event might be the best way to do.

在台灣，學校每一年都會舉辦運動會。一般來說運動會會跟校慶活動結合在一起。賽跑，跳遠，排球，拔河等活動在運動會中都很常見。而除了學校運動會以外，其他像是奧林匹克和亞運都歸類在運動會中。為了宣揚運動精神，讓人了解運動的本質，舉辦個運動會似乎是最好的辦法！

1 我得到冠軍。 **I won the championship.**
   相似短句 我是比賽的冠軍。 **I am the champion of the game.**

2 太多的運動使我的腳受傷。
   Too much exercise hurts my feet.
   相似短句 運動過度會弄傷我的腳。
   My feet gets hurt for having too much exercise.

3 我在跳之前有先暖身。 **I warmed up before leaping.**
   相似短句 我在跳之前會先暖身。
   I do warm-up exercise before I take a leap.

4 我跑得比他還要快。 **I run faster than him.**
   相似短句 我跑得比他快。 **I'm a faster runner than he is.**

5 我今天有田徑比賽。 **I had a track-and-field race today.**
   相似短句 我今天有田徑比賽。
   I am running the track-and-field race today.

依樣畫葫蘆！套進去就能用！

句型1 **儘管我試著～我還是～**
Even though I tried to..., I...

例句 儘管我試著到達終點線，我還是因為脫水而失敗了。
Even though I tried to make it to the finish line, I failed because of dehydration.

句型2 **本來我有計畫要～**
I had planned to...

例句 本來我有計劃要加入籃球隊，但是我因為太矮而被踢出來了。
I had planned to join the basketball team, but I got cut because I was too short.

美分美秒，聽說讀寫Everyday

Unit 29
畢業旅行

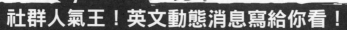

社群人氣王！英文動態消息寫給你看！

Beer, beach and Sunset.

啤酒，海灘與夕陽。

👍 讚 56　　💬 回覆 7

The sky is so blue, and the ocean is so beautiful!

天空好藍，海也好美！

👍 讚 36　　💬 回覆 20

Seize the day! No time for sleeping! Let's play pillow fight!

把握時間！沒時間睡覺了！來打枕頭大戰吧！

👍 讚 130　　💬 回覆 3

I really have no idea why we are still doing the rollercoaster thing at 18? Isn't it something for those screaming kids?

我真不懂為什麼18歲了還在坐雲霄飛車？那不是那些尖叫小孩的專屬遊樂設施嗎？

👍 讚 15　　💬 回覆 12

Can't believe we are going to different cities after this trip, after tonight. Please take care my dear friends. And cheers to our future.

真不敢相信這趟旅行結束後就要各奔前程了。朋友們請多保重，並敬我們的未來。

👍 讚 92　　💬 回覆 3

新手超必備！一個單字嘛欸通！

graduation Ⓝ 畢業　　**trip** Ⓝ 旅行　　　　　**head** Ⓥ 前往

memory Ⓝ 回憶　　**classmate** Ⓝ 同學　　**album** Ⓝ 相冊

route Ⓝ 路程　　**unforgettable** adj. 難忘的

出門超實用！能聽會說一次搞定！

A Hi kids. Now, please divide into ten groups. I need four people in one group to assign you a tent.

B Teacher Nancy, did you just say tent? Aren't we going to stay at a hotel? I already told my mom that we will stay at a hotel.

A 哈囉小朋友們。現在請你們分成十組，我們需要四個人分成一組好分配帳篷。

B 南西老師，您剛剛是說帳篷嗎？我們不是要睡在飯店嗎？我已經告訴我媽說我們要住飯店耶。

A Dear Amy, don't worry. We will set up the tents at Kenting National Museum of Marine biology and Aquarium.

B Oh my gosh! It's my dream to have a sleep over with their dolphins, tropical fish, and whales in the museum!

A 愛咪同學不要擔心。我們會在墾丁海洋生物博物館搭帳篷。

B 我的天啊！跟海豚，熱帶魚還有鯨魚一起在博物館睡覺一直是我的夢想。

A Sounds great, doesn't it? Other then that we will also have scary night strolls, and teach you how to set up a campfire.

B But what is a scary night stroll? Should we prepare anything? And where will we go for a night stroll?

A 聽起來不錯吧。不只如此，我們會有恐怖夜遊活動，還有教你怎麼生營火呢！

B 但什麼是可怕夜遊啊？我們要準備什麼東西嗎？我們要去哪裡夜遊？

A We are going to have adventures in the museum for the night stroll. Each group will receive a treasure map then. But now, please divide into groups and give me the names of your group members.

B I can't wait! Who's going to team up with me? I am a good team player. Pick me!

A 我們即將在博物館裡面舉辦夜遊並展開一場冒險。每個組到時候都會拿到一張藏寶圖。但現在，請你們分組然後給我組員名單。

B 我等不及了！誰要跟我同一隊？我是很好的團隊隊員喔！快選我！

Unit 29 畢業旅行

酸甜苦辣 記下來！

I don't want to graduate...

.Thursday, August 8

Today was the first day of the graduation trip. The traveling route includes Kenting and Green Island. What I look forward to is scuba diving in Green Island and taking a hot spring bath by the sea. I also plan to take lots of pictures of beautiful scenery and make an album to commemorate this journey. Though I look forward to the graduation trip, I don't want to graduate because I really enjoy my school life.

我不想要畢業……

8月8日星期四

今天是畢業旅行的第一天，這次的行程包括墾丁和綠島。我期待的是去綠島浮潛以及在海邊泡溫泉。我也計畫要拍很多漂亮的風景照，並製作相本來紀念這次旅行。雖然我期待畢業旅行，但是我不想畢業，因為我很享受我的學生生活。

增廣見聞 超簡單！

Graduation trip is a tradition for students in Asia countries when they are about to graduate. Students will have chances to organize their trip to visit other places in Taiwan or even go abroad. Some activities like scary night strolls, set a campfire, have BBQ, and live in tents are most seen activities during graduation trip. College or university students will go abroad usually, and really take part in planning their trip and create a memory for a life-time.

畢業旅行是亞洲國家畢業學生一直以來的傳統。畢業生會有機會去規劃自己的旅遊計劃，看是要去台灣其他地方玩或出國。可怕的夜遊、生營火、烤肉或住帳篷都是畢業旅行中很常見的活動。通常大學生會計劃出國旅遊，而他們也真的會參與旅遊計劃的每一步，去創造一生中美好的回憶。

1 我今晚準備畢業旅行的東西。

I prepared for the graduation trip tonight.

相似短句 我今晚為畢業旅行做採買。

I made some purchase for the graduation trip tonight.

2 我們明天要去花蓮。 We will have a trip to Hualien tomorrow.

相似短句 我們前往花蓮，度過假日。

We're heading to Hualien to spend our holidays.

3 我想在心中留下難忘的回憶。

I want to keep the unforgettable memory in my mind.

相似短句 我不想忘記那些珍貴的回憶。

I don't want to forget the precious memories.

4 我不想要畢業。 I don't want to graduate.

相似短句 我想要跟同學和朋友在一起。

I want to stay with my classmates and friends.

5 我要拍很多照片做成相本。

I plan to take lots of pictures to make an album.

相似短句 我拍了很多照片，並放進相簿裡。

I took tons of pictures and put them into an album.

依樣畫葫蘆！套進去就能用！

句型1 我準備～

I prepared for...

例句 我兩天前就為旅行做準備。

I prepared for the trip two days ahead.

句型2 旅遊行程包括～

The traveling route includes...

例句 旅遊行程包括去峽谷、去海邊和逛夜市。

The traveling route includes the gorge, the beach, and the night market.

Unit 30
畫畫

社群人氣王！英文動態消息寫給你看！

She loves painting self-portraits.
她很喜歡畫自畫像。

👍讚 56　💬回覆 7

We were planning to go sketching in the park this morning but it was raining heavily when we woke up.
我們原本打算要去公園寫生，但早上起來窗外正下這傾盆大雨。

👍讚 36　💬回覆 20

He said he wants to be a cartoonist.
I will definitely buy his comic books.
他說他想要成為一名漫畫家。而我一定會買他的漫畫。

👍讚 130　💬回覆 3

My friend is doing sketching as a part time job around 2 to 4 at the Art Village. Come visit her!
我的朋友下午兩點到四點在藝術村幫人畫速寫喔！快來！

👍讚 15　💬回覆 12

The smell of the oil paint is really strong.
油彩的味道好重。

👍讚 92　💬回覆 3

新手超必備！一個單字嘛欸通！

painting ⓝ 繪畫	sketch ⓥ 素描	art ⓝ 藝術
draw ⓥ 畫	painter ⓝ 畫家	model ⓝ 模特兒
object ⓝ 物體	portrait ⓝ 畫像	

出門超實用！能聽會說一次搞定！

A I applied for painting class next week. I would like to paint a picture of my mom as mother's day present.

B Good idea. Do you know what kind of paint to use when painting? Like water color or oil?

A 我報名了下週的畫畫課程，我想要畫一幅我媽的畫像當母親節禮物。

B 好主意！你畫畫時要用哪一種顏料？像是水彩還是油彩？

A I am still thinking about it. Maybe I will try to sketch this time, because it is more appropriate.

B You are right. I love the effect of sketching. It is simple but some how it can present a person's real beauty.

A 我還在考慮呢，或許這次我會用素描，感覺比較恰當。

B 你說得對，我喜歡素描的效果，它雖簡單但卻能夠表現出一個人真正的美。

A Sounds like you are an expert at sketch painting. Why don't you teach me first?

B Okay. Please pick up a pencil. When you do sketches, the way you hold the pencil is one of the keys as well.

A 聽起來你好像是素描專家。要不你先教我吧？

B 好啊，你先挑一支筆，當你在素描時，拿筆的方式也是關鍵之一。

A Well, I guess we have to visit local art supplies first. I don't have pencils for sketch.

B You have a lot of things to buy. Various kinds of pencils and an art paper should be on the shopping list.

A 恩！我想我們大概要先去一趟當地的美材行，我沒有素描用的筆。

B 那你有很多要買的，有很多種類的鉛筆跟繪畫專用紙都要放進購物清單中。

Unit **30** 畫畫

Naked model in my art class!

Wednesday, March 13

We learned how to sketch in art class. Our teacher found a model as our sketch object. The model took off all of her clothes. What an embarrassing thing it was. Almost all of us immersed ourselves in sketching, as if there were nobody in front of us.

美術課的裸體模特兒

3月13日星期三

今天我們在美術課學素描。我們老師找了一個人體模特兒來當素描的主題。那個模特兒把她的衣服脫個精光，真的超級尷尬的！大部分的人都沉浸在畫畫中，好像沒有人在我們前面一樣。

There are several kinds of painting skills: water color, oil, acrylic, and charcoal painting. A workman must have sharpened his tools if he wants to do a good job. Different types of painting require different tools. For example, if we want to use the watercolor, a brush, water paints, and water are enough. Unlike watercolor, if we want to try oil, then an easel, canvas, drawing board, various types of brushes, and oil paints will be needed.

畫畫有很多不同的技法，像是水彩，油彩，壓克力和炭畫。工欲善其事必先利其器，不同的技法當然也需要不同的器具。例如，如果我們要畫水彩，那麼水彩筆、水彩和水就足夠了。但如果是畫油彩的話，我們就需要畫架、帆布、繪圖板跟不同種類的畫筆，另外油彩也是必須的。

來換換口味吧！讓你的表達更豐富！

1 我對繪畫蠻有天份的。　I am quite talented in painting.
相似短句 我對畫畫很在行。　Painting is my thing.

2 我在空閒時間會畫畫。　I draw at my leisure times.
相似短句 我有空時就畫畫。　I draw in my free time.

3 我想要增進我的畫畫技巧。
I want to make progress in painting.
相似短句 我想要增進我的畫畫技巧。
I want to improve my painting skills.

4 我們在美術課上學了素描。
We learned how to sketch in art class.
相似短句 我們在美術課學了素描的技巧。
We learned sketching skills in art class.

5 有人發了有關素描課的傳單。
There came a person dispensing the flyers about the sketch class.
相似短句 有人在發宣傳素描課的傳單。
There were people handing out flyers about sketch class.

依樣畫葫蘆！套進去就能用！

句型1 我鼓起勇氣～
I found my courage to...
例句 我鼓起勇氣跟湯米說我愛他。
I found my courage to tell Tommy that I love him.

句型2 多麼～
What a / an...
例句 多麼漂亮的一個女生！
What a beautiful girl!

Unit 31
照相

社群人氣王！英文動態消息寫給你看！

 I don't know why I barely take pictures with people in it. Maybe it's because I live in a lonely city, crowded with strangers.

中 我不知道為什麼我總是拍無人的照片。大概是因為我住在一個寂寞的城市，擠滿了陌生人。

 讚 56 　回覆 7

 I am going to take photos of all the train stations in Taiwan.

我要去拍全臺灣所有的火車站。

 讚 36 　回覆 20

 I prefer black and white photos.

我喜歡黑白照片。

 讚 130 　回覆 3

 The film for Polaroid is getting more and more expensive. I'm burning my money.

拍立得底片越來越貴了。我根本在燒錢。

讚 15 　回覆 12

 It's so funny watching them take photos of food with that professional heavy SLR camera. It's hilarious! lol

看他們用那麼專業的單眼相機拍食物的樣子真的超好笑，超滑稽的，哈哈。

 讚 92 　回覆 3

新手超必備！一個單字嘛欸通！

photography **n.** 攝影　　　photo **n.** 照片　　　　　view **n.** 視野
digital **adj.** 數位的　　　photographer **n.** 攝影師
single-lens reflex camera **phr.** 單鏡反射照相機；單眼相機

出門超實用！能聽會說一次搞定！

Ⓐ Tom, can you help us take a picture with this beautiful scenery? Thank you.

Ⓑ Okay. One, two, three, say cheese! Hold on, Sara, you got to get closer with Henry, I can't see you through the lens.

Ⓐ 湯姆，可以幫我們跟這幅景象照一張相嗎？謝謝。

Ⓑ 好！一、二、三，笑一個！等等，莎拉你要再靠近亨利一點，我在鏡頭中看不見你。

Ⓐ Is it okay now, Tom? You can just keep shooting, we will change poses by ourselves.

Ⓑ Okay, done. Would you like to take a look of it? We can do it again if those pictures aren't good enough.

Ⓐ 湯姆，這樣可以了嗎？你可以繼續按快門，我們會自己換姿勢。

Ⓑ 好了！你們要不要看一下，如果不夠滿意這些照片的話，我們可以再照一次。

Ⓐ Sure. Okay, I can't see us clear in the picture because of the backlight. You can adjust the exposure rate and see if it gets better.

Ⓑ Okay, let's do it again girls. Give me a vogue model pose and a cool face please.

Ⓐ 好啊。因為背光照片中看不清楚我們。你可以試試調整曝光看會不會比較好。

Ⓑ 好，女孩們我們再拍一次！給我一個時尚雜誌模特兒的姿勢跟酷酷的臉！

Ⓐ Tom, you are so funny. Thank you very much. Shall we go to dinner now? I know there's a famous restaurant owned by a photographer.

Ⓑ I am hungry. But promise me, no more photo shootings during dinnertime, not even selfies.

Ⓐ 湯姆你也太有趣了，真的很謝謝你。那我們可以去吃晚餐了吧？我知道有間有名的餐廳也是一位攝影師開的。

Ⓑ 我好餓。但請答應我，晚餐時間不要再拍照了，連自拍都不可以。

Unit 31 照相

My dream of being a photographer

Thursday, March 28

I am taking a photography course this semester. Everyone should have a single-lens reflex camera. I think it is also necessary to have a digital camera. It is very convenient. I have to work a part-time job to pay for it in twelve installments. It's necessary to invest a lot before becoming a top photographer, there's still a long way for me to go.

我想成為攝影家

3月28日星期四

這學期我在修攝影課。大家都要有單眼相機。我認為擁有一個數位相機也是必備的，它實在是很方便！我只好去打工，來支付十二期支付照相機的費用。要成為一個頂尖的攝影師，大量投資是必要的，我還差得遠呢。

When mentioning about taking pictures, "selfie" is a picture that almost everyone will take, especially women. As camera phones and digital cameras are getting popular and common in our world, the trend of taking a self-portrait photograph gets on as well. Normally, of selfies will be shared on social networks, like Facebook and twitter. The record-breaking selfie this year in 2014, was taken by Ellen at Oscar with several renowned Hollywood actors.

當提到照相時，「自拍」大概是每一個人都會拍的，特別是女孩子。當照相手機跟數位相機漸成主流時，自己拍下自己的肖像的行為也有成長的趨勢。通常，自拍照片都會分享在社群上，例如臉書和推特。2014 年推特點閱率破紀錄的照片，是美國脫口秀主持人艾倫在奧斯卡頒獎典禮上和眾多好萊塢明星拍的。

1 我希望有天能成為一個攝影家。
I want to be a photographer one day.

相似短句 攝影家是我的夢想職業。
Being a photographer has always been my dream.

2 我參加攝影社讓我的攝影技術精進。
To improve my photography skills, I joined a photography club.

相似短句 我參加攝影社，好加強攝影技巧。
I joined a photo club to make my photography skills better.

3 學習攝影花了我很多錢。
Learning photography cost me a lot of money.

相似短句 學習拍好照片要花很多錢。
It's costly to learn to take nice photos.

4 每個人應該都要有一台單眼相機。
Everyone should have a single-lens reflex camera.

相似短句 每個人都該有一台單眼相機。
Single-lens reflex camera is a must have for everyone.

5 我試著用不同的角度取景。
I tried to find a view from different angles.

相似短句 我試著想拍出照片的新視野。
I tried to give my photos a whole new perspective.

依樣畫葫蘆！套進去就能用！

句型1 **我認為～是必要的。**
I think it is also necessary to...

例句 我認為要拍好照片，有好光線也是必要的。
I think it is also necessary to have good lighting to take good photos.

句型2 **為了增進我們的技巧，～**
To practice our skills,...

例句 為了增進我們的技巧，我們加入了本地的攝影俱樂部。
To practice our skills, we joined a local photography club.

Unit 32
看展覽

社群人氣王！英文動態消息寫給你看！

I really don't want to miss the exhibition of Manet.
我好想去看馬內的特展。

 讚 56　　回覆 7

These paintings are all from the Louvre. Although the ticket is quite expensive, the exhibition was really worth the price.
這些畫都是從羅浮宮借來的。票雖然有點貴但是非常值得。

 讚 36　　回覆 20

I bought a bag with Monet's Water Lilies on it. It's so beautiful.
我買了一個印了莫內睡蓮的包包，它超美。

讚 130　　回覆 3

National Palace Museum is always full of tourists. I can't even take a breath when I was trying to pass by the Gallery.
故宮博物院總是充滿了觀光客。在我試圖要穿過展間的時候簡直擠到無法呼吸。

讚 15　　回覆 12

I took my little cousins to see the dinosaur exhibition today. They were so excited.
我今天帶我的小表妹們去看恐龍展，她們超級興奮。

讚 92　　回覆 3

新手超必備！一個單字嘛欸通！

exhibition **n.** 展覽　　highlight **v. n.** 標注；重點　　display **v. n.** 展示
world-renowned **adj.** 世界知名的　　Impressionism **n.** 印象派
capture **v.** 捕捉　　appreciate **v.** 欣賞；表示感激　　painting **n.** 畫作

出門超實用！能聽會說一次搞定！

A Let's buy tickets for the exhibition first. We can use student discounts if I remember correctly.

B But I didn't bring my student ID. But it's my favorite Monet exhibition, so I will go anyway.

A 我們先買展覽的票。我記得可以用學生折扣買。

B 但我沒有帶我的學生證。不過這是我最喜歡的莫內展覽，所以無論如何我還是會去。

A Okay. Shall we go in? His world-renowned artwork "Water Lilies" are the highlight of the exhibition this time.

B That's fantastic! Claude Monet produced over sixty water lily paintings over the time.

A 好的，那我們該進去了嗎？這次的展覽亮點是他世界知名的作品——睡蓮。

B 那超棒的！克勞德‧莫內總共產出超過六十幅睡蓮的作品。

A So can I see sixty paintings this time? I don't think it's possible.

B Of course it's impossible. Eight water lily paintings are placed in Musee de Orange in Paris, and the rest of the paintings are on display in museums around the world.

A 所以我可以一次看到六十個作品嗎？我覺得不太可能吧。

B 當然不可能，八幅畫作放在巴黎橘園美術館，而剩下的則在世界各地博物館展出。

A I see. Is "Impression Sunrise" in exhibition this time? I love that painting as well.

B No, we won't see "Impression Sunrise", but "A woman with a parasol" is on display this time. We are lucky.

A 了解。那「日出印象」有在這次展覽中嗎？我也很愛那幅畫作。

B 沒有，這次看不到「日出印象」，但「撐傘的女人」有在展示中。我們很幸運喔！

Unit 32 看展覽

Part 6 文青正流行

酸甜苦辣 記下來！

An exhibition of Sherlock Holmes

Tuesday, June 24

I went to see an exhibition of the famous detective Sherlock Holmes. The story of Sherlock Holmes was written by Sir Arthur Conan Doyle. I am a fan of his since I was young. I remembered that the first time I read it was in my mom's office. Her colleague handed me this book, and from then on, I became addictive to the series of Sherlock Holmes books. Therefore, when I knew that there will be an exhibition of Sherlock Holmes, I was thrilled! And the exhibition didn't let me down. I was able to see the authentic manuscript and pens of Conan Doyle.

夏洛克福爾摩斯的展覽

6月24日星期二

我去看了有名偵探夏洛克福爾摩斯的展覽。福爾摩斯的故事是柯南道爾所寫，我從小就是他的書迷。還記得我第一次讀他的書是在我母親的辦公室，她同事給我這本書，從那時候開始，我就沈浸在夏洛克福爾摩斯系列小說中。所以當我知道這次會有夏洛克福爾摩斯的展覽時，我超級高興！而且展覽也沒讓我失望，我可以看到柯南道爾的手稿和筆。

增廣見聞 超簡單！

The impressionism comes from the painting 'Impression Sunrise' painted by Claude Monet. The core element of Impressionism is to capture the moment in time. Therefore, the light and color of the moment are what the artists focus on when they were painting. On the other hand, we, as viewers, the impression of the moment that is delivered by light and the color is what we are looking for when appreciating the art works.

「印象派」這個名詞是從莫內的畫作「日出印象」所衍生而來，它的核心理念是捕捉在當下的畫面，因此，畫畫當下的光線和顏色是畫家在作畫時的重點之一。從另一方面來說，身為觀賞者的我們，看畫當下的光線和顏色表現呈現給我們的感覺，就是當我們在觀賞畫作的重點。

1 福爾摩斯的故事是柯南道爾所寫。
The story of Sherlock Holmes was written by Sir Arthur Conan Doyle.

相似短句 福爾摩斯的故事是柯南道爾所寫。
Sir Arthur Conan Doyle wrote the story of Sherlock Holmes.

2 我從小就是他的書迷。 **I am a fan of his since I was young.**

相似短句 我從小就是他的書迷。 I am his fan when I was young.

3 她同事給我這本書。 **Her colleague handed me this book**

相似短句 她同事給我這本書。 Her colleague gave this book to me.

4 而且展覽也沒讓我失望。 **the exhibition didn't let me down.**

相似短句 而且展覽也沒讓我失望。
I was not disappointed with the exhibition.

5 我就沈浸在夏洛克福爾摩斯系列小說中。
I become addictive to the series of Sherlock Holmes books.

相似短句 我就沈浸在夏洛克福爾摩斯系列小說中。
I was obsessed with the series of Sherlock Holmes books.

依樣畫葫蘆！套進去就能用！

句型1 我是～粉絲。
I am a fan of...

例句 我是阿瑟‧柯南‧道爾的粉絲。
I am a fan of Sir Arthur Conan Doyle.

句型2 我還記得……
I remember that...

例句 我還記得我看到手稿時得心情。
I remember the feeling when I saw the manuscript.

Unit 33
看劇場

The man sitting next to me sang every song even Christine's part! Man! I want to listen to the professional performance of The Phantom of the Opera, okay?

坐我隔壁的大叔唱了每一首歌，連 Christine 的部分都唱了！天啊！我只想聽專業版的歌劇魅影不行嗎！

 讚 56　　回覆 7

He said he is an operaholic, but he fell asleep during the show.
他說他熱愛歌劇，卻在中途睡死了。

 讚 36　　回覆 20

I am so looking forward to the next drama from Tainaner Ensemble!
我很期待下一場台南人劇團的戲！

 讚 130　　回覆 3

I got the ticket for Les Miserable!
我買到悲慘世界的票了！

 讚 15　　回覆 12

This drama made me think more and deeper about our lives. It's very worth seeing, and of course it made tonight wonderful.

這齣戲讓我對我們的人生有了更多、更深的思考。非常值得一看，並且它讓我有了個美好的夜晚。

 讚 92　　回覆 3

新手超必備！一個單字嘛欸通！

leading actress **n** 女主角　　musical **n** 音樂劇　　theatre **n** 劇場
leisure **adj** 閒暇得　　supporting role **n** 配角　Broadway **n** 百老匯
amphitheatre **n** 半圓形劇場　inspirational **adj** 激勵人心的

出門超實用！能聽會說一次搞定！

Ⓐ Martha is going to be a leading actress this time in "Les Miserable" I couldn't believe it!

Ⓑ Which role will she play? Fantine or Cosette? This is my first time seeing a musical in theatres. Normally, I watch it on YouTube.

Ⓐ 瑪莎即將成為這次悲慘世界的女主角，我真無法相信！

Ⓑ 她是扮演什麼角色？方婷還是珂賽特？這是我第一次在劇場看音樂劇，通常我都在 YouTube 上面。

Ⓐ I can tell. Cosette is the leading actress, and Fantine, Cosette's mother, is the supporting role.

Ⓑ Never mind. As long as I can see Les Miserable with my own eyes I have no regret.

Ⓐ 我看得出來。柯賽特是主角，而方婷，也就是珂賽特的母親，則是配角。

Ⓑ 沒關係啦！只要我可以親眼看到悲慘世界的演出，那我就此生無憾了。

Ⓐ Okay. You can take a look around the theatre by yourself, then I will introduce it in details.

Ⓑ Well, this theatre is different than what I imagined. It looks old and shabby.

Ⓐ 好吧。你可以自己四處逛逛看看這個劇場，然後我再仔細介紹。

Ⓑ 這個劇場確實跟我想像的不太一樣。這看起好老舊。

Ⓐ This place is called Shakespeas Globe. It was built in the late sixteen century; it was destroyed once, but rebuilt in the 20th century.

Ⓑ No wonder this place is made out of wood. And it is an open-air amphitheatre.

Ⓐ 這個地方叫做莎士比亞環球劇場。這是在 16 世紀後期所建，曾經被破壞掉過，但又在 20 世紀時重建完畢。

Ⓑ 難怪這地方全部以木頭所建成，而且還設有開放圓形劇場。

Part 6 文青正流行

酸甜苦辣 記下來！

I am a gifted child

Monday, April 14

I was chosen as leading actress for a drama competition in school! I am going to tell mommy about this! I feel so lucky that I can be Tracy, the female lead of Hairspray. Because of the movie, I feel much more confidant. I never feel inferiority because of my weight. Sometimes my schoolmates will make fun of me. However, my mom also taught me that I am a gifted child; I shouldn't feel bad for the words they say to me. I am going to watch the movie first before rehearsal tomorrow and also memorize the stage dialogue of the first scene.

我是個聰明的小孩

4月14日星期一

在這次學校戲劇的選秀裡，我被選為女主角。我要趕快跟媽媽說這消息！我覺得好幸運可以演髮膠明星夢的女主角崔西。因為電影，我變得更有信心。我從不因為我的體重覺得自卑。雖然有時候同學會嘲笑我，但是我媽也說了我是個聰明的小孩，我不需要因為其他人說的話覺得傷心。我要在明天第一次彩排前再把電影看一次，還要背第一幕的台詞。

增廣見聞 超簡單！

Going to theatres to enjoy a nice, funny, or inspiring drama or musical is part of the leisure life in Western countries. No matter in London or New York, you can find an area that theatres are all around. In New York, you can go visit the Broadway to buy tickets; on the other hand, in London, you can visit West end, where you can find 40-50 theatres around Leicester square and Covent Garden. It is great to visit theatre areas to experience the culture.

到劇場看一部好的、有趣的或激勵人心的戲劇跟音樂劇已經是日常休閒生活中的一部份。不管你在倫敦或是紐約，隨便都可以找到一個劇院區。在紐約，你可以去拜訪百老匯區，而若是在倫敦，你可以去拜訪西區，在那裡你可以找到 40-50 家戲院圍繞在萊斯特廣場和柯芬園的周邊，有機會去那裡拜訪劇院區體驗文化是很不錯的！

1. 因為電影，我變得更有信心。
   Because of the movie, I feel much more confidant.

   相似短句 因為電影，我變得更有信心。
   The movie boosts my confidence.

2. 我從不因為我的體重覺得自卑。
   I never feel inferiority because of my weight.

   相似短句 我從不因為我的體重覺得自卑。
   My weight never makes me feel inferior.

3. 雖然有時候同學會嘲笑我。
   Sometimes my schoolmates will make fun of me.

   相似短句 雖然有時候同學會嘲笑我。
   My schoolmates will tease me sometimes.

4. 我覺得可以演髮膠明星夢的女主角崔西好幸運。
   I feel so lucky that I can be Tracy.

   相似短句 我覺得可以演髮膠明星夢的女主角崔西好幸運。
   I think I am blessed to be Tracy.

5. 我不需要因為其他人說的話覺得傷心。
   I shouldn't feel bad for the words they say to me.

   相似短句 我不需要因為其他人說的話覺得傷心。
   I don't need to have bad feelings because of those words.

依樣畫葫蘆！套進去就能用！

句型1 被選為～
be chosen as...

例句 他被選為髮膠明星夢的男主角。
He is chosen as the leading actor of Hairspray.

句型2 為……覺得傷心。
feel bad for...

例句 我替她的遭遇感到傷心。
I feel bad for the tragedy that happened to her.

Unit 34
聽音樂會

社群人氣王！英文動態消息寫給你看！

I am attending my sister's piano recital tonight.
我要參加姊姊今天晚上的鋼琴獨奏會。
👍讚 56　💬回覆 7

I haven't been to any concert performed by the National Symphony Orchestra before, thank you for inviting me!
我還沒去過任何一場國家交響樂團的音樂會，謝謝你邀請我。
👍讚 36　💬回覆 20

I can't stand mobile phones ringing during the concert.
我無法忍受音樂會中的手機鈴響。
👍讚 130　💬回覆 3

IT'S MAYDAY!!! I got the first area! I can't believe I can see them so closely!
是五月天！我在搖滾區！真不敢相信可以從這麼近的距離看著他們！
👍讚 15　💬回覆 12

It was a great night and we were all soaked up in her beautiful voice.
這真是一個很美麗的夜晚。我們都沉浸在她美麗的歌聲當中了。

👍讚 92　💬回覆 3

新手超必備！一個單字嘛欸通！

classical adj 古典的	**row** n 排	**seat** n 座位
ticket n 票卷	**concert** n 演唱會	**singer** n 歌手
auditorium n 觀眾席	**wave** v 揮舞	

MP3 Track 034

出門超實用！能聽會說一次搞定！

A Welcome to the 60th memorial music concert of Mozart. We are glad to invite the New York Philharmonic to present the classic pieces.

B Thank you, Robert, for taking me to this music event. I've been looking forward to today since your invitation.

A 歡迎來到莫札特六十周年紀念音樂會！我們很榮幸請到紐約愛樂來替我們表演經典名曲。

B 謝謝你帶我來聽音樂會，羅伯特。從你邀請我那天起，我就開始期待了。

A You are welcome! Alan Gilbert will show up tonight. He did a fantastic job when he took over the position as music director and conductor to the New York Philharmonic.

B I can't agree with you more. Wow, the first song is "Eine kleine Nachtmusik".

A 別客氣。阿倫・吉爾伯特今晚也會現身。自從他接手紐約愛樂的音樂總監跟指揮家的位置後，就一直把他的工作做得很出色。

B 我非常同意。哇！你看第一首是「第 13 號小夜曲」。

A That is the most inspiring piece I simply couldn't forget. I listen to this song when I drive, and at work.

B Sounds like you get inspirations and ideas when you listen to this piece. You are truly an artist.

A 這一部讓我難以忘懷的作品非常激勵人心，我開車工作時都會聽。

B 聽起來你在聽這首歌時，會得到靈感跟點子，你真的是一位藝術家。

A You should give it a try next time. The second piece is "The Marriage of Figaro".

B Oh, the show is about to begin. Let's turn off the phones and be ready for the show.

A 你下次也應該試試邊聽音樂邊找靈感，第二部是「費加洛婚禮」。

B 噢！音樂會要開始了。我們先將手機關機等開場吧！

美分美秒，聽說讀寫Everyday

Unit 34 聽音樂會

酸甜苦辣 記下來！

Yo-Yo Ma is a genius!

Wednesday, April 24

I like classical music. My friend and I went to a concert in the National Concert Hall. We had front row seats, which cost us NT 5000 dollars. The concert was a solo played by Yo-Yo Ma, who is an excellent cellist. I was moved to tears at the end of the concert. I thought Yo-Yo Ma is a genius.

馬友友是個天才

4月24日星期三

我喜歡古典音樂。我跟我朋友去國家音樂會，我們做前排索價 5000 元台幣的座位。這場音樂會是由馬友友獨奏，他是一位優秀的大提琴家。我聽到最後都感動得落淚了，我認為他真是個天才。

增廣見聞 超簡單！

The New York Philharmonic is one of the famous orchestra symphony of the world, organized in 1842. Other than New York Philharmonic, the Berlin Philharmonic Orchestra is also a leading orchestra in the world. Alan Gilbert, is an American violinist and conductor. He is now the music director of the New York Philharmonic. His first debut in New York was 2009, and he had won Grammy Awards for best Opera recording.

紐約愛樂在 1842 年成立，是世界有名的交響樂團之一。除了紐約愛樂，柏林愛樂也是世界首屈一指的交響樂團。阿倫‧吉爾伯特是位美國指揮家和小提琴家。他也是紐約愛樂現任的音樂總監和指揮家，他在 2009 年初登場，曾獲得葛萊美獎最佳歌劇錄製。

來換換口味吧！讓你的表達更豐富！

1 我喜歡古典音樂。　**I like classical music.**
　相似短句 我喜歡古典音樂。　I'm a classical music person.

2 我們坐在前排座位。　**We had front row seats.**
　相似短句 我們坐在前排。　We sat in the front row.

3 我得到兩張免費的門票。　**I got two tickets for free.**
　相似短句 我有兩張免費的票。　I had two free tickets.

4 看一次就夠了。　**Seeing it once is enough.**
　相似短句 這不值得看兩次。　It isn't worth seeing twice.

5 我訂了兩張票。　**I reserved two tickets.**
　相似短句 我預定了兩個位置。　I booked two seats.

依樣畫葫蘆！套進去就能用！

句型1 我得到免費的～
I got... for free.

例句 我得到兩張免費的票。
I got two tickets for free.

句型2 在～的尾聲…
at the end of...

例句 聽眾在音樂劇的尾聲時用力鼓掌。
The audience clapped their hands so hard at the end of the musical.

美分美秒，聽說讀寫Everyday

Unit 35
面試

社群人氣王！英文動態消息寫給你看！

I am attending a job interview next Friday, what should I wear?
我下週五要穿什麼去參加工作的面試呢？
👍 讚 56　💬 回覆 7

Everyone looks smarter than me...I am so nervous.
來面試的其他人看起來都比我聰明……害我好緊張。
👍 讚 36　💬 回覆 20

I think I had answered all the questions quite well. The interviewers seemed to be content with me. Hope I can get the job!
我想我對於考官的提問都回答得滿好的，他們看起來對我相當滿意。希望可以順利得到這份工作！
👍 讚 130　💬 回覆 3

I was so nervous that my brain went totally blank when the interviewers asked me to introduce myself...
我超緊張，緊張到面試官要我自我介紹的時候腦袋整個一片空白……
👍 讚 15　💬 回覆 12

The interviewers kept asking me about how much I knew about their company. How much am I suppose to know!!!
面試官一直問我對於他們公司瞭解多少，我應該要知道多少？！
👍 讚 92　💬 回覆 3

新手超必備！一個單字嘛欸通！

interview ⓝ 面試	**successfully** adv. 成功地	**job** ⓝ 工作
chance ⓝ 機會	**work** ⓥ 工作	**ability** ⓝ 能力
impression ⓝ 印象	**formal** adj. 正規的；符合格式的	

出門超實用！能聽會說一次搞定！

A Hi Jonathon, how are you today? Thank you for coming to join the interview with us. Now, let's talk about you.

B Hi My name is Jonathon. Nice to meet you. I am now 28 years old, and from New Orleans. Currently, I rent a house in the city. My previous job was marketing consultant.

A 哈囉強納森。你好嗎？謝謝你今天參與我們的面試，那麼請你介紹一下自己吧！

B 嗨！我是強納森。很高興認識你。我現在 28 歲，來自紐奧良，現在在市中心租房子。我前一份工作是行銷顧問。

A Okay. Describe your personality to me.

B Well, I am a dedicated worker and a people person. I am a team player, and I enjoy being in contact with the public. My four years working experience with my previous marketing team built up my ability and flexibility to work with other people.

A 好的，請形容你的特質。

B 恩，我是一位認真盡責為人親切的人。我善於團體合作的工作方式，也喜歡與大眾接觸。擁有四年跟行銷團隊合作的經驗，而這造就我有能力和彈性去和他人共事。

A Please tell me about your formal education.

B I graduated from the MBA program delivered by Stanford Business School several years ago. It was a great experience for me. The course offered was quite intensive and challenging which required students to react promptly.

A 請告訴我們一些有關您求學經驗的事。

B 我幾年前從史丹佛商業學院開設的 MBA 課程中畢業。這對我來說是一段很美好的經驗，史丹佛的課程密集且具挑戰性，需要學生適時地做出反應。

A Can you tell me about your work history?

B Yes, when I was in the MBA program, I took an intern position as marketing consultant. After I gradated, I chose to stay at the consultant business, working as a marketing consultant for four years.

A 你可以分享你過去的工作經驗嗎？

B 可以，當我還在 MBA 上課時，我就接下了實習擔任行銷顧問一職！而我在畢業後，我選擇繼續待在顧問業，擔任了四年的行銷顧問。

Unit 35 面試

酸甜苦辣 記下來！

Interview today!!

Monday, September 2

I had worried about today's interview. I picked out a formal deliberately yesterday. I feel that I performed pretty well in the interview today and made a good impression on the interviewers. I hope that I will receive the notification quickly. If I could get this job, I would try my best to fulfill my ambitions.

今天要面試！

9月2日星期一

我很擔心今天的面試，我昨天謹慎地挑選了一件正式的套裝。我覺得我今天表現得還不錯，而且讓面試官有對我很好的印象，我希望我很快就能收到通知。如果我得到這份工作，我一定會努力實現我的抱負。

增廣見聞 超簡單！

How to dress for job interview: A great interview experience is important, but first impressions can also affect the impression for your potential employer. Impression is first judged by your look and what you are wearing. Different kinds of jobs require different outfits. In general, for business formals, you need a blazer, a tie, and sometimes a striped cardigan may be suitable for winter. As for women, a suit is not always the only choice. Simple and classical dresses with decent hairstyle works as well.

如何準備面試穿著？一場成功的面談固然重要，但你給人的「第一印象」也是影響未來僱主決定的關鍵之一。第一印象是從一個人的外表以及穿著來定義，不一樣的工作性質也需要不一樣的面試穿著。一般來說，要看起來有正式的商業氣質，你會需要西裝外套跟一條領帶，有時條紋針織毛衣也適合在冬天面試。而對女孩子來說，套裝不一定是唯一的選擇，有時候一套簡單而經典的洋裝配上莊重的髮型也行得通！

1 我今天有個面試。　**I had an interview today.**
　相似短句 我今天去面試。　**I went for an interview today.**

2 面試進行得不錯。　**The interview went successfully.**
　相似短句 面試進行得很順利。　**The interview went quite well.**

3 我可能會得到那個工作。
　I had a big shot at getting the job.
　相似短句 我有很大的機會能得到那份工作。
　　　　　There's a great chance that I could get the job.

4 我將會更努力工作的。　**I will work harder.**
　相似短句 我會努力工作，證明自己的能力。
　　　　　I'll work harder to prove my ability.

5 我得到這個工作了！　**I got this job.**
　相似短句 我今天得到這份工作了。　**I got the job offer today.**

句型1 **給～好印象**
made an good impression on...
例句 開闊的辦公室給我好印象。
The open office made a good impression on me.

句型2 **我有很大的機會～**
I had a big shot at...
例句 我有很大的機會能得到冠軍。
I had a big shot at winning the championship.

Unit 36
加薪

社群人氣王！英文動態消息寫給你看！

Yeah, I got a raise this month!
我這個月被加薪了！
👍讚 56　💬回覆 7

I am going to take my girlfriend to a nice dinner this weekend for celebrating my raise.
週末要帶我女友去吃好吃的料理，慶祝我被加薪。
👍讚 36　💬回覆 20

After a year of hardworking, I finally got raised!
辛苦了一整年終於被加薪了。
👍讚 130　💬回覆 3

I have no idea why people get so thrilled when they get their salary raised. It's just a little money, why so freaking happy about that?
我真不懂大家幹嘛對加薪那麼高興，錢又不多，到底幹嘛那麼嗨？
👍讚 15　💬回覆 12

Not only got raised but also a lot more work to do...coffee please.
雖然加薪了但工作變得更多了……請再給我一杯咖啡。
👍讚 92　💬回覆 3

新手超必備！一個單字嘛欸通！

raise ⓝ 加薪	**promote** ⓥ 提升；升職	**promotion** ⓝ 升職
colleague ⓝ 同事	**co-worker** ⓝ 同事	**payday** ⓝ 發薪日
salary ⓝ 薪水	**meal** ⓝ 餐點	

出門超實用！能聽會說一次搞定！

A Look at this news! Large corporations outside have raised 5% of the salary for every employee. I don't know if I should feel encouraged or not.

B Things do not seem well in our company. I've worked here for five years, and they only raise 1% of the salary each year.

A 看這新聞！大型企業紛紛幫員工加薪5%。我不知道我該不該覺得有被激勵到。

B 在我們公司看來這事並不樂觀。我在這裡工作五年，他們每年只提高了1%的薪水。

A Will you consider to negotiate your salary package? Five years is not a short period of time. You ought to get what you deserve.

B You are right. I do prepare to have a negotiation with the boss to get a pay raise. After all, the price of consumer product is getting higher. And it does not make sense if our salary remains the same.

A 你會考慮重新談你的薪水嗎？五年不算短耶，你應該得到應有的報酬。

B 你說的對，我確實有在準備跟老闆談加薪。畢竟外面物價高漲，而我們的薪水維持不變是不合理的。

A You speak my mind. However, I don't have that much experience as you do in this company. I guess I will wait for the right time.

B Do not look down on yourself. From what I see, you are the person who has got talent. I don't mean that you need to get another better-paid job, but my suggestion is that looking for second options is always good.

A 你說中我的心聲！但是我的經驗不如你那麼多，我應該要等更好的時機。

B 別看輕你自己。在我看來，你是有能力的人。我不是要催促你去找另一個更好的工作，但還是建議有個備案總是好的。

A Thank you. I will have to do research on salary scale more to prepare for the next job interview.

B Yes. First, research based on company, know their profit-scale; and second, research on similar positions to get to know how much others are being offered are two important topics for you.

A 謝謝。我想我需要再研究一下薪水範圍以準備下份工作的面試。

B 是的！第一步，搜尋公司知道他們的營收，第二，是研究相似職位，知道他們的薪水多少，這是兩個重要的研究主題。

Unit 36 加薪

酸甜苦辣 記下來！

Finally!!

Monday, November 18

I usually work overtime. Today my boss decided to give me a pay raise. He also promoted me to a manager. My colleagues all asked for a big treat. John, the administrative manager, will go celebrate with us tomorrow as well.

終於！！

11月18日星期一

我常常在加班，今天老闆決定要給我加薪，而且把我升職為經理，我的同事都要求我要請他們。行政部門的經理，約翰，明天也要一起來慶祝。

增廣見聞 超簡單！

The demand to get pay raise is not an uncommon issue in Taiwan these days. It is because the overall expense in our life increases without our salaries gaining along with it. Our government recently published a policy for corporations that they could get deduction on taxes by raising the salary for their employees. However, this may have a short-term effect only. For a long-term plan, government will assist companies to become more competitive and increase their profitability in all sorts of method.

加薪需求在台灣已經不是罕見議題，這導因於平均物價金額上漲，而薪水卻沒有因物價同步改變。我們的政府在近期發佈了一項政策，讓企業主可以透過替員工加薪而得到免稅獎勵，這在短期或許能發揮效果，但就長期而言，政府仍需要透過不同方式幫助企業增加競爭力以及獲利能力。

來換換口味吧！讓你的表達更豐富！

1 我加薪了！　**I got a raise.**
　相似短句　我最近加薪了。　I got a pay raise lately.

2 我老闆將我升為經理。　**My boss promoted me to a manager.**
　相似短句　我今天升職成經理了。　I got a promotion to manager today.

3 公司的同事都要我請客。
My colleagues asked for a big meal.
　相似短句　所有同事都要我請吃大餐。
　　　　　　All my co-workers wanted a big meal on my treat.

4 今天是發薪日。　**Today is payday.**
　相似短句　我今天可以拿到薪水。　I can get my salary today.

5 我的薪水蠻高的。　**My salary is quite high.**
　相似短句　我的薪水還不錯。　I get a good salary

依樣畫葫蘆！套進去就能用！

句型1 **寧願～也不～**
rather... than...

例句　我寧可保有自己的生活，也不要領高薪工作到累死。
I would rather have my own life than work to death with higher salary.

句型2 **升職為～**
promoted to...

例句　我不懂為什麼提姆被升職為專案經理。
I didn't understand why Tim got promoted to the project manager.

Unit 37
減薪

社群人氣王！英文動態消息寫給你看！

This doesn't make sense! I work hard but got cut while others did nothing and got raised?

這沒道理啊！我認真工作卻被減薪，其他人什麼都沒做卻被加薪？

👍 讚 56　💬 回覆 7

We get paid less due to the economic crisis. Feeling so bad.

因為經融危機的關係我們都被減薪了。日子真難過。

👍 讚 36　💬 回覆 20

After seeing my pay cheque… okay, I will have to wait a while for my Chanel.

看到了我的薪水後……好吧，我可能要再等一陣子才能買香奈兒了。

👍 讚 130　💬 回覆 3

After all, less is better than nothing. (sigh)

薪水少，總比沒有工作好啊。（嘆氣）

👍 讚 15　💬 回覆 12

Considering to find a part-time job. My boss is paying me less than before.

正在考慮要找個兼職了。我老闆付我的薪水越來越少。

👍 讚 92　💬 回覆 3

新手超必備！一個單字嘛欸通！

decrease ⓥ 減少	**salary** ⓝ 薪水	**notice** ⓝ 通知
pay cut ⓟʰʳ 減薪	**crisis** ⓝ 危機	**bankruptcy** ⓝ 破產
part-time ⓐⁱ 兼職的	**financial** ⓐⁱ 財務上的；經濟上的	

出門超實用！能聽會說一次搞定！

A There's a rumor that our company will dock 7% of salary which I find is hard to believe. Though I know we did not gain profit this year.

B I can only accept that there's no bonus for employees. But speaking of deducting salary, maybe we are not in the worst situation comparing with other people.

A 雖然公司今年沒有獲利，但很難令人相信的是，有傳言說公司要減薪7%。

B 我只能接受員工沒有紅利。不過說到減薪，或許這還不是我們會遇到最慘的情況。

A What makes you think that? I cannot imagine how I can get through this Chinese New year without bonus, and to get deduction on wages at the same time.

B Well, three friends of mine got laid off, and the other one is on unpaid leave. Seriously, I think we are lucky that we still have our jobs.

A 你怎麼會這麼想？我根本不能想像沒有紅利又同時被減薪該怎麼過新年。

B 因為我身邊有三個朋友被解僱，一個朋友在放無薪假，所以說真的，我認為我們有工作，還算幸運的。

A True. Now I see the deduction on wages sounds better than being laid off or an unpaid leave.

B However, sometimes I really want to go abroad and visit somewhere. I can't do it because I don't have any annual leaves.

A 確實，現在我理解減薪聽起來似乎比解僱跟無薪假好多了。

B 不過，有時後我真的很想出國去哪個地方走走，但就是因為我沒有假，所以一直無法去。

A I hear you. You don't have to worry about that. I will report to the boss later; saying that you really want to go on a vacation.

B Don't be silly, Tom. If I leave the company, then no one can help you cover all those bad records, such as being late to work.

A 我聽到囉！不要擔心，我等等就跟老闆報告說你想要去放假。

B 別傻了湯姆！如果我離開公司，就沒有人幫你掩蓋那些个好的記錄了，例如遲到。

Unit 37 減薪

酸甜苦辣 記下來！

Difficult Times

Thursday, December 19

The company is going to the extent of bankruptcy. It is next month that our company will cut salaries. I am going to live a hard life in the following years, and it's inevitable for me to take a part-time job. It is really difficult to live with such little salary.

艱困的時期

12月19日星期四

公司快破產了，下個月公司要減薪。接下來幾年我將會過得很辛苦，不可避免地我得兼一份差。靠著微薄的薪水過活真的很辛苦。.

增廣見聞 超簡單！

The economic crisis in 2008 had resulted in a lot of unpaid leave policies even in large corporations. A lot of corporations published this policy in order to reduce cost on human resource. Unpaid leave means that the employee is able to retain his / her position in the company without getting paid. The start of economic crisis is the result of the domino effect when people who took out outstanding numbers of mortgages were actually unable to make payment of the mortgages.

2008年的金融海嘯導致很多公司實施無薪假，就算是大公司也不例外，有很多公司利用這項政策來降低公司人事成本的開銷。無薪假的意思是：員工可以在沒有領薪水的前提下保有職位。金融海嘯始於骨牌效應，當人們借貸高額房貸，但其實根本無力償還時，就會引發金融海嘯。

來換換口味吧！讓你的表達更豐富！

❶ 今天我收到減薪通知。 **I got the decreased-salary notice.**
相似短句 我最近被減薪了。 I got a pay cut recently.

❷ 公司營運得不好。 **The company is doing much worse.**
相似短句 公司有財務危機。
The company is going through a financial crisis.

❸ 這份工作讓我抓狂。 **This job makes me mad.**
相似短句 這份工作讓我抓狂。 This job is driving me crazy.

❹ 我兼了一份差事。 **I took a part-time job.**
相似短句 我開始在家工作。 I started to work at home.

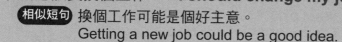

❺ 我應該要換個工作。 **I should change my job.**
相似短句 換個工作可能是個好主意。
Getting a new job could be a good idea.

依樣畫葫蘆！套進去就能用！

句型1 **我將會～**
I am going to...

例句 我將會更加努力工作，保住我的飯碗。
I'm going to work harder to keep my job.

句型2 **為了要～**
so as to...

例句 公司為了要刪減開支，決定要解雇十個人。
The company decided to fire 10 people so as to slash down the cost.

Unit 38
裁員

社群人氣王！英文動態消息寫給你看！

Feeling sad for my colleague for being fired. Farewell and take care.

為我被裁員的同事感到難過，請多保重。

👍 讚 56　💬 回覆 7

I can't take it anymore. I really hope my boss can fire those irresponsible people.

我再也無法忍受了。多希望老闆可以開除那些不負責任的傢伙！

👍 讚 36　💬 回覆 20

My boss was one step ahead firing me when I was considering to quit.

我正想著要辭職的時後老闆就把我裁員了。

👍 讚 130　💬 回覆 3

Okay, yes, I got fired. Please don't say anything if you aren't buying me a drink or offering me a new job.

好的、是的，我被開除了。除非你要請我喝一杯或幫我介紹工作不然不要說多餘的話。

👍 讚 15　💬 回覆 12

Dear God, please tell me what I can do. I got three kids to feed but I just lost my job. Please guide me through the difficulties. Amen.

親愛的上帝，請告訴我我該怎麼做？我有三個孩子要養但我被裁員了。請帶領我走過這些困難。阿門。

👍 讚 92　💬 回覆 3

新手超必備！一個單字嘛欸通！

lay off phr. 裁員	**company** n. 公司	**boss** n. 老闆
worker n. 員工	**fire** v. 開除	**department** n. 部門
colleague n. 同事	**administrative** adj. 行政的	

168

出門超實用！能聽會說一次搞定！

A Hey Michael! Have you thought about how you would react if you got laid off?

B Yes, I have. Some of my friends got laid off last week. It's hard not to think about it when you see your friends around are all in such terrible conditions.

A 嘿麥可。你有想過如果哪天被解僱你會怎麼樣嗎？

B 有啊，我有些朋友上週被解僱，看到朋友這麼悲慘的狀況很難不去想像。

A I feel sorry for them. Did they tell you the reason why they got laid off, though it may be hard questions for them.

B Yes. I am glad they shared their experiences with me. All of them are in the same company, and they are all at similar age.

A 我替他們感到遺憾，他們有跟你說為什麼被解僱嗎？雖然這對他們來說可能是很難回答的問題。

B 有的，我很開心幸好他們願意分享經驗。他們全部都在同一間公司，年齡也都相仿。

A Are you applying that the age is the main reason they got laid off? It's unfair. The work experience and knowledge and so on are real treasures for a company.

B Good guess. Yes, they said that their boss got six freshmen to take over their jobs with much lower wage.

A 你是在暗示說年紀是導致解僱的主要原因嗎？這不公平。工作經驗跟知識等，才是公司最大的寶藏啊！

B 猜得對。是的，他們的老闆找來了六個新鮮人以更低的薪資接替他們的工作。

A Poor them. Let's get back to the question. I will pretend that I still have my job. I will wear my suits; get up early as usual, pretending that I go to work everyday.

B You will be seen through. Mine is more interesting. I will make a good use of the severance and start my own small business.

A 他們真可憐。回到剛剛試想被裁員的問題，我會假裝我還有工作。我會每天穿西裝，一樣早起，假裝我每天都有去上班。

B 你會被識破的。我的答案比較有趣，我會好好利用解僱金，然後自己開創我的小事業。

Part 7 勞工拼經濟

酸甜苦辣 記下來！

It doesn't make sense!

Friday, February 21

The company is downsizing. It doesn't make sense that the company has laid off ten workers. I really don't want to be laid off. We have to take actions against the company superiors to protect our own rights. I hope that we don't have to protest against the company in the street, or the company shall pay for what they have done.

這沒道理阿！

2月21日星期五

公司正在縮減規模。公司一次裁掉了十個人，真是沒道理。我真的不希望被裁員。我們必須採取行動抵制公司高層，以保護自身的權益。希望不要鬧上街頭抗議一途，否則公司將會為他們做的事付出代價。

增廣見聞 超簡單！

There are a lot of reasons that results in being laid off. The case in the conversation is an example. Normally, it occurs when a company is facing financial difficulty, so they have to downsize. Thus, getting laid off has nothing to do with employee's personal performances. However, to get fired has a completely different meaning. To get fired means the person's work performance isn't reaching the expectation or simply because the person is not complying with company culture.

有許多原因可能導致失業，文中對話所述也是一個例子，但大部分的時候，解僱員工是因為公司正面臨財務危機而需要縮小規模，所以被解僱通常跟員工個人表現無關。但是被炒魷魚就不是這樣了，被炒魷魚表示這個人可能工作表現不如預期，或是純粹只因為這個員工不適合這間公司文化。

來換換口味吧!讓你的表達更豐富!

❶ 公司將要裁員。 **Our company will lay off workers.**
> 相似短句 老闆計畫要裁員。 The boss is planning to fire people.

❷ 行政單位是第一波裁員的對象。
The layoff would begin with administrative personnel.
> 相似短句 公司會先解雇行政部門的人。
> The company would sack people in administration department first.

❸ 我今天加班。 **I worked overtime today.**
> 相似短句 我今天得加班。 I had to work late today.

❹ 我習慣在這裡工作。 **I'm used to working here.**
> 相似短句 我習慣在這裡和所有同事一起工作。
> I'm used to this company and working with all the colleagues.

❺ 我真的不希望被裁員。 **I really don't want to be laid off.**
> 相似短句 希望我不要被裁員。 I hope I won't get fired.

依樣畫葫蘆!套進去就能用!

句型1 從～開始
begin with...
> 例句 裁員會從資淺的員工開始裁。
> **The sack begins with less experienced employees.**

句型2 ～真沒道理。
It doesn't make sense that...
> 例句 老闆解雇替他那認真的秘書,真沒道理。
> **It doesn't make sense that the boss fired his hard-working secretary.**

Unit 39
地攤買東西

Part 8 小資省錢趣

Look what I bought from the street vendor!

看看我在地攤上買到什麼！

👍 讚 56　💬 回覆 7

I bought two dresses and a pair of shoes only for 500 NTD!

我只花了五百元買到兩件洋裝和一雙鞋！

👍 讚 36　💬 回覆 20

The street vendors are selling everything! From clothing to kitchen implements.

地攤真是什麼都有在賣耶，從衣服到廚具都有。

👍 讚 130　💬 回覆 3

I don't like to buy stuff from the street vendors, because the quality of the goods there is not very nice.

我不是很喜歡買地攤貨，因為品質沒有很好。

👍 讚 15　💬 回覆 12

The street vendors are so interesting and so cheap that I always end up buying too much every time I go there.

地攤真的超好逛又超便宜，我每次都買好多東西。

👍 讚 92　💬 回覆 3

新手超必備！一個單字嘛欸通！

budget ⓝ 預算；經費	**stall** ⓝ 貨攤；攤販	**cheap** adj. 便宜的
stuff ⓝ 東西	**vendor** ⓝ 小販；叫賣者	**street** ⓝ 街道
save ⓥ 節省		

172

出門超實用！能聽會說一次搞定！

Ⓐ Do you know where I can buy some cheap kitchen utensils? I just moved in to my new place, so I need a new set.

Ⓑ You can try the market under Tassel Bridge. The market opens every Saturday morning, 6-12pm.

Ⓐ 你知道我要到哪裡購買便宜的廚房用具嗎？我剛剛到新家，需要一套全新的用具！

Ⓑ 你可以試試看特梭橋下的市場。每週六早上 6 到 12 點開。

Ⓐ Hi there, can I check this set of glass cups? How much is it? It's beautiful.

Ⓑ Hi there, sure, please be our guest. You have really good tastes. Those glasses are from Italy.

Ⓐ 你好，我可以看看這一套玻璃杯嗎？多少錢啊？這套好漂亮。

Ⓑ 嗨您好，沒問題，想看就看吧。你的品味真好，那些是從義大利來的。

Ⓐ You have a lot of good stuff. No matter if it's vintage, or modern home-deco products.

Ⓑ I have ran this business for so many years. I know where to get the best stuff to sell.

Ⓐ 你有好多好東西呢，不管是復古的或是摩登的家飾。

Ⓑ 我從事這行業已經有很多年了。我知道要去哪裡找到好東西賣。

Ⓐ Oh, you haven't told me how much it costs. I am willing to pay 20 dollars for that set.

Ⓑ Good guess! 20 dollars is exactly what I had in mind and I will give you more discount since you have good taste.

Ⓐ 喔，你還沒告訴我這賣多少錢，我願意付 20 元買下整組。

Ⓑ 猜對了！20 元剛好跟我想的一樣，而且我會再給你一些折扣，因為你識貨。

酸甜苦辣 記下來！

Shopping at a Stall

Tuesday, December 3

I was planning to buy a pair of shoes. Things at a stall are much cheaper than those in the department store. There happened to be a shoes stall on the way that caught my attention. The street vendor suggested that I should buy the high-heeled shoes in coffee. I don't like wearing high heels, so I bought a pair of black boots instead. It cost me 1000 NT dollars.

地攤買東西

12月3日星期二

我想要買一雙鞋子，地攤貨通常都比百貨公司的便宜。路上剛好有一個地攤引起了我的注意力，攤販老闆一直建議我要買那雙咖啡色的高跟鞋。我不喜歡穿高跟鞋，所以我反而買了一雙黑色的靴子。我花了一千元。

增廣見聞 超簡單！

In flea markets or vintage markets, goods are usually presented on a small stall or simply spread out on the ground. If you want to look for something vintage or some second-hand products, then the flea market or vintage market will be the good choice. Also, you may try a garage sale. Typical items in a garage sale are things that are unwanted from households, including old books, toys, clothes, and even home appliances sometimes.

在跳蚤市場或古物市場，商品通常都是擺在小攤子上，要不然就是直接攤在地上賣。如果你想要找一些復古的商品，或是還很具價值的二手貨，那麼跳蚤市場或是古物市場將會是不錯的選擇。又或者你會想試試車庫拍賣，通常會在車庫拍賣中出現的大多是賣方家中不會再使用的用品，包括書、玩具、衣服，有時候也會有家電用品。

1 我想要買一雙鞋子。　**I was planning to buy a pair of shoes.**

(相似短句) 我想買雙鞋。　I was thinking of buying a pair of shoes.

2 我的預算有限。　**My budget is limited.**

(相似短句) 我沒打算花太多錢買東西。
I am not planning to spend too much on it.

3 地攤的東西比百貨公司的便宜多了。
Things at a stall are much cheaper than those in the department store.

(相似短句) 地攤賣的東西比百貨公司賣的便宜。
Stuff are cheaper at stalls than in department stores.

4 路上有一家賣鞋子的地攤引起我的注意力。
There was a shoes stall on the way that caught my attention.

(相似短句) 我想要去看看入口處賣鞋的攤子。
I wanted to go check out a shoes stall at the entrance.

5 我什麼都沒買。　**I bought nothing.**

(相似短句) 我沒買東西。　I didn't buy anything.

依樣畫葫蘆！套進去就能用！

(句型1) ～建議～
suggest that...

(例句) 我建議在你衝動付賬之前，我們先去吃東西。
I suggest that we go grab something to eat before you pay on impulse.

(句型2) 我以為～
I thought...

(例句) 我以為地攤所有東西的價格都比較便宜。
I thought the price of everything at a stall should be lower.

Unit 40
跳樓大拍賣

社群人氣王！英文動態消息寫給你看！

It's a bargain!
真的太划算了。

👍 讚 56　💬 回覆 7

Everything in the shop is 70% off!
所有的商品都三折！

👍 讚 36　💬 回覆 20

The bookstore is closing and I got 10 books for 500 NTD!
那間書店要關門了，我用五百元就買到十本書！

👍 讚 130　💬 回覆 3

The shoe store is going to have a sale, any one wants to take a look with me?
那家鞋店即將有拍賣，有人要跟我一起去看看嗎？

👍 讚 15　💬 回覆 12

There is a sale at the store on the corner. No wonder it is crowded with people.
轉角的那家店正在大拍賣，難怪會有那麼多人。

👍 讚 92　💬 回覆 3

新手超必備！一個單字嘛欸通！

sale ⓝ 拍賣	shop ⓝ 商店	get rid of 𝗽𝗵𝗿 清除掉
goods ⓝ 商品	reasonable 𝗮𝗱𝗷 合理的	discount ⓝ 折扣
department store ⓝ 百貨公司	clearance sale 𝗽𝗵𝗿 清倉大拍賣	

出門超實用！能聽會說一次搞定！

A Wow, Shelly, take a look at that! They are offering 90% off on all jewelry, including bracelet, earrings, necklace, and rings.

B No way. Which brand is it? If it is not a famous brand then I don't think it's that attractive to me.

A 哇，雪莉！看看那個！他們所有珠寶都下殺一折，包括手環，耳環，項鍊跟戒指。

B 不會吧！是什麼牌子？如果不是有名的牌子，就不太吸引我了。

A Okay. Looks like there are various brands in it. The most famous brand is Swarovski.

B It's impossible for Swarovski to put product on sale. Those might be imported goods; otherwise it's not possible to get such cheap prices.

A 恩，看起來有很多各式各樣的牌子在裡面，最有名的是施華洛世奇。

B 施華洛世奇不可能將產品做大特價。那些商品有可能是進口商品，不然不可能賣到這麼便宜的價錢。

A Yes. They did specify it. Now I see that's why they are cheap, because they don't charge custom fees.

B Okay. If that's the case, then we can believe those are real, instead of counterfeits.

A 是啊，他們確實有寫。那這樣我知道為什麼這麼便宜了，因為他們不用收關稅。

B 好吧，如果是這樣我們可以相信這是正品而不是贗品。

A Should we go in now? My girlfriend's birthday is next week. I need to buy a present for her.

B I won't tell her that her present was actually imported goods, not from the store as she imagined.

A 我們現在可以進去了嗎？我女友的生日是在下週，我需要買禮物給她。

B 我絕對不會告訴她禮物是進口品，而非她想像中從店裡買的。

Part 8 小資省錢趣

酸甜苦辣 記下來！

You get what you pay for

Sunday, November 24

Department stores are having clearance sales. I read the "on sale" ads and decided to go shopping. The discounts were reasonable; I bought a shirt and a skirt. There were lots of people in the department store, and I was annoyed with the crowd. It's necessary to look over things on clearance sales because there might be some stains on those clothes. I had a bad experience once.

一分錢一分貨

11月24日星期日

百貨公司正在大特價，我看到拍賣的廣告所以打算去逛逛，因為折扣算是蠻合理的，所以我買了一件裙子跟一件衣服。百貨公司到處都是人，我被人潮惹惱了。一定要好好檢查跳樓大拍賣時的商品，因為上面可能會有些污漬，我就曾經有這種不好的經驗。

增廣見聞 超簡單！

Building jumping clearance sale is the term to describe a big sale in Taiwan. The term in Taiwanese means that the clearance sale is way too cheap to even make profit, even the boss can't stand it and might need to jump off a building. However, it is funny that this clearance sales slogan could be used for marketing to attract people's attention. It is possible to see a store hanging a red cloth and says "clearance sale" throughout the year. Or, "closing sale" is another way to attract customer's attention.

「跳樓大拍賣」是台灣用來敘述大特價的狀況。這名詞是代表：因為大特價太便宜沒得賺，所以老闆要跳樓，常用來譬喻清倉特價。但有趣的是，清倉特價其實可以作為行銷手法用來吸引人們的注意，所以你有可能看到某店家一整年都掛著紅布條寫的跳樓大拍賣。或者，倒店特價也是吸引客人注意力的另一個方式。

❶ 我買了很多東西。　**I bought lots of things.**

　相似短句 我在那間精品店買了很多東西。
　　　　　I did a lot of shopping at the boutique.

❷ 那間店正在打折。　**The shop is having a sale.**

　相似短句 那間店在舉行春季拍賣。　The store is having a spring sale.

❸ 街角的鞋店正在舉辦清倉大拍賣。
　The shoe shop around the corner is having a clearance sale.

　相似短句 那間百貨公司這週正在舉行清倉大拍賣。
　　　　　The department store is having a massive clearance sale
　　　　　this week.

❹ 這家鞋店正試著盡量把貨賣掉。
　The shoe shop is trying to get rid of as many goods as possible.

　相似短句 為了清理庫存，這家店正舉行清倉拍賣。
　　　　　The shop is having a stock clearance to get rid of overstock.

❺ 折扣後的價錢還蠻合理的。　**The discounts were reasonable.**

　相似短句 我會買，因為折扣還不賴
　　　　　I would buy them because the discount was not bad.

依樣畫葫蘆！套進去就能用！

句型1 我利用～
I took advantage of...

例句 我利用信用卡拿到額外的八五折。
I took advantage of the credit card and got 15% extra discount.

句型2 我被～惹惱了。
I was annoyed with...

例句 我被沒禮貌的店員惹惱了。
I was annoyed with the rude clerk.

Unit 41
買保養品

社群人氣王！英文動態消息寫給你看！

I bought a lot of moisturizing lotion for the winter.
我買了很多保濕乳液好過冬～

👍讚 56　💬回覆 7

Skin whitening products are so expensive. Hope they really work.
美白保養品好貴喔！希望真的有效！

👍讚 36　💬回覆 20

My skin got so dark after the summer vacation. It's time to whiten it!
暑假之後我的皮膚曬得好黑，是時候來美白了！

👍讚 130　💬回覆 3

There are so many choice of the facial moisturizing sets. I like A set but it's a little bit expensive.
有好多種臉部保濕組合可以選喔。我很喜歡 A 組但是它有點貴。

👍讚 15　💬回覆 12

The weather is so dry in Canada. Is there any recommending brand for facial moisturizing and body lotion?
加拿大的天氣好乾。臉部保濕乳液和身體乳有什麼推薦的品牌嗎？

👍讚 92　💬回覆 3

新手超必備！一個單字嘛欸通！

cosmetic adj. 化妝品的	pretty adj. 秀麗的	beautiful adj. 漂亮的
lotion n. 化妝水	buy v. 購買	pricey adj. 昂貴的
makeup n. 化妝品	care product phr. 保養品	

出門超實用！能聽會說一次搞定！

A Why does my face get really dry after I shower? It's really uncomfortable for me.

B Which kind of facial cleaner do you use? If you use facial cleaner that is designed for oily skin, then it will cause this kind of situation.

A 為什麼我洗完澡後臉很乾？這真的很不舒服。

B 你用哪一種洗面乳？如果你用的洗面乳是針對油性肌膚設計的，那就會造成你現在的情況。

A Isn't it about the skin care issue? Maybe its time to purchase skin care products.

B Don't try to find excuses for yourself. Okay. Let's see what kind of products are suitable for you.

A 這不是跟肌膚保養有關的原因嗎？也許是時候該購入肌膚保養的產品了。

B 別為你自己找藉口，我們來看看那種產品適合你。

A For dry skin, you have to pick the toning lotion, cream and intensive supplement that is moisturizing enough.

B Do you have any recommending brands? There are too many kinds of products on the market.

A 對乾性肌膚，你可以選擇化妝水、乳液，精華液，這些都足夠保濕。

B 你有推薦哪個牌子嗎？市場上有太多種類的產品了。

A Yes, I do. But I suggest you should go try it first and see if those skin care products work for you.

B Great. Let's go get some samples, so that I can decide which ones are most suitable for me.

A 當然囉，但我建議你應該先試試它，看那些肌膚保養產品是否適合你。

B 太好了，我們去拿些試用品吧，這樣我就能決定哪一款適合我使用了。

Unit 41 買保養品

酸甜苦辣 記下來！

I want to be beautiful

Wednesday, May 1

I'm so attracted by the cosmetic ads on TV. I want to be as beautiful as those models. I felt so comfortable while applying the lotion on my face. It's the most comfortable lotion that I have ever used, so I bought 5 bottles at a time.

我想要變漂亮

5月1日 星期三

電視上的化妝品廣告讓人很心動，我想要和那些模特兒一樣漂亮。化妝水擦在臉上的感覺冰冰涼涼的，真是舒服！這是我用過最舒服的化妝水，所以我一次買了五瓶。

增廣見聞 超簡單！

When purchasing skin care products, people should really be careful of the ingredients in it. For example, it recently became a topic that whether skin care products with or without alcohol is harmful for our skin. Some experts claim that skin care products with alcohol may cause radical damage to our skin, but some are against that point of view, and say there are good alcohol. Thus, as a consumer, although what we care more is probably the effect of the product, it's still better to check the ingredient first and test out some samples before we buy it.

當我們在買保養品時，應該要去注意一下裡面的成分。舉個例子，最近保養品中有沒有酒精、酒精對肌膚有沒有傷害一直是個被討論的議題。有專家認為含酒精的保養品會帶給肌膚嚴重的傷害，但有些專家則反對這樣的觀點，因為他們認為酒精還有好壞之分。所以，作為一個消費者，雖然我們重視的是產品成效，但在購買前還是看看成分，並且用試用包測試一下比較保險。

來換換口味吧！讓你的表達更豐富！

❶ 電視上的化妝品廣告讓人很心動。
I'm so attracted by the cosmetic ads on TV.
> 相似短句 電視上的化妝品廣告讓人好心動。
> The cosmetics ads on TV are so inviting.

❷ 我想要跟模特兒一樣漂亮。
I want to be as beautiful as those models.
> 相似短句 我想要看來和那些模特兒一樣漂亮。
> I want to look like one of those pretty models.

❸ 化妝水擦在臉上的感覺真是舒服。
I felt so comfortable while applying the lotion on my face.
> 相似短句 化妝水擦在臉上感覺真舒服。
> It felt great to have the lotion on my face.

❹ 我買了一整組。 **I bought the whole set.**
> 相似短句 我把整組都買回家了。 I took the whole set home with me.

❺ 保養品都很貴。 **The care products are pricey.**
> 相似短句 保養品通常很貴。 The care products usually cost a lot.

依樣畫葫蘆！套進去就能用！

句型1 這是我用過最～的～
It's the most... that I had ever used.

> 例句 這是我用過最貴也最有效的保養品。
> **It's the most expensive but effective care product that I had ever used.**

句型2 ～花了我～
It cost me... to...

> 例句 這罐高級化妝水花了我兩百元美金。
> **It cost me $200 to buy this high-end toner.**

Unit 42
買名牌

Part 8 小資省錢趣

社群人氣王！英文動態消息寫給你看！

She only wears Dior perfumes.
她只擦迪奧的香水。

👍 讚 56　　💬 回覆 7

Why is everyone so crazy about Louis Vuitton?
為什麼大家如此熱衷於路易威登呢？

👍 讚 36　　💬 回覆 20

I bought a Prada for my mom when I visited Italy last month.
上個月去義大利的時候，我幫我媽買了一件普拉達。

👍 讚 130　　💬 回覆 3

His fountain pens are all Mont Blanc! No wonder why they looks so elegant and special.
他的鋼筆全都是萬寶龍的！難怪每一枝看起來都那麼高雅又特別。

👍 讚 15　　💬 回覆 12

I couldn't decide which Chanel bag I should get, so I bought both. They are both beautiful, aren't they? – feeling satisfied.
我無法決定應該要買哪一個香奈兒包，所以就兩個都買了。它們都好漂亮對吧？——覺得滿足。

👍 讚 92　　💬 回覆 3

新手超必備！一個單字嘛欸通！

money n. 金錢	**purse** n. 包包	**available** adj. 有貨的
latest adj. 最新的	**season** n. 一季	**keen** adj. 敏銳的
sight n. 眼光	**fashion** n. 流行時尚	**style** n. 風格

出門超實用！能聽會說一次搞定！

A I am going to Paris starting next weekend for a week. Do you need me to buy anything for you?

B Yes, of course. I would like some bags and snacks from Paris. Let me check the price on the Internet.

A 我下週末要去巴黎。你要我幫你買什麼東西嗎？

B 當然要啊！我想要一些包包跟零食。我先在網路上看價錢。

A No, you don't have to. I will tell you how much those cost when I am back. You don't need to pay first.

B Okay. I want a Chanel purse, a Prada handbag, and a pair of Gucci sunglasses.

A 不用啦！等我回來，我會告訴你那些東西多少錢，不需要先給我錢。

B 好，那我要一個香奈兒皮夾，一個 Prada 肩背包，還有一副 Gucci 太陽眼鏡。

A Wow. I thought you have those things already. Those are not cheap items.

B Yeah, I do. But you know we can get them 20% cheaper if we buy the products in Paris, because we can get tax reimbursement.

A 哇，我以為你已經有這些東西了，那些可不便宜。

B 是啊我有。但是你知道在巴黎，我們可以用八折的價錢買到，因為我們可以申請退稅。

A Alright, can you print out the item numbers, and the pictures of those things? Otherwise I don't know which ones you want.

B It's easy. You can search those brands on the Internet and you can see the most updated items, and that's what I want.

A 好吧，那你可以列印商品型號和照片給我嗎？不然我不知道哪個是你要的。

B 很簡單啊，你就上網搜尋那些牌子，然後你會看到最新　季的產品，我就是要那些。

Unit 42 買名牌

酸甜苦辣 記下來！

LV new arrival!!

Monday, July 15

I love shopping! LV has new purses available. I have a keen sight on fashion. I often take a look at those new purses in the boutique. Though the price of a LV purse is very expensive in Taiwan, I still like it. It's said that there are lots of boutiques along the Champs Elysees in Paris. I hope I will have a chance to have a boutique trip in Paris someday.

LV 有新貨到！！

7月15日星期一

我好愛逛街哦！！LV 又有新的包包上市了。我對流行有敏銳的眼光。我常去精品店看看那些新包包。雖然 LV 包包在台灣都很貴，我卻還是很喜歡。聽說沿著香榭大道兩旁有很多名牌精品店，希望哪天我有機會來個巴黎精品遊。

增廣見聞 超簡單！

Buying luxury brand products in Paris or Hong Kong may be a good choice because we can get tax reimbursement. Another choice will be at an outlet. Outlets in the United States and European countries are common. Products and items at the outlet are mostly classic bags, and out of season products. If the price is the primary concern for you, then an outlet will be a great choice for you. Also, we don't have to worry that we might buy a bag that is fake.

在巴黎或香港買名牌或許是個很好的選擇，因為可以用退稅價格計算。另一個好選擇則是過季商品店。「暢貨中心」在歐美國家是很常見的商店，在暢貨中心的商品通常是品牌的經典商品以及非當季流行的商品。如果價格是你的主要考量，那麼暢貨中心對你來說就是個好地方；而且，在暢貨中心還可以不用擔心自己買到假貨呢！

來換換口味吧！讓你的表達更豐富！

1 這件裙子很適合我。　**The skirt fits me well.**
　(相似短句) 這件毛衣很襯我的膚色。
　　　　　　The sweater goes well with my skin color.

2 我試了其他的顏色。　**I tried the other color.**
　(相似短句) 我試了其他款式的襯衫。　I tried other kind of shirts.

3 我用完了我的錢。　**I lost my last dollar.**
　(相似短句) 我的錢花完了。　I ran out of money.

4 LV出新款包包了。　**LV has new purses available.**
　(相似短句) 那是 LV 這一季最新的包包。
　　　　　　That's LV's latest purse this season.

5 我對流行有著敏銳的眼光。　**I have a keen sight on fashion.**
　(相似短句) 我對造型很有眼光。　I have a great sense of style.

依樣畫葫蘆！套進去就能用！

(句型1) **聽說～**
It's said that...
(例句) 聽說這些品項的價格比台灣的低了五成。
It's said that the prices of the items were 50% lower than in Taiwan.

(句型2) **我從來不知道～**
I had never known that...
(例句) 我不知道他們的鞋子這麼貴。
I had never known that their shoes were so pricey.

Unit 43
週年慶

社群人氣王！英文動態消息寫給你看！

I hate annual sale. It makes me spend so much money.

我討厭週年慶。它讓我花了好多錢。

👍讚 56　💬回覆 7

The department store is crowded with people during the annual sale. –being scared.

週年慶的時候百貨公司總是塞滿人潮。被嚇壞了。

👍讚 36　💬回覆 20

My husband bought so many toys for the kids. They must love the annual sale.

我先生買了好多玩具給孩子們，他們一定愛死週年慶了。

👍讚 130　💬回覆 3

My mom is obsessed with the annual sale. She spent a whole day buying a truck of new stuff.

我媽很沉迷於百貨公司週年慶。她花了一整天買了一卡車的東西。

👍讚 15　💬回覆 12

There are too many kinds of discounts during the annual sale, which is really complicated and got me really exhausted.

週年慶時的各種折扣辦法和優惠活動實在太複雜了，讓我覺得好累。

👍讚 92　💬回覆 3

新手超必備！一個單字嘛欸通！

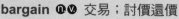

bargain n v 交易；討價還價		**bracelet** n 手環
accessory n 配件	**offer** v 給予；提供	**publish** v 出版
catalog n 目錄	**advertisement** n 廣告	**department store** n 百貨公司

188

出門超實用！能聽會說一次搞定！

A Guess what? It's October now! It's time of the annual sale! I've been waiting for it since July.

B Really! Do you have any DMs in hand? I would like to see what I can buy this year.

A 猜猜看怎麼了，現在是十月了！周年慶的季節！我從七月就開始期待了。

B 真的嗎！你現在手上有 DM 嗎？我想看看今年有什麼我可以買的東西。

A Here! Look at this one, the jacket usually costs us $6000, but now we can have it by spending only 2000 dollars.

B What a good bargain! Hey check this! The bracelet and other accessories are all on sale as well!

A 在這裡，你看，這件外套通常要價 6000，現在我們只需要 2000 就能擁有它。

B 這真是個好折扣！看一下這個，這條手環跟其他配件也都在打折。

A Let's check online DMs of other department stores. Maybe they offer cheaper prices.

B You are right! The on sale items may be different in different department stores.

A 我們看一下其他間百貨公司的線上 DM，也許有更便宜的價格。

B 對耶，這些折扣商品在別間百貨公司可能有不同的價格。

A The bracelet you just saw is cheaper in this department store, but my jacket is more expensive here.

B That means we need to go to two places today. Let's go to get your jacket first!

A 你剛剛看的手環在別間百貨公司比較便宜，但我的外套就貴多了。

B 那表示我們今天需要去兩個地方囉，咱們先去買你的外套吧。

Part 8 小資省錢趣

酸甜苦辣 記下來！

A Big Sale!!

Saturday, November 14

I went to department store with my mom today. We arrived at the time before the department store opened. You must not believe what I saw. The queue has extended two blocks away from the department store. We were astonished at such scene. Then I figured there's a cosmetic brand was having a big sale which offered 300 skin care sets with 90% discount. Luckily, mom doesn't like that brand, so I am safe. At least, this year mom didn't ask me to line up for things she wants.

大特價！！

11月14日星期六

今天我和媽媽一起去了百貨公司，我們在它還沒開之前就到了。你一定不會相信我看到什麼，排隊隊伍已經延長到兩個街區之外。我們對這景象感到非常驚訝。後來發現是因為有個化妝品品牌推出三百組限量一折的優惠組合。幸運的，我媽並不喜歡那品牌，所以我逃過一劫，至少今年我媽都沒有叫我幫她排她想要的商品。

增廣見聞 超簡單！

In Taiwan, the annual sales are usually during October and November. Each department store will publish catalogs of their own, therefore, the same item may have different prices at different lacations. Interestingly, "DM" is the abbreviation of 'direct mail' which in Taiwan, means the mail that contains advertisement or other sales information. But actually, it's an incorrect usage in English. Brochure, catalog, or flyers are the correct words to use.

在台灣，特價季節通常是在十月和十一月份。每一間百貨公司會公佈自己的特價型錄，所以同樣的商品在不同百貨公司可能會有不同的價格。有趣的是「DM」這個詞是「直接派信」的縮寫，泛指直接發佈的訊息或是廣告特價的信件，但事實上，「DM」在英文中並不是一個正統的用法；小冊子，型錄或是傳單都是正確的單字以表示同一種東西。

來換換口味吧！讓你的表達更豐富！

① 今年我媽都沒有叫我幫她排她想要的商品。
Mom didn't ask me to line up for things she wanted this year.
(相似短句) 不用幫我媽排她想要的商品。
I don't have to get in line to buy things that my mom wanted.

② 你一定不會相信我看到什麼。 **You must not believe what I saw.**
(相似短句) 你也許會懷疑我待會要說的話。
You may have doubt about what I am going to say.

③ 排隊隊伍已經延長到兩個街區之外。
The queue has extended two blocks away from the department store.
(相似短句) 排隊隊伍已經延長到兩個街區之外。
The length of the queue has extended to two blocks long
from the department store.

④ 我們在百貨公司還沒開之前就到了。
We arrived before the department store opened.
(相似短句) 我們在百貨公司還沒開之前抵達。
We arrived before the opening time of the department store.

⑤ 我媽跟我對這景象感到非常驚訝。
Mom and I were astonished at such scene.
(相似短句) 我媽跟我對這景象感到非常驚訝。
Mom and I were surprised by such scene.

依樣畫葫蘆！套進去就能用！

(句型1) 為～感到驚訝。
be astonished at...
(例句) 我對於這產品的價格感到驚訝。
I am astonished at the price of this product.

(句型2) 被要求……
be asked to...
(例句) 她被要求出示信用卡。
She was asked to present her credit card.

美分美秒，聽說讀寫Everyday

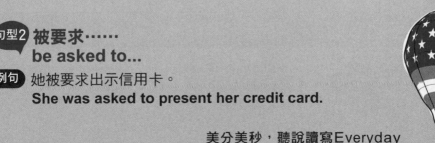

Unit 44
殺價

社群人氣王！英文動態消息寫給你看！

I am really bad at dealing with price.
我很不擅長殺價。

👍讚 56　💬回覆 7

I asked for a discount and got these jeans for 30% off!
我問他們可不可以打折，他們就幫我打了七折～
👍讚 36　💬回覆 20

Saw a girl driving a hard bargain at the stall. That was very impressive.
在攤商前看到一個女孩狠狠殺價了一番，她超厲害。
👍讚 130　💬回覆 3

Some people say it's better not to bargain for the sellers are also struggling for lives; while some people say if you don't bargain you will be cheated.
有人認為不應該殺價，一位賣家也是在為生活努力著；另一方面也有人說，如果不殺價，就等於是被詐欺了。
👍讚 15　💬回覆 12

If the seller is not willing to give me discounts, I will walk away without hesitation. This works out that they often ask me to come back and make the deal.
如果賣家不願意給我折扣，我通常轉頭就走。這招滿有用的，他們常常因此把我請回去並且同意我之前提出的價格。
👍讚 92　💬回覆 3

新手超必備！一個單字嘛欸通！

bargain ⓥ 殺價	**windbreaker** ⓝ 風衣	**discount** ⓝ 折扣
expensive adj. 昂貴的	**seller** ⓝ 銷售員	**vendor** ⓝ 小販
price ⓝ 價格	**lower** ⓥ 降低	

出門超實用！能聽會說一次搞定！

Ⓐ Man, this is way too expensive. We are all buying clothes at your store. Could you give us any discounts?

Ⓑ No, I am sorry. The dress and that pair of jeans are already on sale, so I am sorry that I cannot give you more discounts.

Ⓐ 老闆，這真的太貴了！你看我們全部都準備要在你店裡買衣服了！可以給我們折扣嗎？

Ⓑ 不，很抱歉。那件洋裝和那條牛仔褲都已經是特價商品了，所以我不能再給折扣。

Ⓐ But this shirt is not on sale, and the jeans are put on sale only because of the stains on it.

Ⓑ Yes, I know, so I reduced the price by 50% on the jeans. Rest of the on sale items are 30% off only.

Ⓐ 但是這件襯衫沒有特價，而且這條牛仔褲特價也是因為上面有污漬啊！

Ⓑ 是啊我知道，所以這條牛仔褲我降價一半，那剩餘的特價商品只有七折。

Ⓐ But what about the rest of us? Each of us is spending nearly 5000 dollars here, and the total is about 60000 dollars. Are you sure no bargains at all?

Ⓑ Alright, alright. What about I give each of you $500 worth coupon, and then you can use the coupon next time when you visit the store?

Ⓐ 那我們剩下的人呢？我們每一個人都花了將近五千元，所以總共是六萬元。你確定沒有殺價空間嗎？

Ⓑ 好吧好吧。那不然我給你們每個人五百元折價券，下次來店裡消費可以使用？

Ⓐ Sorry, that's unacceptable. It would be better if you could reduce the price by $500 for each of us on this purchase, because we don't live here, we are from Taipei.

Ⓑ Deal! $500 per person, no more bargains! Thank you.

Ⓐ 抱歉，這無法接受。何不直接給我們降價 500 元，因為我們並不住這裡，我們從臺北來的。

Ⓑ 成交！五百元一個人，不能殺價。謝謝你們。

美分美秒，聽說讀寫Everyday

Unit 44 殺價

酸甜苦辣 記下來！

Men don't get the pleasure of bargaining

Friday, July 12

I enjoy bargaining. I shopped at a uniform price shop today. When I bargained with the clerk for a pair of glasses, she looked at me distantly. My boyfriend never bargains, he is really a freak. He never knows the pleasure of bargaining which is just what we women enjoy. I will go shopping with my female friends next time. It will be more interesting.

男人不懂得殺價的樂趣

7月12日星期五

我很喜歡殺價。我今天去逛不二價店逛逛，當我跟店員議價一副眼鏡的時候，她冷眼看待我。我男朋友從來不殺價的，他真是個怪胎。他不瞭解我們女人為什麼這麼享受殺價的感覺，我下次要跟我女生好朋友出去逛，那會更好玩的！

增廣見聞 超簡單！

How to get a good bargain? Follow your mom to the market, then you will have an idea about bargainings. It is interesting that to bargain is common in traditional markets and night markets. To bargain like a Pro, first, don't be shy. Second, know the price first. If you don't know the bottom line or normal price of the product then you wont even have the chance to bargain. Last, although customers who complain are customers who buy products, we still have to respect the seller.

怎麼學會殺價？跟著媽媽走一趟傳統市場你就知道了！在傳統市場跟夜市殺價是一件很有趣的事，但要殺價要殺得漂亮，首先不能害羞。第二必須先知道一般價格。因為如果你不知道底線，或不知道一般價格在哪裡，你可能連殺價的機會都沒有；最後，雖然會嫌貨才是買家，但我們還是必須尊重賣家。

來換換口味吧！讓你的表達更豐富！

① 媽媽為了一件風衣殺價。　**Mom bargained for a windbreaker.**
> 相似短句 我媽媽想要那件外套多一點折扣。
> My mom wanted more discount on the coat.

② 媽媽覺得那件風衣太貴了。
Mom found the windbreaker too expensive.
> 相似短句 媽媽不想花這麼多錢買外套。
> Mom didn't want to pay so much for the coat.

③ 我和賣家議價。　**I bargained with the seller.**
> 相似短句 我和小販議價。　I bargained with the vendor over the price.

④ 店員降價了。　**The clerk lowered the price.**
> 相似短句 店員提供了更好的價格。　The clerk gave me a better price.

⑤ 她給我折扣。　**She offered me a discount.**
> 相似短句 她提供的折扣還不差。
> The discount she offered was not bad.

依樣畫葫蘆！套進去就能用！

句型1 為了～殺價
bargained for...
> 例句 我爸爸為了一條領帶殺價。
> **My dad bargained for a tie.**

句型2 他永遠不懂～的樂趣。
He never knows the pleasure of...
> 例句 他永遠不懂花小錢購物的樂趣。
> **He never knows the pleasure of getting a bargain price.**

社群人氣王！英文動態消息寫給你看！

The hairdryer I just bought today is a flaw product. I will return it tomorrow.

我今天才買的吹風機是瑕疵品。我明天要拿回去退貨。

👍讚 56　💬回覆 7

That's too bad! The shop doesn't have any return service!

太走運了吧！那家店竟然不接受退貨！

👍讚 36　💬回覆 20

Thankfully I got full refunds.

還好我拿到了全額的退費。

👍讚 130　💬回覆 3

I mistakenly bought something I don't need. Hope I can get refunds.

我不小心買了我不需要的東西，希望我可以拿回去退費。

👍讚 15　💬回覆 12

I returned the product and they promised to send me a new one this Tuesday. But it's now Friday!

我把商品退回去之後他們說週二會寄新的給我，但是現在已經是週五了。

👍讚 92　💬回覆 3

新手超必備！一個單字嘛欸通！

crack ⓝ 裂縫	**imperfection** ⓝ 不完美	**return** ⓥ 退還
refund ⓝ 退款	**break down** 🅟🅗🅡 故障	**ask for** 🅟🅗🅡 要求
buy ⓥ 購買	**customer** ⓝ 顧客	

出門超實用！能聽會說一次搞定！

A Hi, I would like to ask for refund. The size of the dress does not fit me. It's too large.

B Okay. Let me see. Do you have the receipt and credit card with you? I need to check that first.

A 哈囉，我想要退貨。這件洋裝尺寸不適合我，我穿起來太大了。

B 好，我看一下。你有帶收據跟信用卡嗎？我需要先確認過。

A Sure. This is the receipt and my credit card. When will I get the refund?

B Sorry, ma'am, You are not allowed to get a refund at our store anymore.

A 沒問題，這是我的收據跟信用卡。所以我什麼時候可以得到退費？

B 小姐抱歉，你無法在我們的商店做退貨。

A What's the matter? I didn't do anything at all. Why can't I get a refund? There must be something wrong with the system.

B We find that you constantly buy clothes and other appliances and has used various reasons to get refunds after purchases.

A 有什麼問題嗎？我什麼都沒做啊！為什麼我不能退貨？還是系統有什麼問題？

B 我們發現你持續的購買衣物和其他家電，然後購買後用不同的原因申請退貨。

A Well, I just don't feel satisfied with the thing I purchased. I don't think it's an illegal thing to do.

B No, it's not illegal, but we have the right to refuse your request for a refund. You can still exchange the product if you wish to.

A 我就是對我買的商品不滿意啊。我不覺得我在做違法的事。

B 不，你沒有違法，只是我們有權力拒絕你申請退貨。你還是可以換貨，如果你想要的話。

Unit 45 退貨

酸甜苦辣 記下來！

How stupid I was to buy that air conditioner!

Friday, August 16

The weather was so hot that I decided to buy an air conditioner. However, the air conditioner broke down right after I bought it. Mom suggested that I should get a refund on the conditioner right away. I can't believe the salesman backed out on his words! How I wish I hadn't bought the conditioner! I'm going to argue with the salesman tomorrow and give him a lesson that the customer is always right.

我怎麼會這麼笨去買那台冷氣機！

8月16日星期五

天氣實在是太熱了，所以我決定要買冷氣機。但是那台冷氣機在我買了以後，就馬上故障了！我媽媽叫我馬上去退貨。我真的不敢相信那個銷售員竟然反悔他説過的話。我真希望我從來沒有買那個冷氣機，我明天要去跟那個銷售員理論，告訴他「顧客永遠是對的」的道理。

增廣見聞 超簡單！

To request for refunds may not be easy in Taiwan; but in the United States, and other European countries, it is easy and convenient to request refunds, as easy as purchasing the item. However, some people will take advantage of this kind of service. They may purchase the gown for a dinner party, and return it after they're done with the purpose. This kind of people, are so called "Wardrober". In order to prevent this kind of people, some brands choose to refuse requests from this kind of customer.

申請退貨在台灣可能不是件簡單的事，但在美國和其他歐洲國家，申請退貨非常方便簡單，就跟購物一樣。但是，有些人會反過來利用這樣的便利，他們會為了晚會買禮服，在完成目的後就退還該衣物，像這樣的人通稱為「wardrober」。而為了杜絕這種人，有些品牌乾脆就直接拒絕這種客人的退貨請求。

來換換口味吧！讓你的表達更豐富！

1. 這個花瓶上有裂痕。　**There is a crack on the vase.**

相似短句 花瓶上有個瑕疵。　There's an imperfection on the vase.

2 我想要退貨。　**I want to return it.**

相似短句 我要求退款。　I ask for a refund.

3 那台冷氣機在我買了以後馬上故障。
The air conditioner broke down right after I bought it.

相似短句 那台暖氣在我買回去的隔天後就不能用了。
The heater was not working the next day after I bought it.

4 我應該要拿這台冷氣機去退錢。
I should get a refund on the conditioner.

相似短句 我要退回這台暖氣並且退款。
I need to return this heater and get a refund.

5 我真希望我從來沒買這台冷氣！
How I wish I hadn't bought the conditioner.

相似短句 我不該因為低價就買這台暖氣的。
I shouldn't have bought this heater for its low price.

依樣畫葫蘆！套進去就能用！

句型1 我多希望我從沒～
How I wish I hadn't...

例句 我多希望我從買那個便宜的東西，因為它完全沒有用處。
How I wish I hadn't bought this bargain, because it was completely useless.

句型2 衝動之下～
on an impulse.

例句 我當初應該在衝動之下付賬前冉想一下。
I should have thought twice before I paid on an impulse.

Unit 46
過新年

社群人氣王！英文動態消息寫給你看！

My brothers and I are always excited to receive red envelopes.
我弟和我一直都很期待收到紅包。
👍 讚 56　💬 回覆 7

It's my turn to give out red envelopes this year. I am bankrupt.
今年換我要包紅包給別人了。荷包大失血。
👍 讚 36　💬 回覆 20

Playing Mahjong on New Year's Eve is a tradition of our family.
除夕夜打麻將是我們家的傳統。
👍 讚 130　💬 回覆 3

Long hours of traveling and traffic jams are driving everyone crazy. Can't wait to dump myself into my soft and cozy bed.
長途勞頓與交通壅塞整個讓大家都快瘋了。等不及想躺回我柔軟又舒服的床上。
👍 讚 15　💬 回覆 12

We made lots of delicious new year cuisines together. It's always nice to share the best food with the people you love.
我們一起做了很多美味的新年菜餚。和所愛的人一起吃好吃的食物是件好幸福的事。
👍 讚 92　💬 回覆 3

新手超必備！一個單字嘛欸通！

holiday ⓝ 假日	clean up 🔤 清掃	set off 🔤 施放
firecracker ⓝ 鞭炮	red envelope ⓝ 紅包	family ⓝ 家庭
reunion ⓝ 團圓	Chinese New Year ⓝ 新年	

出門超實用！能聽會說一次搞定！

A Happy Chinese New Year! When are you coming back? I am looking forward to see you on New Year's Eve.

B Yes, I will be back on that day. And I have a surprise for you guys. I will bring my girlfriend this time.

A 新年快樂！你什麼時候會回來？期待能在除夕夜看到你。

B 恩，我會在那天回來。而且我要給你們一項驚喜，這次我會帶女朋友回來。

A That's wonderful! But doesn't she have to join her family to celebrate the New Year?

B She is from Poland. I met her a few months ago. She would like to experience the Chinese New Year in our family.

A 那太棒了！但是她不用和她家人一起慶祝新年嗎？

B 她從波蘭來。我幾個月前認識她的。她想要在我們家體驗一下中國新年。

A Did you tell her that we have to prepare red envelop for young people and the elders in the family?

B Yes, I did tell her the tradition, but I didn't ask her to prepare any. She's not one of the family members after all.

A 你有告訴她我們家必須準備紅包給年輕人和長者嗎？

B 有，我有跟她講習俗。但我並沒有要求她準備什麼。她畢竟不是我們的家庭成員。

A Son, I am just kidding! And no worries, I plan to prepare a red envelop for her to welcome her.

B Oh dad! Thank you very much. How much do you plan to put inside the red envelop this year?

A 兒子，我只是開玩笑的。別擔心，我計畫準備一份紅包來歡迎她。

B 喔老爸！太感謝你了。你今年的紅包要包多少阿？

Unit 46 過新年

酸甜苦辣 記下來！

Here comes the Chinese New Year

Tuesday, February 4

I'm looking forward to the Chinese New Year. Next Sunday is Chinese New Year's Eve. Dad and mom started cleaning up the house and purchasing the goods for the New Year. Cleaning up the house always drives me crazy. We are returning to Dad's hometown before Chinese New Year's Eve. My grandparents will be very happy to see us. The best thing during Chinese New Year is that I can get a lot of red envelopes and wear new clothes.

新年來了！

2月4日星期二

我真期待過新年。下個星期天就是除夕夜了，爸爸媽媽都開始要大掃除，並添購年貨。大掃除每次都會讓我抓狂。我們在除夕之前就會回到爸爸的故鄉，祖父母看到我們一定會很開心，新年最棒的就是我能拿到很多紅包又可以穿新衣服。

增廣見聞 超簡單！

What must you say when receiving red envelopes? "Gong Xi Fa Cai" is a must. Giving red envelopes is one of the traditions during Chinese New Year. Red represents luck, energy, and happiness. Chinese people especially love red, such as red cloth, red envelope and wearing red clothes are different kinds of situation where red is used. Therefore, giving a person red envelop with money inside, means we hope to bring happiness and blessing to that person. And be aware that opening up the red envelop in front of the person who give it to you is impolite.

在收紅包的時候，你要說什麼呢？「恭喜發財」是一定要說的。在中國新年時，給紅包是傳統習俗之一，因為紅代表的是幸運、能量和快樂。中國人也特別喜歡紅色，會用在不一樣的情境中，像是紅布條、紅包或是紅色衣服。給別人的紅包裡面放錢，是表示我們希望可以將期望和祝福傳達給那個人，但要注意不要當著給你紅包的人的面開啟紅包，這是一件很不禮貌的事。

來換換口味吧！讓你的表達更豐富！

❶ 我好期待過年。
I'm looking forward to the Chinese New Year.
相似短句 過年是我最喜歡的假日。
Chinese New Year has always been my favorite holiday.

❷ 大掃除讓我快要抓狂了。
Cleaning up the house always drives me crazy.
相似短句 替家裡大掃除總是要花很多時間。
It always takes us a long time to clean up the house.

❸ 人們都放鞭炮。　People set off firecrackers.
相似短句 放鞭炮真好玩。　Firecrackers are so much fun.

❹ 我拿到五個紅包。　I got five red envelopes.
相似短句 我給了七個紅包。　I gave out seven red envelopes.

❺ 我們回家團圓。　We came back for the family reunion.
相似短句 全家團聚是過年最棒的事情。
Family reunion is the best part of Chinese New Year.

依樣畫葫蘆！套進去就能用！

句型1 **新年最棒的就是～**
The best thing in Chinese New Year is that...
例句 新年最棒的就是所有的親戚得以聚首。
The best thing during Chinese New Year is that all the relatives get to see one another.

句型2 **所以～**
so that...
例句 我們起了個大早，所以我們能及時抵達外婆家吃午餐。
We got up early so that we could arrive at Grandma's house for lunch in time.

Unit 47
元宵節

社群人氣王！英文動態消息寫給你看！

I had a cartoon designed lantern when I was a kid. It could even play music!

我小時後有個卡通造型的燈籠。它還會唱歌。

 讚 56　　回覆 7

I used to carry the lantern and explore the darkened park with my friends.

我以前會和朋友一起提燈籠去黑暗的公園裡探險。

 讚 36　　回覆 20

I adore sesame dumplings more than peanut dumplings.

比起花生湯圓我更喜歡芝麻湯圓。

讚 130　　回覆 3

The fireworks will start from 7pm but it's already crowed at 5pm!

煙火七點才開始，但是五點的時候這裡已經塞滿人潮。

讚 15　　回覆 12

My little sister is so obsessed with the lantern riddles. She keeps asking me to give her more.

小妹妹很喜歡燈謎，她一直要求我給她更多燈謎。

 讚 92　　回覆 3

新手超必備！一個單字嘛欸通！

rub **v** 搓　　　　　riddle **n** 謎題　　　　　lantern **n** 燈籠
light up **phr** 點燃　　Lantern Festival **phr** 元宵節
temple **n** 廟　　　　stuffed dumplings **phr** 湯圓

出門超實用！能聽會說一次搞定！

Ⓐ Mommy, I got a good news for you! I won the distinction award this year in lantern design festival!

Ⓑ Congratulations, honey! What's the theme this year? Where can I see your lantern?

Ⓐ 媽咪，我有一個好消息要告訴妳！我在今年的天燈設計節贏得了卓越獎。

Ⓑ 恭喜親愛的！今年主題是什麼？我在哪裡可以看到妳的天燈？

Ⓐ The theme is "Horse", which is the animal of the year in Chinese Animal Zodiac. You can see my lantern in Taipei lantern festival.

Ⓑ No problem! I will tell your daddy about that. What about you come back home next week, and we can go together?

Ⓐ 天燈主題是今年十二生肖之一的馬。妳可以在台北天燈節看到我的天燈。

Ⓑ 沒問題！我會告訴妳爹地的。不如妳下禮拜回家吧，或許我們可以
一起去。

Ⓐ Let me check the calendar. Sorry, mom, I have another plan next weekend, so I have to stay at school.

Ⓑ It's okay! Don't forget to cook some rice balls during the celebration of lantern festival.

Ⓐ 讓我確認一下日曆。媽抱歉我下周末有另一個計畫，所以我必須待
在學校。

Ⓑ 沒關係！別忘了在元宵節煮些元宵來吃。

Ⓐ I know. Mom, sorry again that I cannot go back next week. I really want to share the joy with you and dad.

Ⓑ Don't worry, honey. We are happy that you told us in the first place when you won the prize, and we are happy for you.

Ⓐ 我知道。媽，我再次為下周無法回去感到抱歉。我真的很想跟妳
和爸分享這份喜悅。

Ⓑ 別擔心，親愛的。我們非常高興妳在第一時間告訴我們妳得獎了，
我們替妳感到開心。

Unit 47 元宵節

酸甜苦辣 記下來！

Rub the stuffed dumplings

Tuesday, February 25

Mom taught us how to rub stuffed dumplings by hand. My favorite activity on Lantern Festival is rubbing stuffed dumplings. Nowadays, there are many different flavors of stuffed dumplings. After eating stuffed dumplings, we went out with lanterns. There were lots of people playing riddles in front of the temple.

搓湯圓！

2月25日星期二

媽媽教我們怎麼用手搓出湯圓，元宵節我最喜歡的活動就是搓湯圓了。現在有非常多種口味的湯圓。吃完湯圓以後我們提著燈籠出門，在廟前面有很多人在猜燈謎。

增廣見聞 超簡單！

In Taiwan, there are lantern design competitions held before the lantern festival. The winner can not only win money awards, but also have their lanterns displayed in the lantern carnival. During lantern festival, watching lanterns is a must. Second, Guessing lantern riddles is also the thing to do. People can write riddles and let others guess. Third, enjoying eating "Yuan xiao", which represents reunion and happiness because of its round shape, is important, too.

在台灣的元宵節前夕，通常會舉辦元宵燈籠設計比賽，得勝者不僅可獲得獎金，還可以將作品展示在元宵燈會中。在元宵節時，欣賞燈籠是必要的，而猜燈謎則是另外一個元素；每個人都可以寫謎語讓其他人猜。再來，吃元宵也很重要，因元宵的外形是圓形，表示團圓和幸福。

① 媽媽教我們用手搓湯圓。
Mom taught us how to rub stuffed dumplings by hand.
相似短句 我媽媽教我們如何自己做湯圓。
My mom taught us how to make stuffed dumplings by ourselves.

② 我們提燈籠去外面。　**We went out with lanterns.**
相似短句 我們手提燈樓出門去。
We went out with lanterns in our hands.

③ 民俗舞蹈很有趣。　**The folk dance was interesting.**
相似短句 民俗舞蹈看來真有趣。　Folk dancing was fun to watch.

④ 我們玩猜燈謎。　**We played riddles.**
相似短句 我們開始猜燈謎。　We started the lantern riddle game.

⑤ 我和鄰居一起放天燈。　**I flew sky lanterns with neighbors.**
相似短句 我和鄰居聚在一起放天燈。
My neighbors and I gathered together and lighted up sky lanterns.

依樣畫葫蘆！套進去就能用！

句型1 我最喜歡的活動是～
My favorite activity is...
例句 我最喜歡的活動是猜燈謎大會。
My favorite activity is the lantern riddle party.

句型2 我開始～
I'm starting to...
例句 我開始期待明年的元宵節了。
I'm starting to look forward to the Lantern Festival next year.

Unit 48
清明掃墓

社群人氣王！英文動態消息寫給你看！

There will be a family gathering on the Tomb Sweeping Day.
清明節那天也會有家族聚會。
👍讚 56　💬回覆 7

It rains a lot around the Tomb Sweeping Day.
清明時分常常下雨。
👍讚 36　💬回覆 20

I have not attend tomb sweeping for 6 years.
我已經六年沒有回去掃墓了。
👍讚 130　💬回覆 3

Although I only do tomb sweeping once a year, I am always missing my grandpa.
雖然每年我只來掃一次墓，但我一直都很想念外公。
👍讚 15　💬回覆 12

We have to get up very early in the morning to go tomb sweeping tomorrow.
我們明天要很早起床去掃墓。
👍讚 92　💬回覆 3

新手超必備！一個單字嘛欸通！

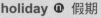

holiday **n** 假期　　　　tomb **n** 墓；墓碑　　　　hometown **n** 家鄉
worship **v** 敬仰；祭拜　cemetery **n** 公墓；墓地　ancestor **n** 祖先
Tomb-sweeping Day **phr** 清明節　　sacrificial offerings **phr** 供祭品

出門超實用！能聽會說一次搞定！

A It's the tomb sweeping festival this Saturday. We will have a three-day holiday. Do you have any plans for it?

B I will go back to Kaohsiung on Thursday night because the tombs of our ancestors is located in Kaohsiung.

A 這周六是清明節。我們會有連續三天的假期。你有任何計畫嗎？

B 我星期四晚上會回去高雄，因為我們家祖墳在那。

A I see. Ours is located at Yangming Mountain, so all I have to do is get up as early as possible to avoid the traffic jam.

B Why didn't you try to finish tomb sweeping last week or even earlier, so that you don't have to worry about traffic jam.

A 了解。我們的在陽明山，所以我必須起的越早越好以避免塞車。

B 為何你不試著在上周或者更早掃完，這樣你就不用擔心塞車問題了。

A I know. My colleagues gave the same suggestion, but my husband can only get off from work from China during the time of the festival.

B I see. Do you need to prepare materials for making spring rolls and run cakes?

A 我知道。我的同事給我相同的建議，但是我老公只能在節日期間要求離開大陸。

B 了解。你有需要準備春捲和潤餅的材料嗎？

A No. My husband's mother will buy those from the traditional market. We don't have that much time to prepare it.

B That's an option. By the way, if you want to, I can bring some run cakes that are homemade for you.

A 不用。我婆婆會從傳統市場採買。我們並沒有這麼多時間來準備這些。

B 那是一個選項。順帶一提，如果你願意，我可以帶些我們自己做的潤餅給你。

Unit 48 清明掃墓

酸甜苦辣 記下來！

Tomb-sweeping Day

Thursday, April 4

Tomb-sweeping Day is one of our continuous holidays. Many people have to go tomb sweeping on that day. My family got up very early to sweep our family's tomb in the south. It was kind of late, but we still took sacrificial offerings to my ancestors' tombs. Because of the traffic jam, we didn't get home until 3:00 p.m.

清明節

4月4日星期四

清明節是我們連續假期的其中一天，很多人在那一天都要去掃墓。我們家起了個大早要到南部去掃墓。雖然有點晚了，但我們還是帶著祭品去掃墓。因為塞車，我們到下午三點多才到家。

增廣見聞 超簡單！

Tomb sweeping, also known as "Qingming" festival is for people to pay respect to their ancestors. Tomb sweeping festival is also called "Cold food day" which explains why we have run cakes and spring roll as food on that day. During Qingming festival, family will reunite together to clean the dust, and sweep the grass off the tombs. Tombs are aggregated in one place, thus highway toll is free in Taiwan on that day in order to prevent traffic jam.

掃墓節，也被稱為清明節，是讓人們對祖先表示緬懷之意的節日。掃墓節也可被稱為寒食節，這也解釋了為什麼在清明節當天我們會吃潤餅和春捲。在清明節期間，家族會團聚在一起替祖先清理墓上的灰塵和雜草，而因為墳墓大多都被集中在同一區，所以當天高速公路不會收費，以避免交通更加阻塞。

Part 9 全國瘋節慶

1 清明節是我們連續假期的其中一天。
Tomb-sweeping Day is one of our continuous holidays.

（相似短句）五天的假期包含了清明節。
Tomb-sweeping Day is included in the 5-day holiday.

2 很多人都要在那天去掃墓。
Many people have to go tomb sweeping on that day.

（相似短句）很多人都要回家鄉掃墓。
A lot of people travel back to their hometown to do tomb sweeping.

3 我們起了個大早回南部掃墓。
We got up very early to sweep our Family's tomb in the south.

（相似短句）為了回南部掃墓。我們早早就起床了。
To get back to the south and sweep our family's tomb, we woke up early in the morning.

4 我們用水果祭拜祖先。　**We worship our ancestors with fruits.**

（相似短句）我們通常用水果祭祖。
We usually bring fruits when worshipping our ancestors.

5 回家的路上塞車了。　**There was a traffic jam on our way home.**

（相似短句）我們回家的路上塞車了。
We got stuck in traffic when we went back.

依樣畫葫蘆！套進去就能用！

（句型1）**很多人必須～**
Many people have to...

（例句）很多人必須在清明節時花很多時間回家鄉。
Many people have to travel so far to their hometown for Tomb-sweeping Day.

（句型2）**提供一個機會～**
provided an opportunity...

（例句）這個節日提供一個機會讓家族團聚。
The festival provided an opportunity for family reunions.

Unit 49
母親節

社群人氣王！英文動態消息寫給你看！

I made chocolate for my mom on Mother's Day.
我做了巧克力送給媽媽當母親節禮物。

👍 讚 56　💬 回覆 7

I did the cooking and my sister did the cleaning. Mom said she hopes that everyday was Mother's Day.
我負責做飯，妹妹打掃了家裡。我媽說她希望每天都是母親節。

👍 讚 36　💬 回覆 20

My mom was so surprised when she saw us bringing her a bouquet of carnations. Happy Mother's Day.
我媽看到我們拿出康乃馨花束的時候超驚訝的。母親節快樂～

👍 讚 130　💬 回覆 3

I have no idea why my brother picked Mother's Day to hang out with his friends.
我不懂我弟怎麼會選母親節跟朋友出去玩。

👍 讚 15　💬 回覆 12

We took grandma to a nice dinner to celebrate Mother's Day.
我們帶外婆去餐廳吃飯慶祝母親節。

👍 讚 92　💬 回覆 3

新手超必備！一個單字嘛欸通！

gift **n** 禮物　　　surprise **n** 驚喜　　　carnation **n** 康乃馨
please **v** 使……開心　　handmade **adj** 手做的；手工的
Mother's Day **phr** 母親節

Ⓐ Jenny, look! Those are paintings and hand-made presents that you made at school for mother's day when you were a child.

Ⓑ Mom, that's embarrassing! Can you tell what I was drawing? Is this you and dad?

Ⓐ 珍妮你看！那些是你還是小孩時在母親節畫的塗鴉和手做的禮物。

Ⓑ 媽，那真是太尷尬了！你可以説説我在畫什麼嗎？是你和爸？

Ⓐ Come on, Jenny. Those paintings are cute, and it represents your genuine love.

Ⓑ Alright, mom, please put those things down. I am going to give you a present. It's a pearl necklace.

Ⓐ 別這樣，珍妮。這些塗鴉非常可愛，而且它代表了真誠的愛。

Ⓑ 好吧媽，請把那些放下，我現在要送你一份禮物。這是珍珠項鍊。

Ⓐ How sweet of you. Thank you very much, Jenny. This is quite expensive, isn't it?

Ⓑ Well, dad is the main sponsor of this necklace, and the rest came out from my own pocket.

Ⓐ 喔，你真是貼心。非常謝謝你，珍妮。這非常貴，是吧？

Ⓑ 恩，爸是這條項鍊主要的贊助者，其他剩餘部分來自我自己的零用錢。

Ⓐ My baby girl has grown up. But you know the best gift from you is that I can have you by my side on this special day.

Ⓑ Mom, I love you. I wish you could always be happy, and stay healthy.

Ⓐ 我的寶貝女兒已經長大了。但是你知道，其實最好的禮物，就是你陪著我過這特別的一天。

Ⓑ 媽，我愛你。我希望你可以快樂常駐，保持健康。

酸甜苦辣 記下來！

My handmade gift for mom

Sunday, May 12
Mother's Day is coming. I only have two hundred dollars in my account, and my brother has ten in his. But I'm worried because it seems that I can't buy anything nice with two hundred and ten dollars. I am going to make handmade carnations for Mom. I believe the best gift is being a hard working child. Mom was touched when I told her that I love her.

我要給媽媽的手工禮物

5月12日 星期日
母親節快要到了。我只有兩百元的積蓄，而我弟弟有十元。但是我擔心兩百一十元是買不到什麼好東西的。所以我打算手做康乃馨給媽媽。我相信最好的禮物就是當一個用功的小孩。媽咪聽到我說我愛她的時候，感動的哭了。

增廣見聞 超簡單！

Would you be curious about the job description of being a mother? This job requires you to constantly exerting your stamina, 24 hours a day, seven days per week, no break, and on holidays, like New Years, dragon boat festival, or moon festival, the workload is even more than usual. Therefore, buying a small gift, taking moms to a nice restaurant, sending her a card, buying her a bunch of flowers, or simply spending time with her are all sorts of things you can do to express your appreciation to your mother.

你會好奇「母親」是個怎樣的角色嗎？這份工作需要你每天 24 小時投入精力，一周七天，沒有休息時間，而在新年假期，端午節或中秋節時工作量還會加倍。所以買點小禮物、帶媽媽上餐館、寄卡片或買一束花給她，或是純粹花時間陪她等等的做法，都可以表示對母親的謝意。

❶ 母親節要到了。　**Mother's Day is coming.**
> (相似短句) 母親節就要到了。　Mother's Day is around the corner.

❷ 我妹妹跟我要一起買禮物給媽媽。
My sister and I planned to buy Mom a gift.
> (相似短句) 我和妹妹計畫要買禮物，給媽媽一個驚喜。
> My sister and I planned to surprise Mom with a gift.

❸ 我打算手做康乃馨給媽媽。
I am going to make handmade carnations for Mom.
> (相似短句) 我要做康乃馨當禮物，送給媽媽。
> I'm planning to make carnations by myself for Mom as a gift.

❹ 我相信最好的禮物就是認真唸書。
I believe the best gift is being a hard working child.
> (相似短句) 我認為認真讀書就是給雙親最大的禮物。
> I think studying hard is the best gift for parents.

❺ 我們到外面吃。　**We ate out.**
> (相似短句) 我們在餐廳慶祝。　We celebrate it in restaurant.

依樣畫葫蘆！套進去就能用！

句型1 為了～
In order to...,...
> (例句) 為了以晚餐給媽媽一個驚喜，我們打電話給傑米叔叔要求幫忙。
> **In order to surprise my mom with dinner, we called uncle Jamie to help.**

句型2 我相信最好的禮物是～
I believe the best gift is...
> (例句) 我相信最好的禮物是讓你的父母知道你有多愛他們。
> **I believe the best gift is to let your folks know how much you love them.**

美分美秒，聽說讀寫Everyday

社群人氣王！英文動態消息寫給你看！

This is the first time for me making rice dumplings! They look so nice. I must be a genius. lol

第一次包粽子就上手！我一定是天才！哈哈

👍 讚 56　💬 回覆 7

**No more rice dumplings please…
I have been eating them since last week.**

拜託不要再給我粽子了，我已經從上週吃到現在……

👍 讚 36　💬 回覆 20

The Dragon boat competition was so exciting.

划龍舟比賽真是太精采了！

👍 讚 130　💬 回覆 3

**People mountain people sea…
I couldn't even see a dragon boat!**

人山人海……我連一艘龍舟都看不到。

👍 讚 15　💬 回覆 12

When I was a kid I used to get fragrant sachets made by my grandma.

我小時候祖母會做香包給我。

👍 讚 92　💬 回覆 3

新手超必備！一個單字嘛欸通！

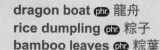

dragon boat phr. 龍舟	**race** n. 競賽	**river** n. 河
rice dumpling phr. 粽子	**participate** v. 參加	**wrap** v. 包裹
bamboo leaves phr. 粽葉	**Dragon Boat Festival** phr. 端午節	

出門超實用！能聽會說一次搞定！

Ⓐ Our company will join the dragon boat race this year on dragon boat festival. We are now preparing for it.

Ⓑ You are so lucky. I never had the chance to join dragon boat races. When are you going to attend the race?

Ⓐ 我們公司會參加今年端午節的划龍舟比賽。我們正在為這進行準備。

Ⓑ 你還真幸運！我從來都沒有機會參加划龍舟比賽。你什麼時候要去參賽？

Ⓐ Unlike you, comparing to attending a dragon boat race, I would rather choose to sit aside and enjoy the race while having rice dumplings.

Ⓑ Sounds like you don't really like to be the one who's on the boat! Can I go see how you guys practice for that?

Ⓐ 我跟你不同，與參加划龍舟比賽相比，我寧願選擇坐在旁邊吃粽子看比賽。

Ⓑ 聽起來你沒有真的想在那艘船上。我可以去看你們如何練習嗎？

Ⓐ Sure. We will be at the riverside park this Friday night. Why not come and join us?

Ⓑ Wonderful! I will bring some rice dumplings for you and your colleagues. We made it by ourselves.

Ⓐ 當然。我們這周五晚上會在河濱公園。何不過來加入我們呢？

Ⓑ 太棒了！我會帶些粽子去給你和你的同事。我們自己做的喔。

Ⓐ I appreciate that. But I guess it's not suitable to have rice dumplings right after training. Some coke and beer will be alright.

Ⓑ You're right. Then I will bring rice dumplings to you on the day of dragon boat race.

Ⓐ 感激不盡。但是我猜訓練過後不太適合吃粽子。一些可樂和啤酒或許不錯。

Ⓑ 你說的對。那我會在划龍舟比賽當天帶粽子給你。

酸甜苦辣 記下來！

Dad is the best!

Saturday, June 22

Dad participated in a dragon boat race. He wanted us to be there cheering for him. Mom was even yelling loudly through a megaphone when we watched the race on the bank. They came in second at last, and the whole team won twenty thousand dollars as a reward.

爸爸最棒了！

6月22日星期六

爸爸參加了划龍舟比賽，他希望我們到場去幫他加油。當我們在河堤上看比賽的時候，媽媽甚至還用大聲公大聲吼叫。他們最後得了第二名，而且全隊得了兩萬元的獎金。

增廣見聞 超簡單！

The origin of dragon boat race is associated with Qu Yuan, who drowned himself in the river as a protest against the corrupted dynasty. When people heard that Qu Yuan had drowned himself in the river, they all came out, rowed the boat to save Qu Yuan. It is said that the winning team can bring happiness to other people. How to define the winner? There will be a team member sitting in the front of the dragon-shaped boat. The one of any boat to who get the flag first, is the winner.

龍舟競賽的起源和屈原有關，他犧牲自己跳入河中溺斃，以表示對腐敗朝廷的抗爭，當人們聽到他溺水的消息後都紛紛出動，跳上船去救屈原。而龍舟競賽背後的涵意就是勝利者必須幫助自己和別人都一切順利。那該怎麼定義勝利者呢？龍舟上會有一位旗手負責坐在龍舟最前面，誰划得快先搶到旗就是贏囉！

① 今天河邊有划龍舟比賽。
There was a dragon boat race along the river.

相似短句 划龍舟比賽在那邊的河裡舉行。
The dragon boat race was held on the river over there.

② 表哥有參加划龍舟比賽。
My cousin participated in a dragon boat race.

相似短句 我表哥參加划龍舟比賽。
My cousin was on the dragon boat racing team.

③ 河邊有很多看比賽的人。
Lots of people watch the race along the river.

相似短句 河岸滿滿都是看比賽的人。
There was full of people watching the race along the river.

④ 媽媽教我們怎麼把米包進竹葉裡。
Mom taught us how to wrap rice in the bamboo leaves.

相似短句 我媽媽教我們怎麼包粽子。
My mom taught us how to wrap up rice dumplings.

⑤ 大家看完比賽後都很感動。
Everyone was moved after watching the dragon boat race.

相似短句 這是場刺激的比賽，大家都很盡興。
The race was so exciting that everyone was having fun.

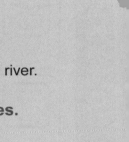

依樣畫葫蘆！套進去就能用！

句型1 **太～以至於～**
so... that...

例句 雨太大了，以至於他們延遲了比賽。
The rain was so heavy that they put off the race.

句型2 **～得到第幾名……**
came in...

例句 新來的組別得到了第三名，還不賴。
The new team came in third place, which wasn't so bad.

Unit 51
七夕情人節

社群人氣王！英文動態消息寫給你看！

We went to see the fireworks at the river bank.
我們去河邊看煙火。

👍讚 56　💬回覆 7

We went on a day trip to celebrate the Chinese Valentine's Day.
我們一起出遊慶祝七夕。

👍讚 36　💬回覆 20

Everyone was surprised that I didn't know the story of the Chinese Valentine's Day.
大家都很驚訝我不知道七夕的傳說。

👍讚 130　💬回覆 3

Since I have no girlfriend, I have no idea what to do tomorrow. Any suggestions?
我沒有女朋友，所以我不知道明天要幹嘛。有任何建議嗎？

👍讚 15　💬回覆 12

I am having a fight with my boyfriend so I am not planning to celebrate any Valentine's Day.
我跟男友正在冷戰中，所以我不想過任何情人節。

👍讚 92　💬回覆 3

新手超必備！一個單字嘛欸通！

take-away ⓝ 外帶	**restaurant** ⓝ 餐廳	**celebration** ⓝ 慶祝
recommend ⓥ 推薦	**preference** ⓝ 偏好	**couple** ⓝ 情侶
custom ⓝ 習俗	**mythology** ⓝ 神話	

出門超實用！能聽會說一次搞定！

Ⓐ Oh baby, what would you want to have for dinner on Valentine's day? We have to book the restaurant now.

Ⓑ Thank you babe, but its only June now. Wouldn't it be way too early to book the restaurant for Valentine's Day?

Ⓐ 喔寶貝，你情人節當天晚餐想吃什麼啊？我們現在就必須要訂餐廳了。

Ⓑ 謝謝你寶貝，但現在才六月而已。難道不會太早預訂情人節餐廳嗎？

Ⓐ Not at all. Do you remember last year we had to do take-away, because there were no tables for us at the restaurant?

Ⓑ Yeah, you reminded me! But I find it acceptable. I don't need a big celebration on Valentine's Day.

Ⓐ 一點也不。你記不記得去年因為餐廳沒位子，所以我們必須外帶？

Ⓑ 對，你提醒了我！但我認為這是可以接受的。我不需要在情人節盛大地慶祝。

Ⓐ Anyway, you haven't answer my question. And, what kind of present do you want for Valentine's Day?

Ⓑ I would like to try Italian food! There is a restaurant strongly recommended by Collin!

Ⓐ 無論如何，你還沒回答我的問題。還有你情人節想要什麼禮物啊？

Ⓑ 我想要試試義大利美食！這裡有間柯林強烈推薦的餐廳。

Ⓐ Deal! What about the gift? Do you have any preferences?

Ⓑ No. As long as you are not going to propose with a diamond ring on that day, I am fine with anything, even if we are not going anywhere.

Ⓐ 好阿！那禮物呢？你有什麼偏好嗎？

Ⓑ 不。如果你那天並沒有打算用鑽戒求婚，任何東西我都可以，甚至是我們哪也不去。

酸甜苦辣 記下來！

It's weird...

Saturday, November 14

My wife hasn't mentioned anything about Valentine's Day, which is weird. Normally, she will make plans for it. For example, last year, we stayed at the luxury hotel near Taipei 101 for night. The night view from the room was truly fantastic! And the year before last year, she chose an island villa in Bali. We spent five days there doing nothing but swimming and enjoying seafood. I think I should be the one who prepares Valentine's Day celebration. This might be the reason why she's being so cold to me recently.

好奇怪……

7月24日星期四

好奇怪！我老婆還沒有提到任何有關情人節的事。通常，都是她計畫一切。舉例來說，去年我們在101大樓附近的高級酒店過了一晚。從房間看出去的夜景真的非常棒！而前年，我老婆挑了巴里島海島度假村，我們在那裡待了五天。除了游泳跟吃海鮮之外，什麼也沒做。我想今年應該換我來準備情人節的慶祝了，這可能是她最近都對我如此冷淡的原因吧！

增廣見聞 超簡單！

Chinese Valentine's day is called "Qixi" festivals which falls on the seventh day of July in Chinese Lunar Calendar. This is an important festival for couples. There are many kinds of celebrations in different places, such as girls praying to Zhi Nu to better skilled in sewing, but now, most customs have disappeared. Only the love story between the cowherd and the weaver girl in the Chinese mythology remains, and is well remembered. You can even find the stars, which represents the cowherd and the weaver girl in the sky.

每年農曆的七月七號是中國情人節，也叫做七夕情人節，對情侶來說是很重要的節日，本來在各地都有許多不同的慶典，例如女孩們會向織女祈求自己可以有一雙很會織布的手。但時至今日，很多習俗都已消失不見，只剩下牛郎跟織女的浪漫愛情故事仍被傳頌著，你也可以在星空中找到牛郎跟織女的星星喔！

1 好奇怪！我老婆還沒有提到任何有關情人節的事。
My wife hasn't mentioned anything about Valentine's Day, which is weird.

(相似短句) 我認為我老婆完全沒有跟我提及任何有關情人節的事是非常詭異的。
I find it weird that my wife didn't discuss anything about Valentine's Day with me.

2 從房間看出去的夜景真的非常棒！
The night view from the room was truly fantastic!

(相似短句) 我們非常享受從房間裡看出去的夜景！
We enjoyed the night view from our room so much.

3 我們在那裡待了五天。除了游泳跟吃海鮮之外，什麼也沒做。
We spent five days there doing nothing but swimming and enjoying seafood.

(相似短句) 除了游泳跟吃海鮮之外，我們在那裡待了五天，什麼也沒做。
Except swimming and enjoying seafood, we spent five days there without doing anything.

4 這可能是她最近都對我如此冷淡的原因吧！
This might be the reason why she's being so cold to me recently.

(相似短句) 我猜這就是為什麼她最近都對我很冷淡！
I guess this is why she treat me so cold recently.

5 通常，都是她計畫一切。
Normally, she will make plans for our Valentine's Day.

(相似短句) 通常，她會計畫好情人節的慶祝活動。
Normally, she will plan Valentines Day's celebration.

依樣畫葫蘆！套進去就能用！

(句型1) **對誰冷淡……**
be cold to...

(例句) 我丈夫最近對我很冷淡。
My husband is cold to me recently.

(句型2) **除了……什麼也沒……**
do nothing but...

(例句) 我們除了一整天都在整理家裡以外其他都沒做。
We did nothing but clean the house for the whole day.

Unit 52
父親節

社群人氣王！英文動態消息寫給你看！

I played golf with my grandpa on Father's Day morning.
父親節這天早上，我跟爺爺一起去打高爾夫球。

👍 讚 56　　💬 回覆 7

I bought my father a watch as a present and my brother made a cake for him.
我買了一只錶送爸爸，我弟則烤了一個蛋糕。

👍 讚 36　　💬 回覆 20

Happy Father's Day to the best father in the world!
全世界最好的爸爸，父親節快樂。

👍 讚 130　　💬 回覆 3

Oh no! I totally forgot today is Father's Day! I will at least have to make a phone call before it's too late.
糟了我完全忘記今天是父親節！現在至少要在今天結束前打通電話給爸爸。

👍 讚 15　　💬 回覆 12

I took my father parachuting for celebrating Father's Day. Cool eh!
我帶我爸去跳傘慶祝父親節，很酷吧！

👍 讚 92　　💬 回覆 3

新手超必備！一個單字嘛欸通！

day off ⓝ 放假	**suggestion** ⓝ 建議	**camping** ⓝ 露營
thoughtful ⓐ 替人著想的	**pronunciation** ⓝ 發音	
razor ⓝ 刮鬍刀	**accept** ⓥ 接受	**masculinity** ⓐ 男性特質

出門超實用！能聽會說一次搞定！

Ⓐ Mom, do you have any plans on Father's day? Does dad need to work on that day?

Ⓑ Of course, honey. We don't have a day off on Happy Father's day. We can celebrate it earlier on this weekend.

Ⓐ 媽，你父親節有任何計畫嗎？爸那天需要工作嗎？

Ⓑ 當然，親愛的。我們父親節並沒有放假。我們可以在這周末就先慶祝。

Ⓐ Okay. I am free this weekend. I would like to take dad to the shopping mall. I think he needs some new shirts.

Ⓑ No, your father doesn't like to go shopping, so it's not a good idea. Do you have any other suggestions?

Ⓐ 好，我這周末有空。我想要帶爸去購物中心。我想他需要件新的襯衫。

Ⓑ 不，你爸並不喜歡購物，這不是個好主意。你有其它建議嗎？

Ⓐ What about we plan a trip to go camping this weekend? I am sure he would like it.

Ⓑ I thought you hated to go camping. What made you change your mind? You can buy some new shirts for him and that will be alright.

Ⓐ 那我們這周末去露營呢？我確定他會喜歡的。

Ⓑ 我以為你討厭露營。什麼讓你改變想法了？你幫他買些新襯衫也不錯阿。

Ⓐ I just think that I seldom have time to be with you and dad. As long as you two are happy, and there's no harm in going camping.

Ⓑ How thoughtful you are! I am sure your dad will accept the plan. Let's decide where to go first.

Ⓐ 我只是覺得我很少有時間陪你和老爸。只要你們兩個快樂，去露營也無傷大雅。

Ⓑ 你真貼心！我確定你爸他會贊同這計畫的。我們先來決定去哪吧。

Unit 52 父親節

酸甜苦辣 記下來！

I sent a card.

Thursday, July 31

I sent a card to my dad for celebrating Happy Father's day. This is the first time that I can't be with him and my family on such special day. This is what I wrote: Thank you daddy for always supporting me. Without you, I couldn't possibly come to New York to pursue my dream of being a designer. I am lucky that I have such a great dad. I hope you will have loads of fun that day. I am sure mom and brother will surprise you. Love you, dad.

我寄了張卡片。

7月31日星期四

我寄了父親節卡片給我爸爸，這是我第一次不能跟他還有家人一起度過這特別的日子。下面是我寫給爸爸的：謝謝爸爸總是這麼支持我，沒有你，我根本沒辦法到紐約追求我當一名設計師的夢想。我很幸運我有這樣的爸爸，我希望你今天可以過得很開心，我相信媽媽跟弟弟會給你驚喜的！爸！我愛你！

增廣見聞 超簡單！

The date of Happy Father's day is different in each country. For example, father's day in Taiwan is on August 8th, which is a result from the pronunciation of father in Chinese. It is similar to the pronunciation of the date. In fact, most countries celebrate father's day on the third Sunday of June, although the origin is unclear. Interestingly, the gift and card on father's day tends to be more masculin, such as a nice razor, or an electric massage chair.

父親節在不同國家的日期是不一樣的。舉例來說，台灣的父親節是在八月八號，是由於中文「爸爸」的發音跟當天日期的發音很類似。事實上很多國家都在六月的第三個週日舉辦父親節，起源為何仍不清楚。有趣的是，父親節的禮物跟卡片在各國都偏向男性化，例如一把好刮鬍刀或是一張電動按摩椅。

來換換口味吧！讓你的表達更豐富！

➊ 這是我第一次不能跟他還有家人一起度過這特別的日子。
This is the first time that I cannot be with him and my family on such special day.
相似短句 這是我第一次不能跟他一起度過父親節。
This is the first time that I could not stand by his side for Father's day.

➋ 我希望你今天可以過得很開心。
I hope you will have loads of fun that day.
相似短句 希望你今天可以過得開心。
Wish you could be happy that day.

➌ 謝謝爸爸總是這麼支持我。
Thank you daddy for always supporting me.
相似短句 謝謝爸爸這麼支持著我。
Thank you dad for being so supportive for me.

➍ 沒有你，我根本沒辦法到紐約追求我當一名設計師的夢想。
Without you, I couldn't possibly come to New York to pursue my dream of being a designer.
相似短句 如果沒有爸爸的幫忙，我不可能到紐約追求我當一名設計師的夢想。
It is impossible for me to go pursue my dream of being a designer in New York without dad's support.

➎ 我寄了父親節卡片給我爸爸。
I sent a card to my dad for celebrating Happy Father's day
相似短句 我寫了卡片給我爸爸慶祝父親節。
I wrote a card to dad to celebrate Father's Day.

依樣畫葫蘆！套進去就能用！

句型1 **不可能……**
Couldn't possibly...
例句 沒有他，我不可能成為設計師。
I couldn't possible become a designer without him.

句型2 **和誰一起慶祝～**
Celebrate...with sb.
例句 我想跟家人一起慶祝生日。
I want to celebrate my birthday with my family.

Unit 53
中秋節

社群人氣王！英文動態消息寫給你看！

We had a barbecue dinner in the garden tonight.
晚上我們在庭院裡烤肉。

👍 讚 56　　💬 回覆 7

The moon is so bright and round just like a shining coin.
月亮好圓好亮，好像一枚閃閃發光的銀幣。

👍 讚 36　　💬 回覆 20

Can't see the full moon for the bad weather. So disappointed.
因為天氣不好沒辦法看到滿月。
好失望。

👍 讚 130　　💬 回覆 3

Look at the picture I took with my new camera! It can capture the full moon so well!
看我用新相機拍到的照片！他拍出來的月色超美！

👍 讚 15　　💬 回覆 12

Since when having barbecue on the Moon Festival has became a tradition?
從什麼時候開始烤肉變成了中秋節的傳統？

👍 讚 92　　💬 回覆 3

新手超必備！一個單字嘛欸通！

moon cake ⓝ 月餅	**barbecue** ⓥ 烤肉	**eclipse** ⓝ 蝕
lunar ⓐⓓⓙ 月亮的	**trash** ⓝ 垃圾	**fire** ⓝ 火
Moon Festival ⓝ 中秋節		

Ⓐ Do you want to come over and join our BBQ party this Sunday? We will prepare a lot of food and drinks.

Ⓑ Sure, when exactly on Sunday? Because I have three BBQ party invitations on moon festivals!

Ⓐ 這周日你想要過來加入我們的 BBQ 派對嗎？我們準備了很多食物和飲料。

Ⓑ 當然，星期日的什麼時候？因為我中秋節有三場 BBQ 派對的邀約。

Ⓐ That's ridiculous! We will start our BBQ party around 4pm, we will play some games before dinner.

Ⓑ I will be there around 5pm because I have to buy some moon cakes and pineapple pastries first.

Ⓐ 那真是難以置信啊！我們 BBQ 派對大約下午四點開始，晚餐前我們會玩些遊戲。

Ⓑ 我大概下午五點到，因為我必須先去買些月餅和鳳梨酥。

Ⓐ Okay, no problem. Can you also help my buy some pomelos? These might not be enough for all people.

Ⓑ Yes. By the way, my girlfriend will come along with me, is that okay? She's good at starting a barbeque fire.

Ⓐ 好沒問題。那你可以幫我買些柚子嗎？這些可能不夠所有人吃。

Ⓑ 可以。順帶一提，我女朋友會跟我一起去，可以嗎？她非常擅長生火。

Ⓐ Are you serious? There's absolutely no problem to bring your girlfriend, though I don't think we are going to need her help for that.

Ⓑ Okay. I can't wait! It is always good to have friends and parties on autumn moon festival.

Ⓐ 這真是出乎意料。你帶女朋友來絕對沒問題，但我不認為我們會需要她那方面的協助。

Ⓑ 好。我等不及了！秋天中秋節有派對和好朋友的陪伴總是美好的。

酸甜苦辣 記下來！

Barbecu!!!

Thursday, September 26
My friend and I decided to barbecue in my yard for celebrating the Moon Festival. When we were busy building a fire at about eight, a lunar eclipse took place. The news said that it's a rare coincidence. People enjoying the full moon exclaimed in excitement together for the phenomenon. The moon was eclipsed totally and showed up after three minutes. It shone more brightly after the eclipse. But I ended up unhappy because people left lots of trash after barbecuing. We should teach them how to keep the environment clean first.

烤肉！！

9月26日星期四
我和我朋友決定要在我家庭院裡烤肉慶祝中秋節！大約是八點左右，當我們正忙著生火的時候，發生了月全蝕。新聞說這個巧合是很不常見的，賞月的人都一同為這個現象驚呼，月亮完全被遮蔽住，三分鐘過後月亮又再度露出來，月亮在全蝕的之後更為明亮了。但是我最後有點不開心，因為大家烤完肉都亂丟垃圾，我們應該先教育大家如何維持環境的整潔。

增廣見聞 超簡單！

Mid-autumn festival is celebrated both in Taiwan and Vietnam. It usually falls between late September and early October which is the same day as the full moon. There are different versions that explain origins of the moon festival. Edting moon cakes to plan an uprise against the ruling dynasty, is probably the most remembered among all. The Chinese Moon festival today, especially in Taiwan is mostly about barbequeing and eating moon cakes, or pomelos.

中秋節是個台灣和越南都會慶祝的節日，中秋節通常落在九月底和十月初之間，恰好就在月圓當天。中秋節的由來有很多不一樣的版本，吃月餅起義大概是所有故事裡面最普遍和最被記得的。現代台灣的中秋節，大概最重要的就是烤肉、吃月餅跟吃文旦了。

1 對中國人來說中秋節是個很重要的日子。
Moon Festival is a big festival for Chinese.

相似短句 對中國人來說，中秋節很重要。
Moon Festival is an important festival for Chinese people.

2 爸媽的朋友送我們很多月餅。
My parents' friends gave us many moon cakes.

相似短句 爸媽的朋友送我們月餅作為禮物。
Friends of my parents sent us moon cakes as gifts.

3 小孩都很喜歡烤肉。　**Children all love barbecuing.**

相似短句 誰不喜歡烤肉呢？　Who doesn't love barbecue?

4 今晚八點發生月全蝕。
A lunar eclipse took place at eight tonight.

相似短句 今天晚上八點有月全蝕。
There was a lunar eclipse at eight tonight.

5 我們去探訪外婆。　**We visited Grandmother.**

相似短句 我們去鄉下，探望祖父母。
We went to the countryside to visit our grandparents.

依樣畫葫蘆！套進去就能用！

句型1 **發生～**
took place...

例句 那場由烤肉引起的火災意外發生在市中心。
The fire accident caused by barbecue took place in city center.

句型2 **取而代之……**
instead of...

例句 我們沒有烤肉，取而代之的是我們吃火鍋當晚餐。
Instead of having a barbecue party, we had hot pot for dinner.

美分美秒，聽說讀寫Everyday

Unit 54
聖誕節

社群人氣王！英文動態消息寫給你看！

I am surprised to know that Christmas is popular in Japan, even though there are only a few Christians.

我很驚訝即使基督徒不多，聖誕節在日本仍是很受歡迎的節日。

👍 讚 56　💬 回覆 7

My kids are reluctant to go to bed because they want to see Santa Claus.

孩子們不願意去睡覺，因為她們想親眼看看聖誕老人。

👍 讚 36　💬 回覆 20

The plane tickets becomes so expensive around Christmas Holidays.

耶誕假期期間機票變得好貴。

👍 讚 130　💬 回覆 3

The department stores in Taipei designs beautiful Christmas trees every year.

台北的百貨公司每年都會設計很多漂亮的聖誕樹。

👍 讚 15　💬 回覆 12

Christmas is a time when family and friends get together and be thankful for what we possess.

耶誕節是個與家人朋友相聚並且珍惜我們所擁有的一切的日子。

👍 讚 92　💬 回覆 3

新手超必備！一個單字嘛欸通！

believe ⓥ 相信	**socks** ⓝ 襪子	**Santa Claus** ⓝ 聖誕老人
Boxing Day ⓝ 節禮日	**gift** ⓝ 禮物	**opportunity** ⓝ 機會
wonder ⓥ 對……感到驚奇；疑惑		**taste** ⓝ 品味

出門超實用！能聽會說一次搞定！

Ⓐ Merry Christmas, Jack! Did you believe in Santa Claus when you were a child? I did and I still believe in it.

Ⓑ You must be joking. I had once believed in that until I caught my dad putting gifts in the socks.

Ⓐ 聖誕快樂，傑克！你在小時候相信有聖誕老公公嗎？直到現在我都還是相信。

Ⓑ 你一定在開玩笑。我是曾經相信過，直到抓到我爸在我襪子裡放禮物。

Ⓐ So what is the best Christmas present you have ever gotten? The best one I had was a car key of a brand new car from my dad.

Ⓑ Oh my, no wonder you believe that Santa Claus does exist! Mine is probably a pregnancy ultrasound photo.

Ⓐ 所以你拿過什麼最棒的聖誕節禮物？我最棒的禮物是我爸給的新車鑰匙。

Ⓑ 我的天阿，難怪你相信聖誕老人的存在！我想我拿過最好的禮物或許是懷孕的超音波照片。

Ⓐ Congratulations, Jack! You are going to be a father! That is the best present I've ever heard.

Ⓑ Thank you, Kim. I promise that I will never let my kids find out that there's no Santa Claus in the world.

Ⓐ 恭喜，傑克！你要當爸了！這是我聽過最棒的禮物。

Ⓑ 謝謝，金。我保證絕不會讓我孩子發現這世上沒有聖誕老人。

Ⓐ You bet! I am going to check where my wife is. Hope she's not going to lose control on Boxing Day.

Ⓑ Okay. I am going to buy some baby's stuff with my wife. Merry Christmas.

Ⓐ 最好是！我要去確認我老婆在哪。希望她沒有迷失在節禮日。

Ⓑ 恩，我要和我老婆去買些寶寶用品。聖誕節快樂。

（節禮日:英國與大多英聯邦國家在12月26日（聖誕節翌日）慶祝的公眾假期。）

酸甜苦辣 記下來！

Santa Claus

Friday, November 28

Dad asked me what gift I wanted to receive from Santa Claus on Christmas day. I said I want dad to be home on Christmas Eve. Dad didn't reply and then I knew the answer. Dad has been stationed in Germany for half a year. I didn't let dad know that I understand that Santa Claus is a fictional character. Last year, I didn't sleep for the whole night waiting for Santa Claus to come, and it turned out that Santa Claus was my dad. Since then, I knew Santa Claus does not exist. However, I really wish Santa Claus does exist, so that he can hear my wish.

聖誕老公公

11月28日星期五

爸爸問我聖誕節那天想要收到什麼禮物。我說希望爸爸在平安夜那天可以在家。爸爸沒有回答，我就知道答案了。爸爸在德國駐守半年。我沒有讓爸爸知道我理解聖誕老公公是虛擬人物。去年，我整個晚上沒睡覺就是為了等聖誕老公公，結果原來聖誕老公公是我爸爸。從那時候我就知道聖誕老公公並不存在，但是現在我希望聖誕老公公真的存在，這樣他就可以聽到我的願望。

增廣見聞 超簡單！

What to give on Christmas day? Men and women's taste could be really different. If you check the gift idea for men and women on the Internet, then you will understand. For example, the gift for men could be a grilling tool set, Bluetooth interactive helicopter, a nice watch or a bottle of nice whiskey. As for women, a yoga pad, a necklace, or a spa gift basket could be the choices. Anyway, no matter what gifts you give, giving a present on Christmas is just an opportunity to show your love for others.

聖誕節該送什麼？男生女生可大不同了！可以看看網路上分別為男生、女生提供了哪些禮物建議，你就大概可以知道。例如：送給男生的禮物，可以是烤肉工具組、藍牙互動直升機、一隻好的錶或是一瓶很棒的威士忌。但若是女生，一個瑜伽墊、一條項鍊、或是 spa 禮物籃都可以是很好的選擇。總之，不管你送的是哪一種禮物，在聖誕節送禮都是個可以讓你表達愛意的好機會。

來換換口味吧！讓你的表達更豐富！

❶ 從那時候我就知道聖誕老公公並不存在。
Since then, I knew Santa Claus does not exist.

(相似短句) 我從那時候開始就知道聖誕老公公並不存在。
I realize Santa Claus does not exist from then on.

❷ 爸爸問我想要從聖誕老公公那裡得到什麼樣的禮物。
Dad asked me what gift I wanted to receive from Santa Claus on Christmas day.

(相似短句) 爸爸問我想要從聖誕老公公那裡得到什麼樣的禮物。
Dad asks me what my wish to Santa Claus is for Christmas Day?

❸ 我說希望爸爸在平安夜那天可以在家。
I said I wanted dad to be home on Christmas Eve.

(相似短句) 我希望可以和爸爸在平安夜那天相聚。
Wish dad reunited with me on Christmas Eve.

❹ 我沒有讓爸爸知道我理解聖誕老公公是虛擬人物。
I didn't let dad know that I understand that Santa Claus is a fictional character.

(相似短句) 我沒有讓爸爸知道我發現聖誕老公公是虛擬人物。
I hid the truth from my dad that I realize Santa Claus is a fictional character.

❺ 爸爸在德國駐守半年了。
Dad has been stationed in Germany for half a year.

(相似短句) 爸爸在德國服役半年了。
Dad has served in the military in Germany for half a year.

依樣畫葫蘆！套進去就能用！

(句型1) **自從……**
since then...

(例句) 從那時起我知道現實生活中的聖誕老公公是誰。
Since then, I know who is Santa Claus in real life.

(句型2) **駐守在……**
is stationed in...

(例句) 爸爸在阿富汗駐守超過一年。
Dad is stationed in Afghanistan for over a year.

美分美秒，聽說讀寫Everyday

Unit 55
食安風暴

I don't know what to buy nor what to eat since there's nothing left to be trusted.
我不知道可以買什麼吃什麼，因為不知道還可以相信什麼了。
👍 讚 56　💬 回覆 7

I can't buy any milk for almost 3 weeks!
將近三週買不到牛奶！
👍 讚 36　💬 回覆 20

The problem is that the customer is always asking for the cheaper prize but not paying attention to the quality.
問題的癥結點在於，消費者總是在要求更低的價格，沒考慮過相應的品質。
👍 讚 130　💬 回覆 3

Eat real food instead of reprocessed foods, it's safer and healthier.
吃真正的食物而非加工食品，才是健康又安全的上上策。
👍 讚 15　💬 回覆 12

Hope we can improve the concept of food after this lesson.
希望在上了這一課之後，我們能改變對食物的觀念。
👍 讚 92　💬 回覆 3

pastry ⓝ 糕餅	**tainted-cooking-oil** ⓝ 黑心油　**scandal** ⓝ 醜聞
pineapple pastries ⓝ 鳳梨酥	**street stalls** ⓝ 路邊攤販
waste oil ⓝ 飼料油　**contain** ⓥ 含有	**animal feed oil** ⓝ 飼料油

出門超實用！能聽會說一次搞定！

A Hey Frank, do you want to try some pineapple pastries? I bought it from a really famous store yesterday.

B No, thanks Kate. Didn't you see the news these days? Tainted-cooking-oil has been spearding all around for over 10 years.

A 嗨！法蘭克，你想嚐些鳳梨酥嗎？我昨天在家非常有名的店買的。

B 不了，謝謝凱特。你難道沒看到最近幾天的新聞嗎？黑心油到處都是，而且已經超過十年了。

A Are you serious? What does it have to do with my pineapple pastries? Please don't tell me that they contain tainted-cooking-oil.

B That is what I am telling you! There are a lot of food stores; street stalls that misused the oil, including the store which sells pineapple pastries.

A 你是認真的嗎？那這跟我的鳳梨酥有什麼關係？拜託別告訴我這裡面有黑心油。

B 這就是我正要告訴你的！有很多食品店、路邊攤誤用油品，包含賣鳳梨酥的店。

A Can you tell me more about the news? What's inside the tainted-cooking-oil? And how should we avoid them?

B Tainted-cooking oil contains recycled waste oil and animal feed oil in it. It is harmful to human-body.

A 你可以告訴我更多資訊嗎？黑心油裡面有什麼？我們又要如何預防呢？

B 黑心油包含回收的廢棄油及動物食用油。那對人體是有害的。

A I am really disappointed in our government. It looks like there are quite a lot of flaws in the law.

B I agree. I hope this is the last time; otherwise we probably need to start cooking at home.

A 我真的對政府感到很失望。看起來法律有很多的漏洞。

B 我同意。希望這是最後一次，不然我們可能需要自己在家開伙了。

Unit 55 食安風暴

酸甜苦辣 記下來！

pineapple pie from Laura's family

Tuesday, September 2

Laura's family is running a business of pastry shop. Their pineapple pie is the most delicious one in Taipei. Most of my relatives will purchase tons of them when they go back to the United States. However, the food scandal exploded last week and caused great damage to their business. They accidentally used tainted-cooking-oil into their pastry. Laura is exhausted dealing with all the press and news reports. I feel sorry for what happened to their family and also other food industry that is affected by the oil issue. I think the government should take the most responsibility for the food scandal.

羅拉家的鳳梨酥

9月2日星期二

蘿菈家是開糕餅店的，他們家的鳳梨酥是全臺北最好吃的。我大部分的親戚都會買許多鳳梨酥帶回美國。但上週爆發的食安醜聞造成他們生意上很大的損失，他們不小心誤用了黑心油。應付所有新聞媒體讓蘿菈精疲力竭。我替他們家以及其他同樣被油品問題影響的食品業者感到難過，我認為政府應該為食安醜聞負最大的責任。

增廣見聞 超簡單！

2014 has been called as a food scandal year on Wikipedia due to series of food safety issues. Unscrupulous corporations mixed recycled waste oil and animal feed oil together and then sold it to people. There are over thousands of food manufacturers, food stores, or street foods becoming victims. As a result, instead of purchasing breads, soymilk, or eating out all the time, people now prefer cooking by themselves. Kitchen appliances are then becoming popular as well.

2014 年，台灣因為一連串的食安風暴而被維基百科定名為「食物醜聞的一年」。不肖廠商將回收油和飼料油混合並販售出去，有超過千名食品製造商、商店和攤販都變成了受害者。因此，與其在外購買麵包、豆漿或是吃外食，人們現在比較傾向自己烹煮食物，而那些廚房家電也因此變得供不應求。

來換換口味吧！讓你的表達更豐富！

❶ 他們不小心誤用了黑心油。
They accidentally used tainted-cooking-oil into their pastries.
相似短句 他們在製作糕餅時誤用了黑心油。
They misused tainted-cooking-oil when making pastries.

❷ 應付所有新聞媒體讓羅拉精疲力竭。
Laura is exhausted dealing with all the press and news reports.
相似短句 蘿菈十分疲於應付新聞和媒體。
It must be tiring for Laura to deal with the press and news reports.

❸ 我認為政府應該為食安醜聞負最大的責任。
I think the government should take the most responsibility for the food scandal.
相似短句 我認為政府應該負起責任去處理食安醜聞。
I think the government should take the lead for dealing with the food scandal.

❹ 我大部分的親戚都會買許多鳳梨酥帶回美國。
Most of my relatives will purchase tons of them when they go back to the United States.
相似短句 我的親戚們在回美國前都會買很多的鳳梨酥。
My relatives will buy lots of them before they go back to the United States.

❺ 蘿菈家是開糕餅店的。
Laura's family is running a business of pastry shop.
相似短句 蘿菈家是經營糕餅店的。　Laura's family is operating a pastry shop.

依樣畫葫蘆！套進去就能用！

句型1 對～造成傷害。
cause great damage to...
例句 食安醜聞對生意造成很大的傷害。
The food scandal caused great damage to the business.

句型2 為～負起責任。
take responsibility for...
例句 她要為誤用油的原因負責。
She has to take responsibility for why they misused the oil.

Unit 56
停電

社群人氣王！英文動態消息寫給你看！

I can't find flashlights nor candles in my house. What can I do now?
我在家裡找不到手電筒也沒有蠟燭。我現在該怎麼辦？

👍讚 56　💬回覆 7

If it was not for the black out, I would never noticed that there are so many stars in the sky.
如果不是停電，我大概永遠不會注意到天空裡有那麼多星星。

👍讚 36　💬回覆 20

I woke up and found that the power had been cut. What a bad beginning of a day!
我起床的時候發現停電了，真是個很糟糕的開始。

👍讚 130　💬回覆 3

The power shortage is bringing great inconvenience to us.
停電帶來諸多不便。

👍讚 15　💬回覆 12

The power is cut off and my mobile phone is running out of battery. –feeling miserable.
停電了，而且我的手機也快要沒電了。覺得悲慘。

👍讚 92　💬回覆 3

新手超必備！一個單字嘛欸通！

electricity ⓝ 電	cut off phr. 切斷	power ⓝ 電力
darkness ⓝ 黑暗	blackout ⓝ 停電	abruptly adv. 突然地
blow ⓥ 燒斷	identify ⓥ 辨別	

出門超實用！能聽會說一次搞定！

A Last night, our electricity was cut off due to a construction near our house. They accidentally broke the electric wire and cable.

B How did it feel when your life is without electricity? Comparing to water shortage, I can't accept life without electricity.

A 昨晚我們的電力因為附近施工的關係被切掉了。他們不小心破壞了電線和電纜。

B 當你生活中少了電的感覺如何？與缺水相比，我無法接受沒有電的生活。

A I just feel lucky that my laptop and cell phone were fully charged before we were out of electricity.

B Ha! Did they say how long it would take to restore the electricity? You can come to my house if you want.

A 我只是覺得很幸運，因為我的筆電和手機在斷電前都充飽了。

B 哈！他們有說要花多少時間才能恢復電力嗎？如果你要的話你可以來我家。

A Thanks, but I have to take care of my parents. It's dark in the night. We have to rely on flashlights during the night.

B But how can you take showers without electricity? And how would you cook?

A 多謝，但我必須照顧我的父母。晚上非常暗。我們今天晚上必須靠手電筒了。

B 但是你要如何在沒電的情況下洗澡呢？要如何做菜呢？

A Oh dear. We use gas to cook and we use a gas water heater, so there's no problem at all.

B I see. I think you need to prepare more batteries, in case it might take longer to get back to normal life.

A 喔親愛的。我們用瓦斯來煮飯和瓦斯熱水器，所以完全沒有問題。

B 了解。我想你需要多準備些電池，以防還要很久才能回歸正常。

酸甜苦辣 記下來！

A blackout ?!

Saturday, November 2
We hardly ever have blackouts here. What is a blackout? I have never thought about it. Not until the blackout happened did I realize how terrible it was. I got many bumps on my body, for I could only identify things and moved about by touching things in the darkness. I realized the importance of electricity after the blackout. I don't want to have this kind of experience anymore.

停電？！

11月2日星期六
我們這裡從沒有停電過，我根本就不知道停電是怎麼一回事，直到它發生了我才了解到這情況有多糟糕。我只能在黑暗中用摸得來辨認東西，結果我撞得全身都傷，在這之後我終於了解到電的重要性，我不想要再經歷一次這種情況了。

增廣見聞 超簡單！

Can you imagine life without electricity? Electricity is probably the base of our entertainment. Without electricity nothing seems to work. What can you do during a power outage? Here are some interesting things to do: first, you can set up a tent with your child and bring some pillows, snack, and books. Second, have a candlelit dinner. You can have a romantic night and nice conversation with your partner without going to expensive restaurants.

你可以想像沒有電的生活嗎？電力大概是我們一切娛樂來源的基礎，沒有電好像什麼也做不了。到底沒電的時候可以做些什麼呢？這裡推薦你幾個選項：第一，你可以帶些枕頭零食和幾本書，跟你的孩子搭個帳篷世界。第二，你可以來個燭光晚餐，不用到昂貴餐廳也可以跟你的伴侶有個浪漫的夜晚和美好的對話。

來換換口味吧！讓你的表達更豐富！

① 今晚又停電了。　**Electricity was cut off again tonight.**
(相似短句) 今晚又跳電了。　The power blew out again tonight.

② 我只能用摸得來辨別東西。
I could only identify things by touching in the darkness.
(相似短句) 黑暗中，什麼都看不到。
I could see nothing in the darkness.

③ 我瞭解到電的重要性。
I realized the importance of electricity.
(相似短句) 我才發現電對我們如此的重要。
It dawned on me that electricity is so important to us.

④ 以前都沒發生過停電。　**We hardly ever have blackouts here.**
(相似短句) 以前從沒停電過。　Blackout has never happened before.

⑤ 它突然發生了！　**It happened abruptly.**
(相似短句) 事發突然。　It came all of a sudden.

依樣畫葫蘆！套進去就能用！

(句型1) **重新開始～**
start over
(例句) 電力恢復時，電視又重新開始播放。
As the electricity went back, the TV started over.

(句型2) **直到～我才了解～**
Not until... did I realize...
(例句) 直到停電，我才了解手電筒的重要。
Not until the blackout happened did I realize the importance of my light torch.

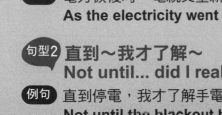

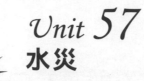

Unit 57
水災

社群人氣王！英文動態消息寫給你看！

I have just saw the flood from TV. It was so terrifying.
我剛剛在電視上看到洪水了，真的好可怕。

 讚 56　　回覆 7

The village is totally damaged due to the flood.
水災讓那個村落幾乎全毀。

 讚 36　　回覆 20

Due to the whole night of heavy rain, I woke up in a floating bed this morning.
整夜的大雨讓我在醒來的時候發現床正在漂浮。

 讚 130　　回覆 3

I caught a fish on the road due to the flood. lol
因為淹水的關係，我在馬路上竟然抓到一條魚，哈哈。

 讚 15　　回覆 12

After the flood, the whole city became a great mess. It's time to clean up!
水退後整個城市一團亂。是該整理一下的時候了。

 讚 92　　回覆 3

新手超必備！一個單字嘛欸通！

flood n 洪水；水災	**furniture** n 家具	**float** v 漂浮
dirty adj 骯髒的	**water level** phr. 水位	**rain** n 雨水
water-splash n 積水	**submerge** v 浸泡；使……浸入水中	

出門超實用！能聽會說一次搞定！

A I have to cancel my trip to Thailand, because water floods are everywhere in Thailand, including Bangkok.

B Yes, I saw it on the news. Our company's factory in Thailand is forced to shut down due to the flood.

A 因為泰國跟曼谷到處都淹水，所以我必須取消去泰國的行程。

B 恩，我在新聞上有看到。我們公司在泰國的工廠也因水災被迫關閉。

A Flooding during monsoon season in Thailand is often heard, but this time, the situation is even worse than before.

B Millions of people are affected by the water flood, even US Navy is flying to Thailand to support.

A 泰國在季風季節發生水災時有所聞，只是這一次情況比之前更加嚴重。

B 數百萬人受到這次水災波及，甚至連美國海軍都飛來泰國救援了。

A The same thing happened in Taiwan as well. Whenever typhoon comes, it will cause water flood in some areas.

B The cause of the flood might be the effectiveness of the draining systems in the city. Our government should put more effort in improving the draining system.

A 同樣的事情也會發生在台灣。每當颱風過境，某些區域就會受到水災肆虐。

B 造成水災的原因可能是城市排水系統的效能。我們政府應多用點心在改善排水系統上。

A Draining system is one thing. Environmental protection is another. The effect of deforestation cannot be ignored.

B Looks like you are not affected by the cancellation of your trip to Thailand, which is good.

A 排水系統是一個原因。環境保護則是另外一項。森林開伐的影響是不容忽視的。

B 看來你沒有受到泰國之旅泡湯的影響，這非常好。

Unit 57 水災

酸甜苦辣 記下來！

The flood!

Monday, May 27
How terrible the flood was! The flood was dirty and smelled disgusting. I was so scared when I saw the water level go up higher and higher. I was shocked when I saw my house flooded with rain water. We could have prevented the disaster if we had done the checkup on the flood system.

淹水！！！

5月27日星期一
淹水真的很恐怖！水看起來很髒而且聞起來很噁心，當我看到水位一直升高時我很害怕，之後雨水整個淹進我們家時我真的嚇呆了。如果我們做好防災系統，是可以防範災難的。

增廣見聞 超簡單！

There are numbers of reason which could cause water floods, such as high rainfall, snow melt, and coastal flooding that are categorized as natural reasons. However, deforestation, poor farming, or poor draining system are human causes of floods. The water flood disaster which occurred in Thailand in 2011 was resulted from natural reason. During the monsoon season, there could be several floods happening. However, the biggest flood disaster is resulted from tropical storms which brings high rainfalls.

造成水災的原因有很多種，高雨量、融雪或是沿海洪災都可以被歸類為自然原因。但是森林砍伐、不當耕作或是排水系統不良則歸類為人類肇因。2011 年在泰國發生的水災是導因於自然原因；其實泰國在雨季時，本來就常有淹水的情況，但是最嚴重的水災則是熱帶氣旋所夾帶的龐大雨勢水量所造成的。

來換換口味吧！讓你的表達更豐富！

① 我們有水患。　**We got flooded.**
　相似短句　水要淹來了。　The flood is coming.

② 水滲進屋子。　**The water seeped into the house.**
　相似短句　水淹進房子了。　The water flew into the house.

③ 家具在飄。　**The furniture was floating.**
　相似短句　家具都泡在水裡了。
　　　　　　The furniture was all submerged in the water.

④ 水很髒而且聞起來很噁心。
The flood was dirty and smelled disgusting.
　相似短句　水很髒，而且味道讓人感到噁心。
　　　　　　The water was nasty, and the smell got people nauseous.

⑤ 我看到房子被雨水淹的到處都是。
I saw my house flooded with rain water.
　相似短句　這水災摧毀了我的屋子的結構和一切。
　　　　　　The flood water wreaked havoc on the structure of my house and everything.

依樣畫葫蘆！套進去就能用！

句型1　～好可怕。
How terrible...
例句　水災好可怕！
How terrible the flood was!

句型2　～很不方便。
It was not convenient to...
例句　颱風天要得到醫療診治很不方便。
It was not convenient to get medical treatment during typhoon days.

Unit 58
火災

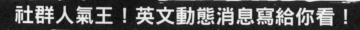
社群人氣王！英文動態消息寫給你看！

No one knows why the building was on fire.
沒有人知道為什麼那棟大樓會起火。
👍讚 56　💬回覆 7

I was having lunch in the restaurant when the kitchen got on fired.
正當我在吃午餐的時候餐廳的廚房竟然燒起來了。
👍讚 36　💬回覆 20

The fire fighters came immediately but it's already too late.
消防人員很快就趕到現場，但一切已經為時已晚。
👍讚 130　💬回覆 3

I check the gas every time before I leave the kitchen.
我每次離開廚房前都會檢查瓦斯有沒有關。
👍讚 15　💬回覆 12

The smoke was so thick that I could not see anything, not even the exit of the theater.
煙濃到我連電影院的出口都看不見。
👍讚 92　💬回覆 3

新手超必備！一個單字嘛欸通！

smoke ⓝ 濃煙	**fire** ⓝ 火災	**fight** ⓥ 對抗
put out phr 撲滅	**victim** ⓝ 災民	**ceiling** ⓝ 天花板
escape ⓝ 逃生工具	**fire alarm** phr 火災警報器	

出門超實用！能聽會說一次搞定！

A Can we remove the fire alarm? It's too sensitive that even a light smoke can cause the alarm.

B No way. We can make adjustments, but it's impossible to remove it. I don't want to regret one day when something really happens.

A 我們可以拿掉火災警報器嗎？它太敏感了，連微量的煙都可以引發警報。

B 不可以。我們可以做調整，但是不能拿掉它。我不想等到哪天真的有事了才來後悔。

A Alright. Several weeks ago, the house located just three blocks away from us was destroyed by late night fire.

B I heard about it. Luckily, people inside the house were all evacuated at the fire place, so no one got injured.

A 好吧。幾周前，離我們這邊三個街區遠的一間房子才在午夜被火災所毀。

B 我有聽說。幸運的是，住在裡面的人都在第一時間逃了出來，所以無人受傷。

A Thank god! But what caused the fire that late at night? No one cooks at midnight.

B It was caused by electrical fire! The houses in that area were built over ten years ago.

A 感謝上帝！但是，是什麼東西在半夜造成了火災？沒人會在半夜煮東西。

B 是電線走火！那區域的房子已經建超過十年以上了。

A I see. I think we have to ask people to come in our house and check the circuit and electric power system.

B I am glad you changed your mind. Don't forget to adjust the settings of the fire alarm system.

A 了解。我想我們必須叫人來家裡檢查線路和電源系統。

B 非常高興你改變心意了。別忘了調整火災警報器的設定。

Unit 58 火災

酸甜苦辣 記下來！

Bad luck

Tuesday, December 31
There was a factory near Mary and John's house. Mary and John's house was caught on fire. The house was burnt down, and they've just bought it only half a year ago. They were terribly frightened when they heard about the fire. I heard that they had two houses in the countryside, but both of the houses were old. Their estimated loss was up to about several million dollars. They really had bad luck.

運氣真不好

12月31日星期二
瑪莉和約翰的房子附近有一間工廠。他們的房子失火了，並且被全部燒毀。他們買這間房子才半年。當他們聽到這個消息時，都嚇壞了。我聽說他們在鄉下有兩棟房子，但是兩間都是舊的。他們估計損害金額達到幾百萬元，他們運氣真的很不好。

增廣見聞 超簡單！

We use fire to cook, to generate electric power, and so on. However, once the fire becomes out of control, it can create a lot of destruction. How to prevent you and your home from fire? Installing a fire alarm in your home is a smart choice. According to the news, there are only 2 minutes to get away from home once the fire starts. With installation of a fire alarm, we can immediately put out the fire hazards. However, don't forget to check the fire alarm every two months to make sure it works.

我們利用火來煮飯，或用火來發電等等。但是火勢一旦失去控制就會造成很大的災害。那麼，要如何預防家裡發生火災呢？安裝火災警報器會是個聰明的選擇。根據新聞，一旦失火，我們只有兩分鐘的時間逃生，安裝火警警報器之後，我們就可以立即撲滅火源。但是千萬別忘記每兩個月就要檢查一次，以確保火警警報器運作正常。

1 整棟大樓都是煙。　**The building was full of smoke.**

相似短句 整動大樓被火吞噬。
The whole building was consumed by fire.

2 消防車前來救火。
The fire fighting trucks came to fight against the fire.

相似短句 消防車火速趕到那裡滅火。
The fire trucks rushed to the building to put out the fire.

3 有些人即時逃出。　**Some people fled in time.**

相似短句 有些人從逃生梯逃出。
Some people got out from the fire escape.

4 火災觸動警鈴。　**The fire initiated the bell.**

相似短句 煙霧漫到天花板時，火災警報器就響了。
The fire alarm rang when the smoke hit the ceiling.

5 災民情緒激動。　**The victims flipped out.**

相似短句 災民變得情緒化且激動。
The victims went emotional and freaked out.

依樣畫葫蘆！套進去就能用！

句型1 ～著火了。
...be caught on fire

例句 電視因為電線問題著火了。
The TV was caught on fire due to electrical problem.

句型2 充滿了～
be full of...

例句 天空因為這場火災充滿了煙霧。
The sky was full of smoke because of the fire.

Unit 59
颱風

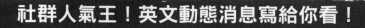
社群人氣王!英文動態消息寫給你看!

Typhoons come quite frequently every August and September.
每年八、九月的時候颱風比較多。
👍 讚 56　💬 回覆 7

I hope our company will agree to have a day off tomorrow since the typhoon is coming.
我希望我們公司明天可以放颱風假。
👍 讚 36　💬 回覆 20

The price of vegetables soared high due to the typhoons.
蔬菜的價格因為颱風而飆漲。
👍 讚 130　💬 回覆 3

My plane is cancelled because of the typhoon. I have to stay at Penghu for another few more days now.
颱風的關係我的班機被取消了,現在我必須在澎湖多待幾天了。
👍 讚 15　💬 回覆 12

Kids are happy because they don't have to go to school tomorrow.
孩子們很開心她們明天不用去學校。

👍 讚 92　💬 回覆 3

新手超必備!一個單字嘛欸通!

serious adj. 嚴重的　　typhoon n. 颱風　　predict v. 預測
hit v. 襲擊　　windy adj. 刮風的　　sandbag n. 沙包
preparation n. 預防措施　　instant noodles phr. 泡麵

出門超實用！能聽會說一次搞定！

A I bet we have a chance of taking a typhoon day off on Monday, then we can enjoy three days off.

B I really don't want to see Typhoons coming. Imagine life without clean water and electricity.

A 我打賭我們有機會在星期一放颱風假，這樣我們就可以享受三天連假了。

B 我真的不想要看到颱風來。想像一下沒有乾淨水和電力的生活。

A Okay. It's weird that typhoons are coming in September. Normally, they come during July and August.

B I don't think the seasons have that great of an effect on the formation of typhoons!

A 恩。颱風在九月來非常奇怪。正常來說，他們會在七月到八月時出現。

B 我想季節對颱風的構成沒有太大的影響力。

A Anyway, I have to make a call back home, asking them to get prepared for the typhoon coming.

B Yes! Your hometown is located near the river. Then they got to get prepared for the possible water flood.

A 不論如何，我必須要打通電話回家，跟他們說準備好颱風的來臨。

B 對！你的家鄉靠近河流。那他們最好為可能的水災做準備。

A Yes, we have to build a fortress by using earth bags and trying to remove things from the ground.

B So are you still expecting the typhoon coming? Think about what might happen to your hometown.

A 沒錯，我們必須用土堆來建造些堤防和試著移走地面上的東西。

B 所以你還仍然期待颱風來嗎？想想你的家鄉可能會發生什麼事情吧。

酸甜苦辣 記下來！

Typhoon is coming!

Wednesday , June 26

There was a serious typhoon today. Typhoon did terrible damages to properties and the environment. It has become more and more windy this afternoon. The Weather Bureau suggested that we should make preparations against the typhoon. For fear that the electricity would be cut off, people stormed into convenience stores to grab candles. I went to grab dozens of instant noodles so that I don't need to worry about eating when the typhoon attacks.

颱風要來了！

6月26日星期三

今天有個強度很大的颱風，它造成財產上跟環境上的嚴重災害。下午的時候風越來越大了，氣象局建議我們要做好防颱措施。因為怕會停電，大家都湧進便利商店買蠟燭。我也買了很多泡麵，這樣我就不用怕颱風來沒東西吃了。

增廣見聞 超簡單！

Typhoon, you can also call it a hurricane, or a tropical storm. There are two to four typhoons that hit Taiwan every year in average during summer and autumn. Have you ever thought about how a typhoon is named? The name of a typhoon actually follows the rule that was published by World Metrology Committee. Typhoon is named based on the rule from year 2000. Since the composition of the name is complex, numbers are used mainly, and the name has became a auxiliary name to remember.

颱風，你也可以稱之為颶風或熱帶氣旋。台灣平均每年都有二至四個颱風在夏季和秋季經過。你有想過颱風到底是如何被命名的嗎？颱風的名字自 2000 年開始，是根據世界氣象組織颱風委員會公佈的規則命名。但因為颱風名字的組成太複雜，所以通常主要使用數字，而名字則作為補充說明使用。

來換換口味吧！讓你的表達更豐富！

1 今天有個嚴重的颱風。　There was a serious typhoon today.
　相似短句 今天有強颱襲來。　A strong typhoon is coming today.

2 颱風要來了。　There is a typhoon coming.
　相似短句 據預測，兩個小時內颱風就會登陸台灣。
　　It's predicted that the typhoon will hit Taiwan in 2 hours.

3 下午風就變得越來越大。
It has become more and more windy this afternoon.
　相似短句 風雨在下午變得更大。
　　The wind got stronger and the rain got heavier in the afternoon.

4 我去買了很多泡麵。
I went to grab dozens of instant noodles.
　相似短句 颱風來襲，我們買了好多東西準備。
　　We made a big purchase for the coming typhoon.

5 我們應該要做好防颱準備。
We should make preparations against the typhoon.
　相似短句 為了防颱，我們在庭院裡堆起沙包。
　　We piled up sandbags in the yard in preparation for the coming typhoon.

依樣畫葫蘆！套進去就能用！

句型1 變得越來越～
It has become more and more...

例句 颱風似乎改變了路徑，讓情勢越來越緊張。
It has become more and more intense because the typhoon seems to have changed its path.

句型2 到目前為止～
So far, ...

例句 到目前為止，沒人在水災中受傷。
So far, no one got hurt in the flood.

Unit 60
地震

社群人氣王！英文動態消息寫給你看！

Earthquake! There is an earthquake! This one is so seriously strong!
地震！有地震！這次晃得好厲害！
👍讚 56　　💬回覆 7

Since there are too much earthquakes, Taiwanese seem to be very used to them and don't feel nervous to the small ones.
因為地震太頻繁了，臺灣人似乎都頗習以為常，對於小地震一點也不感到緊張。
👍讚 36　　💬回覆 20

When earthquakes happen, the first thing we do nowadays is posting the news on Facebook rather than hiding under the table.
地震的時候，現在的我們所做的第一件事情不是躲到桌子下，而是在臉書上分享這則消息。
👍讚 130　　💬回覆 3

The building had fallen suddenly due to the earthquake. That was so scary.
那棟大樓突然就這麼被震倒了，真可怕。
👍讚 15　　💬回覆 12

Everything was destroyed due to the earthquake. Some people even lost their family.
所有的東西都被地震震毀了。有些人甚至失去了家人。
👍讚 92　　💬回覆 3

新手超必備！一個單字嘛欸通！

earthquake **n** 地震　　destroy **v** 毀壞　　nowadays **adv** 現今；時下
donate **v** 捐贈　　victim **n** 遇難者　　tsunami **n** 海嘯
prevention **n** 預防

出門超實用！能聽會說一次搞定！

Ⓐ I donated three thousand dollars to victims of the Great East Japan Earthquake which happened on March 11th.

Ⓑ Me too. I donated a month of my salary to help victims as well. I just couldn't help crying when I saw the news.

Ⓐ 我捐了三千元給 311 東日本大地震的災民。

Ⓑ 我也是。我也捐了一個月的薪水來幫助災民。我看到新聞時就是忍不住淚水。

Ⓐ It was the most powerful earthquake to ever be recorded to hit Japan, and the fourth most powerful earthquake in the world.

Ⓑ I cannot imagine if this happened in Taiwan! The tsunami and earthquake is going to cause serious damage all around.

Ⓐ 那是日本有史以來監測到最強烈的地震，而且在全世界是排名第四強的。

Ⓑ 我無法想像如果這發生在台灣會怎麼樣！海嘯和地震將會對全體造成嚴重的損害。

Ⓐ Looks like all those education on disaster preventions won't work if we were facing such a great calamity.

Ⓑ It is absolutely wrong saying that. There would be a lot more deaths and injured people if they didn't know how to protect themselves.

Ⓐ 看起來如果是面對如此強烈的災難，所有防災教育都無用武之地了。

Ⓑ 這麼說是絕對不對的。如果他們不知道如何自我保護，這裡會有更多的死傷人數。

Ⓐ You are right. But it's just hard to remain calm when encountering emergency situations.

Ⓑ I agree. That is why we have to attend education classes on disaster prevention every year.

Ⓐ 説的沒錯。但是緊急狀況時要維持鎮靜真的就是很困難。

Ⓑ 我同意。這也是為什麼我們必須參加每年的防災教育。

Unit 60 地震

酸甜苦辣 記下來！

Earthquake experiences

Tuesday, March 11

It has been 3 years after the "Great East Japan Earthquake". Mr. Lin asked us to share and discuss our experiences about earthquakes. Most of the classmates said that they are so used to the earthquakes that they don't fear it at all. But I think, for our safety, we should maintain our vigilance against earthquakes.

地震的經驗

3月11日星期二

東日本大地震已經歷時 3 年了，林老師要求我們分享語討論關於地震的經驗。大部分的同學都說他們因為太習慣而不會感到害怕。但我認為，為了安全起見，我們都應該保持對地震的警覺心。

增廣見聞 超簡單！

Remember the South Asia earthquake and tsunami in 2004? Do you remember the earthquake disaster in Sichuan in 2008 that caused a great disaster on an immense scale? And then, what about the earthquake and tsunami in Japan in 2011? Earthquake happens all the time that it is a regular release of energy. However, the earthquakes that release large amount of energy all in a sudden can cause great effect and serious damage such as major disasters mentioned above.

還記得 2004 年的南亞地震跟海嘯嗎？還記得 2008 年四川大地震造成的重大災害嗎？接下來，2011 年日本發生也發生了地震跟海嘯……為了要釋放能量，地震其實一直都在發生，但是當地震在短時間釋放巨大能量時，就可能造成很大的影響和嚴重的災害，像是上述提到的災難。

(左側直書) Part 10 人禍比天災更可怕

來換換口味吧！讓你的表達更豐富！

1 地震發生得很頻繁。　There are too much earthquakes.

> 相似短句 我們時常經歷地震。　We often have earthquakes.

2 那太可怕了！　That was so scary.

> 相似短句 那真是恐怖！　It was horrible.

3 我忍不住的哭了。　I just can't help crying.

> 相似短句 我不由自主的哭了。　I can't help myself from crying.

4 我無法想像。　I can't imagine.

> 相似短句 我無法想像。　I can't get over the fact.

5 那就是我們為什麼必須這麼做的原因！
That's why we have to.

> 相似短句 那就是我們為什麼必須這麼做的原因！
> That's the reason why we have to.

依樣畫葫蘆！套進去就能用！

句型1 習慣於～
be used to...

> 例句 我習慣用我的右手拿筷子。
> I am used to using chopsticks with my right hand.

句型2 由於～
due to...

> 例句 因為他生病了，所以今年沒有去學校。
> Due to him being sick, he didn't go to school
> today.

Unit 61
感冒

社群人氣王！英文動態消息寫給你看！

I got running nose and can't stop coughing. I think I need to see the doctor.
一直流鼻水而且咳嗽咳個不停，我大概需要去看醫生了。
👍讚 56　💬回覆 7

I am running a fever but I don't want to see the doctor. Hope I will be fine after getting enough sleep.
我發燒了但是我不想要去看醫生。希望好好睡一覺起來就好了。
👍讚 36　💬回覆 20

Spring and Autumn is the easiest time to get a cold.
春秋之際是最容易感冒的季節。
👍讚 130　💬回覆 3

I had a headache this morning and I couldn't even get off of bed.
今天早上我整個頭痛欲裂到連床都下不了。
👍讚 15　💬回覆 12

I haven't recovered from the cold yet and now I got a fever. Huh! It's killing me!
我的感冒都還沒好現在又發燒了，噢這真是太折磨人了。
👍讚 92　💬回覆 3

新手超必備！一個單字嘛欸通！

cough **v.** 咳嗽　　headache **n.** 頭痛　　fever **n.** 發燒
medicine **n.** 藥品　　pill **n.** 藥錠　　sick **adj.** 生病的
cold **n.** 感冒　　powdered **adj.** 磨成粉的

出門超實用！能聽會說一次搞定！

A James is not in the office today. I think its probably because the epidemic flu. Sara is off today as well.

B Yes, it is possible. My daughter and son are both in the hospital now and there are already a lot of children in the hospital.

A 詹姆士今天並沒有在辦公室。我猜有可能是流行性感冒的關係。莎菈今天也沒有來。

B 恩，這是有可能的。我的女兒和兒子現在都在醫院，而且那邊已經有很多生病的孩童了。

A It's that serious? Did you bring your parents to take the flu shot? Epidemic flu can be serious.

B Of course I did. In order to prevent things from getting worse, I have asked them to take the shot ever since my two kids got the flu.

A 這麼嚴重？你有帶你的父母去注射流感疫苗嗎？流行性感冒也可以很嚴重的。

B 當然。為了避免事情變得更糟，從我兩個小孩感冒後，我就要求他們去打疫苗。

A Oh, I don't feel well now. I've got high body temperature and a sore throat. Do you have medicine with you?

B Yes, I do. Don't tell me that you got a cold as well! Drink some more water and go back home and take a hot bath.

A 喔，我現在有點不舒服。我有點發高燒和喉嚨痛。你身上有藥嗎？

B 我有。別跟我說你也感冒了！喝點水然後回家沖個熱水澡吧。

A Okay. I am sorry I have to ask for a sick leave this afternoon. You have to take care parts of my work.

B No problem. I hope this is not your excuse to escape from the important meeting this afternoon.

A 好。我為我中午必須請病假感到抱歉。讓你必須兼顧我的工作。

B 沒問題。我只希望這不是為了逃避中午那個重要會議的理由。

Unit 61 感冒

酸甜苦辣 記下來！

Brrr...Got a cold

Thursday, September 12

It rained and I was like a chicken drenched and about to be feathered. I coughed and felt hot. I felt dizzier and dizzier. I thought I must be sick. It's so uncomfortable to catch a cold. The doctor said that I should take a day off and take some rest so that I would make a recovery as soon as possible.

感冒了

9月12日星期四

下雨了，我被淋成落湯雞，我覺得很熱而且一直咳嗽，我覺得頭越來越昏，我想我一定是生病了，感冒的感覺真的很不好受，醫生說我應該要休一天假好好休息，這樣才會盡快康復。

增廣見聞 超簡單！

The flu season runs from December to March in winter. As winter comes, it will be better to make plans to get vaccines for your elder parents or young child. The influenza is different from serious cold, though they share runny/blocked nose, sore throat, and cough symptoms. However, if you got the flu, symptoms are: serious headaches, cold sweats, high temperature, aching joints, or nausea, vomiting, and so on. In general, flu is not a serious issue, but still it depends on the age.

流行感冒通常好發於冬季十二月到三月。當冬天來臨時，最好能盡早計劃替家中的長輩跟小孩接種流感疫苗。流行性感冒跟一般嚴重的感冒是不一樣的，雖然它們都有同樣的症狀，像是流鼻水、喉嚨痛和咳嗽。但是如果你得的是流行性感冒，則症狀還會有：頭痛、冒冷汗、高燒、關節痠痛、噁心嘔吐等等；相較來說，流行性感冒較不嚴重，但還是必須看年紀決定。

① 我淋成落湯雞。 **I was like a chicken drenched.**

相似短句 我渾身濕透了。 I got totally soaked.

② 我咳嗽而且覺得很熱。 **I coughed and felt hot.**

相似短句 我忍不住咳嗽、不停冒汗。

I couldn't help coughing and feeling sweaty.

③ 我頭痛。 **I had a headache.**

相似短句 我感冒，所以頭痛。

I suffered from a headache caused by the fever.

④ 我晚餐後吃藥。 **I took medicine after dinner.**

相似短句 晚餐後我吃了些藥。 I took some pills after dinner.

⑤ 我不喜歡藥粉。 **I don't like powdered medicine.**

相似短句 我比較喜歡藥錠。 I prefer medicinal pills.

依樣畫葫蘆！套進去就能用！

句型1 ～真的很不舒服。
It's so uncomfortable to...

例句 感冒真的很不舒服。
It's so uncomfortable to catch a cold.

句型2 他甚至不敢～
He didn't even dare...

例句 他甚至不敢喝水，因為他仍覺得想吐。
He didn't even dare to drink water because he still feels nauseous.

Unit 62
中暑

社群人氣王！英文動態消息寫給你看！

It's better to carry an umbrella since the sunshine is really strong.
太陽很大，最好帶把傘出門

 讚 56　　回覆 7

I got a heatstroke at the beach and I spent 2 weeks to recover from it.
我在海灘中暑後花了兩個週的時間才恢復。

 讚 36　　回覆 20

Drinking enough water is another way to avoid getting a heatstroke.
補充足夠的水分也是避免中暑的方法。

 讚 130　　回覆 3

Ouch! I got sunburns and my skin feels like burning.
啊啊！我被曬傷了，整個皮膚像是火在燒一樣。

 讚 15　　回覆 12

I didn't know heatstrokes can be so seriously dangerous.
我不知道中暑可能會變得非常危險。

 讚 92　　回覆 3

新手超必備！一個單字嘛欸通！

appetite ⓝ 胃口　　　　**turn on** ⓟⱨⱤ 開啟　　　　**stay** ⓥ 待在
dizzy ⓐⱭⱼ 暈眩的　　　　**take a nap** ⓟⱨⱤ 小憩一會
sunstroke ⓝ 中暑　　　　**air conditioner** ⓝ 冷氣機

A Vicky, are you okay? You look pale and exhausted. Do you want me to take you to the hospital?

B No, I think I am fine. I am just feeling a bit dizzy and exhausted. I should be alright after some rest.

A 薇琪，你還好嗎？你的臉色看起來蒼白無力。需要我帶你去醫院嗎？

B 不用，我想我很好。我只是覺得有些頭暈目眩和疲倦。休息一下應該就好了。

A I don't think so. It's 38 degree Celsius, and you're wearing a coat? You might get a heat stroke.

B Oh my god! Heat stroke, would it be that serious? Should I go to the doctors now?

A 我不這麼認為。現在攝氏 38 度，而你卻穿著外套？你可能是中暑了。

B 喔我的天啊！中暑，有這麼嚴重嗎？我現在應該去看醫生嗎？

A No, it's not as serious as you think. Please take your coat off first, and I will buy you some cold water and sports water to see if we can relieve the symptoms first.

B Thank you so much. I feel much better after drinking cold water and sports drinks. I should go home.

A 不，並沒有你想得這麼嚴重。請你先脫掉你的外套，我會幫你買些冷開水和運動飲料，再來看看我們能不能讓症狀先舒緩些。

B 非常謝謝你。在喝完冷開水和運動飲料後我已經好很多了。我應該回家了。

A Before you go, I am curious about why you wore a coat on such a hot day walking under the sun?

B I don't want to get tanned, but I will not do it again. Thank you anyway, I didn't even notice that I got a heatstroke.

A 在你走之前，我非常好奇為何你要在這麼大的熱天，穿外套走在太陽下？

B 我不想被太陽曬黑，但我絕不會再做一次一樣的事情。總之謝謝你，我甚至沒注意到我中暑了。

酸甜苦辣 記下來！

Soccer exam

Thursday, August 22

I prefer winter to summer. The temperature today is 38°C. We still had to pass the soccer exam in such a hot day. My classmate was sent to the health center because of getting a sunstroke in the afternoon. The nurse said that we had better stay indoors on such a hot day. I really envy him for staying in the health center all afternoon.

足球考試

8月22日星期四

我喜歡冬天勝過夏天。今天的溫度有攝氏38度欸，我們還要再大熱天裡考足球。我同學就因為中暑而被送到保健中心。護士說我們這種天氣最好待在室內，我好羨慕他哦，可以下午都待在保健中心。

增廣見聞 超簡單！

What will happen when you get a heatstroke? There are two kinds of heatstrokes: classic heatstroke and extertional heatstroke. Classic heatstroke shows symptoms such as rapid heart beating, feeling dizzy, headache and so on. Extertional heatstroke happens when a person is having an intense exercise under the heat. We may not notice but it is actually the top three killers for athletes and soldiers in training.

中暑有什麼症狀呢？有兩種中暑：傳統型中暑和運動型中暑。傳統型中暑會伴隨著心臟快速跳動、暈眩、頭痛等等症狀。而運動型中暑則會發生在高溫中密集運動時。我們或許不知道，其實運動型中暑是運動員和軍人在訓練時造成死亡的前三大殺手。

Part 9 全國瘋節慶

來換換口味吧！讓你的表達更豐富！

① 天氣熱死了。　**The weather was hot to death.**
　[相似短句] 這溫度真是熱死人了。　**The heat is killing me.**

② 我沒有食慾。　**I had no appetite.**
　[相似短句] 我不想吃東西。　**I don't feel like eating.**

③ 我只想待在家裡開冷氣。
　I just want to stay home and turn on the air conditioner.
　[相似短句] 我想待在家裡吹冷氣。
　　All I want to do is stay home with the air conditioner on.

④ 我待在家裡休息。　**I stayed at home and rest.**
　[相似短句] 我寧願待在家睡午覺。
　　I'd rather stay home and take a nap.

⑤ 我覺得頭暈。　**I feel dizzy.**
　[相似短句] 我頭暈想睡了。　**I get dizzy and sleepy.**

依樣畫葫蘆！套進去就能用！

[句型1] **我喜歡～勝過～**
　　I prefer... to...
[例句] 我喜歡戶外活動勝過閱讀。
　　I prefer outdoors activities to reading.

[句型2] **我沒有～**
　　I had no...
[例句] 我沒有曬傷的相關經驗。
　　I had no experience of getting sunburned.

Unit 63
過敏

社群人氣王！英文動態消息寫給你看！

 I am allergic to shrimps and crabs so please don't put them in my dishes.

我對蝦蟹過敏，所以請不要放在我點的餐裡。

👍讚 56　　💬回覆 7

 I am allergic to peanuts. They can kill me.

我對花生過敏，甚至可能死掉。

👍讚 36　　💬回覆 20

 I can't stand the air pollution in the city. It makes my nose run badly.

我無法忍受城市裡的空氣汙染。它讓我一直流鼻水。

👍讚 130　　💬回覆 3

 I am allergic to the rapid change of the temperature.

我對急遽的溫度變化過敏。

👍讚 15　　💬回覆 12

 I am itchy all over. What did I just eat?

我全身發癢，我剛剛到底吃錯什麼？

 👍讚 92　　💬回覆 3

新手超必備！一個單字嘛欸通！

allergy n. 過敏	**dust** n. 灰塵	**sneeze** v. 打噴嚏
dripping n. 水滴；滴下	**itch** v. 發癢	**sensitive** adj. 敏感的
rash n. 疹子	**running nose** phr. 流鼻水	

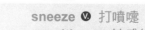

出門超實用！能聽會說一次搞定！

Ⓐ Dinah, come over here and join us! I brought some homemade cookies today. Let's enjoy some afternoon team time.

Ⓑ Hurray! Thank you, Hana. You know I always feel hungry after 4 in the afternoon.

Ⓐ 黛娜，過來這裡加入我們！我帶了些手工餅乾。讓我們來享受午後小隊時光。

Ⓑ 呀呼！感謝你，漢娜。你知道嗎？我每次中午四點後都會肚子餓。

Ⓐ How's the taste? This is my first time baking cookies. Laura and I spent the whole day together to make the cookies.

Ⓑ Hold on. My throat is itchy, and I feel itchy all over my body! May I ask what are the ingredients inside?

Ⓐ 嚐起來如何？這是我第一次烤餅乾。蘿拉和我花了一整天一起做這些餅乾。

Ⓑ 等等。我喉嚨有點癢，我覺得我全身都在癢！我可以問一下這裡面放了什麼？

Ⓐ The cookies contain baking soda, milk, flour, salt, chocolate and a really small portion of peanut butter. Oh my god, your lips are swelling.

Ⓑ Okay, I see why I became like this. I am allergic to peanut butter. Can someone send me to the hospital?

Ⓐ 餅乾包含小蘇打、牛奶、麵粉、鹽巴、巧克力和些微的花生醬。喔天阿，你的嘴唇腫起來了。

Ⓑ 恩。我知道為什麼我會變成這樣了。我對花生醬過敏。有人可以送我到醫院嗎？

Ⓐ I can take you to the hospital! I am sorry, Dinah. I didn't tell you what was inside first.

Ⓑ It's fine. Don't worry too much. By the way, the cookie tasted great! Can you bake some other flavors next time?

Ⓐ 我可以送你到醫院。我很抱歉黛娜。我並沒有先告訴你裡面有什麼。

Ⓑ 沒關係的。別太擔心。順帶一提，餅乾很好吃！下次你可以烤些別種口味的嗎？

Unit 63 過敏

酸甜苦辣 記下來！

My nose

Tuesday, November 5

I have nose allergies. I sneeze all the time if the air is dirty. It embarrasses me a lot when I sneeze constantly in public. I wanted to see a doctor to treat my allergy. One of my co-workers took flowers to our office; as a result, I sneezed and got a running nose constantly. Today I went to see an allergist. He treated me with a new drug and asked me to spray some medicine into my nose before I go to bed.

我的鼻子

11月5日星期二

我有鼻子過敏症，只要空氣有點不乾淨，我就會一直打噴嚏。在公眾場合中一直打噴嚏真的讓我很尷尬，所以我想找醫生治療過敏。有一次我同事帶花來辦公室，結果我就不停地流鼻水跟打噴嚏。今天我去看了個過敏科的醫生，他用一種新藥幫我治療，並叫我睡覺之前要噴一點藥在鼻子裡。

增廣見聞 超簡單！

Food allergy resultes in disorder of the immune system when eating certain kinds of foods. One of the most common food allergies is peanut, which is a member of the bean family. The other one is seafood. Symptoms of allergy are varied, including itching throat, eyes, or skins, and swelling of the lip, tongue or even worse, it can cause death. To avoid food allergy, the best way is to avoid the allergen food or any other things that can cause your allergy.

食物過敏，是因為食用特定食物而導致的免疫系統失調。導致過敏最普遍的食物是堅果類家族中的花生；另一種會導致過敏的則是海鮮。過敏出現的症狀有很多種，包括喉嚨、眼睛跟皮膚發癢，或是嘴唇、舌頭腫脹，更糟的甚至可能造成死亡。避免食物過敏最好的方法就是避開過敏原，或其他任何可能導致過敏的食物跟東西。

來換換口味吧！讓你的表達更豐富！

1 我有鼻子過敏症。 **I have nose allergies.**
（相似短句）我對灰塵過敏。 **I am allergic to dust.**

2 我會一直打噴嚏。 **I sneeze all the time.**
（相似短句）因為過敏，我一直打噴嚏。
I sneeze all the time because of allergy.

3 我鼻水流個不停。 **I had a running nose.**
（相似短句）我的鼻水流個不停。 **My nose is dripping snot like water.**

4 我只要碰到灰塵，皮膚就會癢。
Every time when I touch dust, my skin itches.
（相似短句）曬到陽光，我的皮膚就會發癢。
My skin gets itchy under the sun.

5 我的皮膚很敏感。 **My skin is very sensitive.**
（相似短句）我的皮膚很容易起疹子。 **I get skin rash easily.**

依樣畫葫蘆！套進去就能用！

（句型1）**結果～**
as a result,...

（例句）我沒戴口罩就打掃房間，結果我的鼻水流不停。
I cleaned up my room without wearing a gauze mask; as a result, I got a running nose.

（句型2）**每次～**
Every time....

（例句）每次我吃海鮮，皮膚就會癢。
Every time I eat seafood, my skin gets itchy.

特別 附錄

寫英文抄好用～
即時速查！

01 年 / 月 / 日

寫日記的時候，紀錄日期是最基本的。用英文紀錄日期的順序與中文不同，要先寫出月份，之後是日期，最後是年份，其中日期與年份可以直接以數字表示，而日期與年份之間必須以逗點區隔開來。另外括號中的寫法是直接以數字做紀錄，如果你不是寫正式的文章，用數字表示就可以了！以下是年月日的寫法。

基本句型

2015年1月1日　　　　　　_____ 1, 2015

 Tips　只要在劃線處套上替換字，輕鬆表達不同意思！

 ## 隨查即用！

2015年1月1日	January 1, 2015 (01 / 01 / 2015)
2015年2月1日	February 1, 2015 (02 / 01 / 2015)
2015年3月1日	March 1, 2015 (03 / 01 / 2015)
2015年4月1日	April 1, 2015 (04 / 01 / 2015)
2015年5月1日	May 1, 2015 (05 / 01 / 2015)
2015年6月1日	June 1, 2015 (06 / 01 / 2015)
2015年7月1日	July 1, 2015 (07 / 01 / 2015)
2015年8月1日	August 1, 2015 (08 / 01 / 2015)
2015年9月1日	September 1, 2015 (09 / 01 / 2015)
2015年10月1日	October 1, 2015 (10 / 01 / 2015)
2015年11月1日	November 1, 2015 (11 / 01 / 2015)
2015年12月1日	December 1, 2015 (12 / 01 / 2015)

02 星期

寫日記的時候常會提到時間，提醒自己事情發生的日子，最常用的就是「今天是星期……」、「我星期……去看電影」，這是一定要會的喔！

基本句型

今天是_____　⟶ Today is _____.
明天是_____　⟶ Tomorrow is _____.
昨天是_____　⟶ Yesterday is _____.

Tips 只要在劃線處套上替換字，輕鬆表達不同意思！

隨查即用！

今天是星期一。	⟶ Today is Monday (Mon.).
今天是星期二。	⟶ Today is Tuesday (Tues.).
今天是星期三。	⟶ Today is Wednesday (Wed.).
今天是星期四。	⟶ Today is Thursday (Thur.).
今天是星期五。	⟶ Today is Friday (Fri.).
今天是星期六。	⟶ Today is Saturday (Sat.).
今天是星期日。	⟶ Today is Sunday (Sun.).
明天是星期一。	⟶ Tomorrow is Monday (Mon.).
明天是星期二。	⟶ Tomorrow is Tuesday (Tues.).
明天是星期三。	⟶ Tomorrow is Wednesday (Wed.).
明天是星期四。	⟶ Tomorrow is Thursday (Thur.).
明天是星期五。	⟶ Tomorrow is Friday (Fri.).
明天是星期六。	⟶ Tomorrow is Saturday (Sat.).
明天是星期日。	⟶ Tomorrow is Sunday (Sun.).
昨天是星期一。	⟶ Yesterday is Monday (Mon.).
昨天是星期二。	⟶ Yesterday is Tuesday (Tues.).
昨天是星期三。	⟶ Yesterday is Wednesday (Wed.).
昨天是星期四。	⟶ Yesterday is Thursday (Thur.).
昨天是星期五。	⟶ Yesterday is Friday (Fri.).
昨天是星期六。	⟶ Yesterday is Saturday (Sat.).
昨天是星期日。	⟶ Yesterday is Sunday (Sun.).

03 日子

　　雖然在記錄日期的時，可以直接寫出數字，但是如果要唸出來的話，就必須以序數讀出，以下為一到三十一的序數寫法：

1st	2nd	3rd	4th	5th	6th	7th
8th	9th	10th	11th	12th	13th	14th
15th	16th	17th	18th	19th	20th	21st
22nd	23rd	24th	25th	26th	27th	28th
29th	30th	31st				

04 驚嘆詞、狀聲詞

　　寫日記常常會寫到驚嘆詞……用最道地的發語詞能讓日記內容更豐富哦！

Aha!	啊！有了！〔找到東西、想到事情〕	Ahh!	阿！〔被嚇到、撞到、驚呼〕
blah	等等……，之類的……〔簡略事情〕	brrr...	打顫聲〔形容一個人很冷會發出的喘息聲〕
drat	嘖！彈舌聲〔不耐煩、不悅〕	duh	喔，是喔〔不屑、問題太簡單不想回應〕
eek!	額！〔大大地驚訝、噁心〕	gee!	天阿！〔開心的驚呼〕
gosh	喔！〔輕柔的驚呼〕	ha-ha	哈哈！〔笑聲〕
hey	嘿！欸！〔叫人、提醒〕	hmm	嗯……〔思考、疑惑〕
huh?	蛤？〔疑惑、質疑〕	humph	哼〔不同意、討厭〕
oops	哎唷～〔撞到、驚嘆〕	oh dear	我的老天阿！〔感嘆、大大地驚呼〕
ouch	噢！〔感到痛、表不悅〕	phew	呼～呼氣聲〔放鬆、紓解〕
wahoo	哇呼～～〔大開心、歡呼〕	well	這個嘛……〔疑惑、思考〕
shh	噓！〔使……安靜、閉嘴〕	yuck	額～～〔噁心、討厭〕

05 天氣

天氣是千變萬化的，以下列出各式各樣描述天氣的句子，讓你的日記中不再只有晴天、雨天、陰天的變化了！

基本句型

今天 ＿＿＿＿＿＿＿。 ➲ It's ＿＿＿＿＿ today.

Tips 只要在劃線處套上替換字，輕鬆表達不同意思！

隨查即用！

今天下雨。	➲ It's rainy today.
今天是晴天。	➲ It's sunny today.
今天有雲。	➲ It's cloudy today.
今天下雪。	➲ It's snowy today.
今天有風。	➲ It's windy today.
今天陽光普照。	➲ It's bright today.
今天很熱。	➲ It's hot today.
今天很涼爽。	➲ It's cool today.
今天很寒冷。	➲ It's cold today.
今天很溫暖。	➲ It's warm today.
今天很潮濕。	➲ It's humid today.
今天很乾燥。	➲ It's dry today.
今天好天氣。	➲ It's fine today.
今天天氣很糟。	➲ It's nasty today.
今天天氣舒適。	➲ It's comfortable today.

06 情緒

寫個人日記常常將自己的內心情緒與感覺紀錄下來，所以個人情緒的表達方式是一個要會的句型，以下就是各種情緒的表達方式：

基本句型

我很 ＿＿＿＿＿＿。　➲ I was ＿＿＿＿＿＿.

隨查即用！

我很沮喪。	➲ I was down.
我很興奮。	➲ I was excited.
我很高興。	➲ I was happy.
我很欣喜。	➲ I was cheerful.
我很愉快。	➲ I was delightful.
我很無聊。	➲ I was bored.
我很傷心。	➲ I was sad.
我很不高興。	➲ I was unhappy.
我很擔心。	➲ I was worried.
我很消沉。	➲ I was depressed.
我很生氣。	➲ I was angry.
我被嚇壞了。	➲ I was frightened.
我很害怕。	➲ I was scared.

07 個性

在敘述家人、朋友、同事的時候，一定會提到他們的個人特質，因此也需要學會怎麼形容個性的短句。其中要注意的是，個性是一種本質的形容，所以通常是以現在式表示。

基本句型

他是個 _____ 的人。 ➲ He is a / an ____ person.

Tips 只要在劃線處套上替換字，輕鬆表達不同意思！

隨查即用！

他是個隨和的人。	➲ He is an easygoing person.
他是個外放的人。	➲ He is an extroverted person.
他是個內斂的人。	➲ He is an introverted person.
他是個謹慎的人。	➲ He is a cautious person.
他是個很好的人。	➲ He is a kind person.
他是個溫柔的人。	➲ He is a gentle person.
他是個聰明的人。	➲ He is a smart person.
他是個搞笑的人。	➲ He is a funny person.
他是個膽小的人。	➲ He is a timid person.
他是個無理的人。	➲ He is a rude person.
他是個魯莽的人。	➲ He is a reckless person.
他是個愛批判的人。	➲ He is a critical person.
他是個貼心的人。	➲ He is a sweet person.
他是個天真的人。	➲ He is a naive person.
他是個有才華的人。	➲ He is a talented person.
他是個獨立的人。	➲ He is an independent person.
他是個懶惰的人。	➲ He is a lazy person.
他是個樂觀的人。	➲ He is an optimistic person.
他是個幼稚的人。	➲ He is a childish person.
他是個陰險的人。	➲ He is a tricky person.
他是個害羞的人。	➲ He is a shy person.

08 專長

不管是介紹自己或認識別人時，都不免會提到各自的專長、熟悉的領域，想要稱讚或描述某個人的時候，只要套用這個句型就可以囉！

基本句型

他很擅長 _____ 。 ➲ He is good at _____ .

 只要在劃線處套上替換字，輕鬆表達不同意思！

隨查即用！

他很擅長足球。	➲ He is good at soccer.
他很擅長籃球。	➲ He is good at basketball.
他很擅長排球。	➲ He is good at volleyball.
他很擅長網球。	➲ He is good at tennis.
他很擅長羽毛球。	➲ He is good at badminton.
他很擅長高爾夫球。	➲ He is good at golf.
他很擅長游泳。	➲ He is good at swimming.
他很擅長交際。	➲ He is good at socializing.
他很會討價還價。	➲ He is good at bargaining.
他很擅長攝影。	➲ He is good at photography.
他很擅長繪畫。	➲ He is good at painting.
他很擅長烹飪。	➲ He is good at cooking.
他很擅長園藝。	➲ He is good at gardening.
他很擅長唱歌。	➲ He is good at singing.
他很擅長跳舞。	➲ He is good at dancing.
他很擅長數學。	➲ He is good at Math.
他很擅長英文。	➲ He is good at English.
他很擅長國文。	➲ He is good at Chinese.
他很擅長科學。	➲ He is good at Science.
他很擅長地理。	➲ He is good at Geography.
他很擅長歷史。	➲ He is good at History.

09 興趣

每個人的興趣都不盡相同，因此所用的單字會更多樣，通常是一種行為、動作，快點學會基本句型，就能輕鬆講你最喜歡做的事。

基本句型

他很喜歡 _____。 ➲ He loves to _____.

隨查即用！

他喜歡玩線上遊戲。	➲ He loves to play on-line games.
他喜歡網路聊天。	➲ He loves to chat on the Internet.
他喜歡踢足球。	➲ He loves to play soccer.
他喜歡晨泳。	➲ He loves to swim in the morning.
他喜歡裝飾房間。	➲ He loves to decorate his room.
他喜歡塗鴉。	➲ He loves to do some graffiti.
他喜歡學習語言。	➲ He loves to learn different languages.
他喜歡閱讀。	➲ He loves to read.
他喜歡唱歌。	➲ He loves to sing.
他喜歡探索世界。	➲ He loves to explore the world.
他喜歡旅行。	➲ He loves to travel.
他喜歡逛街。	➲ He loves to go shopping.
他喜歡跟朋友去玩。	➲ He loves to hang out with his friends.
他喜歡看電影。	➲ He loves to see movies.
他喜歡聽音樂。	➲ He loves to listen to music.

10 場所

要使日記裡的文意更加完整，必須加上動作發生的地點，以下列舉了數個現代生活中的常見場所，多加利用便能敘述更完整的語意。

基本句型

我在 _____看到她。 ➲ I saw her in the _____.

隨查即用！

我在餐廳看到她。	➲ I saw her in the restaurant.
我在運動場看到她。	➲ I saw her in the stadium.
我在理髮店看到她。	➲ I saw her in the barbershop.
我在美容沙龍看到她。	➲ I saw her in the beauty salon.
我在健身中心看到她。	➲ I saw her in the fitness center.
我在飯店大廳看到她。	➲ I saw her in the hotel lobby.
我在醫院看到她	➲ I saw her in the hospital.
我在停車場看到她。	➲ I saw her in the parking space.
我在機場看到她。	➲ I saw her in the airport.
我在火車站看到她。	➲ I saw her in the train station.
我在劇院裡看到她。	➲ I saw her in the theater.
我在公園看到她。	➲ I saw her in the park.
我在圖書館看到她。	➲ I saw her in the library.
我在郵局看到她。	➲ I saw her in the post office.
我在銀行看到她。	➲ I saw her in the bank.
我在診所看到她。	➲ I saw her in the clinic.
我在超級市場看到她。	➲ I saw her in the supermarket.
我在百貨公司看到她。	➲ I saw her in the department store.
我在捷運站看到她。	➲ I saw her in the MRT station.

11 節慶

特殊節慶總是會發生有趣的事情，所以我們一定要知道節日的寫法，這樣紀錄生活的時間點就能很明確的表現出來。

基本句型

今天是 ＿＿＿＿＿＿。　⟳ It's ＿＿＿＿＿＿＿.

隨查即用！

今天是除夕。	⟳ It's Chinese New Year's Day.
今天是元宵節。	⟳ It's Lantern Festival.
今天是情人節。	⟳ It's Valentine's Day.
今天是愚人節。	⟳ It's April Fool's Day.
今天是兒童節。	⟳ It's Children's Day.
今天是清明節。	⟳ It's Tomb-sweeping Day.
今天是勞動節。	⟳ It's Labor Day.
今天是母親節。	⟳ It's Mother's Day.
今天是父親節。	⟳ It's Father's Day.
今天是七夕。	⟳ It's Chinese Valentine's Day.
今天是中秋節。	⟳ It's Moon Festival.
今天是教師節。	⟳ It's Teacher's Day.
今天是雙十節。	⟳ It's Double Tenth Day.
今天是萬聖節。	⟳ It's Halloween.
今天是聖誕節。	⟳ It's Christmas.
今天是平安夜。	⟳ It's Christmas Eve.

加碼贈送

文法充電站！
邊做題目邊學，印象最深刻

應該很多人想到英文文法就皺眉頭，本書特別精選出大家使用時容易出錯，卻又一定要會的文法，透過文法觀念小測驗，邊做題目邊驗證的方式，讓學習盲點無所遁形。

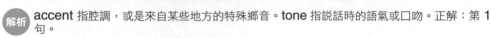

【文法觀念小測驗！】
名詞篇

請選出正確的句子，答完記得對照解析，驗證是否正確！

01 那女人的口音告訴我們她是北方人。

☐ The woman's **accent** tells us that she is from the North.

☐ The woman's **tone** tells us that she is from the North.

解析 accent 指腔調，或是來自某些地方的特殊鄉音。tone 指說話時的語氣或口吻。正解：第 1 句。

02 那些背包客正在找過夜的住處。

☐ Those backpackers are looking for overnight **accommodations**.

☐ Those backpackers are looking for overnight **housing**.

解析 accommodation 指暫時棲身的地方。housing 則是住宅的統稱。正解：第 1 句。

03 你對車禍的描述與目擊者的說法差異很大。

☐ Your **account** of the car accident is very different from the witness's.

☐ Your **explanation** of the car accident is very different from the witness's.

解析 account 指以口頭或書面的方式「描述」人物或事件。explanation 指「解釋」事件發生背後的原因。正解：第 1 句。

04 我的頭痛快把我折磨死了。

☐ The **pain** in the head is killing me.

☐ The **ache** in the head is killing me.

解析 ache 指持續性的、隱約的疼痛。pain 指的則是突然間身體或精神上感到的極大痛苦。正解：第 1 句。

05 因為我下週休假，我的代理人將代表我出席會議。

☐ Since I'll be on leave next week, my **agent** will attend the meeting on behalf of me.

☐ Since I'll be on leave next week, my **deputy** will attend the meeting on behalf of me.

解析 agent 指代表客戶或是某一家公司處理業務或買賣的代理商。deputy 指的是在公司中暫代主管職務的代理人。正解：第 2 句。

【文法觀念小測驗！】
代名詞篇

請選出正確的句子，答完記得對照解析，驗證是否正確！

01 我們一定要全面地檢討這件事。

☐ We must review this incident in **its** entirety.
☐ We must review this incident in **it's** entirety.

解析 it's 為代名詞 it is 的縮寫式，its 為代名詞所有格。正解：第 1 句。

02 天助自助者。

☐ God helps **those** who help themselves.
☐ God helps **who** help themselves.

解析 those 為表示 those people 的指定代名詞，為句中的先行詞；who 為引導名詞子句的關係代名詞。 正解：第 1 句。

03 把這兒當自己家。

☐ Make **you** at home.
☐ Make **yourself** at home.

解析 祈使句省略主詞 you，句中若接受動作的對象為 you，則需使用反身代名詞。正解：第 2 句。

04 我會帶我朋友到那兒去，你也可以帶你的去。

☐ I'll bring my friends there and you can also bring **your friends**.
☐ I'll bring my friends there and you can also bring **yours**.

解析 句子前文出現過的名詞，後文再次出現時應用所有代名詞取代，以避免重復。正解：第 2 句。

05 我爸媽一直以來都很支持我。我愛他們兩位。

☐ My parents have been very supportive to me. I love them **both**.
☐ My parents have been very supportive to me. I love them **all**.

解析 指定代名詞 both 用於表示「兩者」的情況下，而 all 則用於「兩者以上」的情況。正解：第 1 句。

動詞篇

請選出正確的句子，答完記得對照解析，驗證是否正確！

01 你要在巴黎待多久？

☐ How long are you going to **stay** in Paris?
☐ How long are you going to **live** in Paris?

解析 stay 表示到某地「暫住」；live 則表示「居住」在某地過生活。正解：第 1 句。

02 行動勝於言辭。

☐ Actions **speak** louder than words.
☐ Actions **say** louder than words.

解析 speak 表示「說話、發表言論」，亦可作「傳達」解；say 則用來表示「說；講述」。正解：第 1 句。

03 不用送我了。

☐ Don't **disturb** to see me out.
☐ Don't **bother** to see me out.

解析 disturb 表示用事情「妨礙」某人，有搞亂之含意；bother 表示用事情「煩擾」某人，有造成他人麻煩之含意。正解：第 2 句。

04 我的家鄉自我離開後改變了許多。

☐ My hometown has **reformed** a lot since I left.
☐ My hometown has **changed** a lot since I left.

解析 reform 表「改革」，指將不好的地方加以改善革新；change 指「改變」，指將原來的樣子改變為其他樣子。正解：第 2 句。

05 我們在評估你的工作表現後才會決定是否要給你加薪。

☐ We'll decide whether to give you a raise after **estimating** your work performance.
☐ We'll decide whether to give you a raise after **evaluating** your work performance.

解析 estimate 表數字方面的「估計、估算」；evaluate 表「為…估價」或「為…評價」。正解：第 2 句。

【文法觀念小測驗！】
動詞時態變化篇

請選出正確的句子，
答完記得對照解析，驗證是否正確！

01 如果明天下雨的話，戶外典禮將會延後舉行。

☐ The outdoor ceremony will be put off if it **rains** tomorrow.
☐ The outdoor ceremony will be put off if it **will rain** tomorrow.

解析 一般性的假設語氣時，雖然假設狀況是發生在未來，條件子句的動詞仍須以現在式取代未來式。正解：第 1 句。

02 在他終於回到家鄉時，他的女友早就已經嫁給別人了。

☐ His girlfriend **has already married** someone else when he finally returned hometown.
☐ His girlfriend **had already married** someone else when he finally returned hometown.

解析 在過去某時間之前發生且結束的動作，用過去完成式。正解：第 2 句。

03 如果當時我有足夠的錢的話，我就會買那輛車了。

☐ I would have bought the car if I **had had** enough money at that time.
☐ I would have bought the car if I **have had** enough money at that time.

解析 與現在事實相反的假設，用過去簡單式；與過去事實相反的假設，用過去完成式。正解：第 1 句。

04 明天此時我們就會是在峇里島度假了。

☐ We **will be enjoying** our vacation in Bali at this time tomorrow.
☐ We **will enjoy** our vacation in Bali at this time tomorrow.

解析 表示未來某時間將正發生或進行的動作時，要用未來進行式。正解：第 1 句。

05 過去我從來沒遇過像他這麼好心的人。

☐ I never **met** such a kind person like him before.
☐ I **have** never **met** such a kind person like him before.

解析 過去簡單式用在描述發生在過去的事實。現在完成式用來說明從過去到現在的經驗。正解：第 2 句。

形容詞篇

請選出正確的句子，答完記得對照解析，驗證是否正確！

01 我的祖母是個體型嬌小卻果敢的女性。

☐ My grandmother is a **small** but resolute woman.

☐ My grandmother is a **little** but resolute woman.

解析 small 指尺寸或外型小的。little 指年紀或份量小的。正解：第 1 句。

02 回教女人不能在公共場合露出她們的臉。

☐ Muslim women cannot have their faces **uncovered** in public.

☐ Muslim women cannot have their faces **open** in public.

解析 open 表示「開啟的」。uncovered 指的是「沒有遮住的」。正解：第 1 句。

03 在過去，同性戀被認為是不正常的。

☐ Homosexuality was considered **subnormal** in the past.

☐ Homosexuality was considered **abnormal** in the past.

解析 abnormal 指「不正常的」或「反常的」。subnormal 則為「低於正常值以下的」如智能不足 subnormal intelligence。正解：第 2 句。

04 你可以告訴我昨天為何在會議上缺席嗎？

☐ Can you tell me why you were **missing** from the meeting yesterday?

☐ Can you tell me why you were **absent** from the meeting yesterday?

解析 absent 表示「缺席的，沒有出現的」，missing 指的是「不見了的」或「失蹤的」。正解：第 2 句。

05 我真的很討厭那個人。連聽到他的名字都讓我作噁。

☐ I really hate that person. Even hearing his name makes me **sick**.

☐ I really hate that person. Even hearing his name makes me **ill**.

解析 sick 除表示「生病的」之外，尚有「感到噁心的」之意。ill 則單純表示「生病的」。正解：第 1 句。

【文法觀念小測驗！】
副詞篇

請選出正確的句子，答完記得對照解析，驗證是否正確！

01 男孩從單槓上跌了下來，並且傷得很重。

☐ The boy fell off the monkey bar and was **bad** injured.

☐ The boy fell off the monkey bar and was **badly** injured.

解析 bad 作副詞解時，通常放在形容詞或句子後面修飾之；badly 放在形容詞前後皆可。正解：第 2 句。

02 大聲說出來。不要在我們面前咬耳朵。

☐ Talk **aloud**. Don't whisper before us.

☐ Talk **loudly**. Don't whisper before us.

解析 aloud 表示「發出聲音地」；loudly 則表示「大聲地，吵鬧地」。正解：第 1 句。

03 我們沒有足夠時間慢慢吃頓飯。咱們吃快點吧！

☐ We don't have enough time for a slow meal. Let's eat **fast**.

☐ We don't have enough time for a slow meal. Let's eat **fastly**.

解析 fast 為形容詞與副詞同形。正解：第 1 句。

04 我們的客服人員不斷地接到關於這項產品的客訴。

☐ Our customer service has **constantly** received complaints about the product.

☐ Our customer service has **continually** received complaints about the product.

解析 constantly 表「不斷地」做同一動作或發生同一件事；continually 則為「不停地」持續同一動作。正解：第 1 句。

05 瑪莉和史蒂芬分手之後就展開了另一段戀情。

☐ Mary broke up with Steven, and started another relationship **later**.

☐ Mary broke up with Steven, and started another relationship **afterward**.

解析 later 表時間上的「稍晚、之後」；afterward 則用於一件事發生在另一件事「之後」。正解：第 2 句。

介系詞篇

請選出正確的句子，答完記得對照解析，驗證是否正確！

01 你這次又想幹什麼好事？

□ What are you up **to** this time?

□ What are you up **for** this time?

解析 be up for 表示「對某事或物熱烈期待或渴望」，而 be up to 則是指「打算做某事」之意。正解：第 1 句。

02 那年輕女孩嫁給這老人完全是因為貪圖他的錢。

□ The young girl married the old man simply because she was out **for** his property.

□ The young girl married the old man simply because she was out **of** his property.

解析 be out of 指某物「用完了」。be out for 指對某物「有所企圖」。正解：第 1 句。

03 你能相信賴瑞在一年之內就把他父親的遺產揮霍光了嗎？

□ Can you believe that Larry ate **up** his father's inheritance within a year?

□ Can you believe that Larry ate **into** his father's inheritance within a year?

解析 eat into 表示「用盡或耗費（資源、預算等）」。eat up 則用來表示「吃完某樣東西」。正解：第 2 句。

04 主持人將會致謝詞作為派對的結束。

□ The host will end **up** the party with a thank-you speech.

□ The host will end the party **with** a thank-you speech.

解析 end with 是指「以某事做為結尾」。end up 則是指「在意料之外演變成某種情況」。正解：第 2 句。

05 我爸媽從不會當著其他人的面責備我。

□ My parents never come down **with** me in the presence of others.

□ My parents never come down **on** me in the presence of others.

解析 come down on 是「責備、處罰」某人的意思。而 come down with + 病名，則是指「染上（某病）」。正解：第 2 句。

【文法觀念小測驗！】
連接詞篇

請選出正確的句子，答完記得對照解析，驗證是否正確！

01 彼得和約翰都沒有獲邀參加艾美的婚禮。

☐ **Neither** Peter **nor** John was invited to Amy's wedding.

☐ **Both** Peter **and** John weren't invited to Amy's wedding.

解析 both ... and ... 表示「A 與 B 兩者都…」，用在肯定句；neither ... nor ... 則表示「A 與 B 兩者都不…」，用在否定句。正解：第 1 句。

02 我也許身體有殘疾，但我並不是個廢人。

☐ I may be handicapped, **but** I am not a good-for-nothing.

☐ I may be handicapped, **and** I am not a good-for-nothing.

解析 but 連接語意相反的詞類或句子。and 連接語意相似的詞類或句子。正解：第 1 句。

03 我不會道歉，因為我沒有做錯事。

☐ I won't apologize **because** I didn't do anything wrong.

☐ I won't apologize **so** I didn't do anything wrong.

解析 because 引導表示原因的子句。so 引導表示結果的子句。正解：第 1 句。

04 雖然他中了樂透，卻仍一如往常的努力工作。

☐ **Although** he won the lottery, he still works hard as usual.

☐ **Although** he won the lottery, **but** he still works hard as usual.

解析 although 引導表示「雖然…」之子句，but 引導表示「但是…」之子句。兩個連接詞不會同時出現在一個句子中。正解：第 1 句。

05 在她道歉之前，我是不會跟她說話的。

☐ I won't speak to her **until** she apologizes.

☐ I won't speak to her **when** she apologizes.

解析 when 表示「當…之時」，即當 A 發生時，B 也同時發生。而 until 則表示「直到…」，即 A 的狀態會持續到 B 發生為止。正解：第 1 句。

【文法觀念小測驗！】

冠詞篇

請選出正確的句子，答完記得對照解析，驗證是否正確！

01 我們現在正飛在太平洋上方。

☐ We are now flying over **the Pacific Ocean**.

☐ We are now flying over **Pacific Ocean**.

解析 指地名、山川或海洋時，必須使用定冠詞 the。正解：第 1 句。

02 他今天忙得無法吃午餐。

☐ He was too busy to have **a dinner** today.

☐ He was too busy to have **dinner** today.

解析 除非是描述這是怎麼樣的一頓晚餐，如 a candlelit dinner（燭光晚餐）否則晚餐或早、午餐之前皆不需冠詞。正解：第 2 句。

03 預防勝於治療。

☐ **Prevention** is better than **cure**.

☐ **The prevention** is better than **the cure**.

解析 prevention 為「表示各種預防方式」之統稱，並沒有指定是哪一種預防措施，因此不需定冠詞。後面 cure 也是如此。正解：第 1 句。

04 機會是不等人的。

☐ **The opportunities** wait for no men.

☐ **Opportunities** wait for no men.

解析 此句泛指所有的機會，並沒有特別指定哪些或哪個機會，故不需用定冠詞。正解：第 2 句。

05 那個你在派對上介紹給我認識的傢伙一直約我出去。

☐ **The** guy you introduced to me at the party kept asking me out.

☐ **A** guy you introduced to me at the party kept asking me out.

解析 指稱特定對象時，必須使用定冠詞。本句省略的關係代名詞 who 引導形容詞子句，即可知是特定的人。正解：第 1 句。

【文法觀念小測驗！】
贅詞篇

請選出正確的句子，答完記得對照解析，驗證是否正確！

01 如果你餓的話，我可以幫你弄一份煙燻鮭魚三明治。

☐ I can make you a smoked **salmon fish** sandwich if you're hungry.

☐ I can make you a smoked **salmon** sandwich if you're hungry.

解析 salmon 指鮭魚，本身就是魚，後面的 fish（魚）是一個多餘的名詞。正解：第 2 句。

02 要不要在咖啡裡加點冰塊？

☐ Do you want some **ice cubes** in your coffee?

☐ Do you want some **frozen ice cubes** in your coffee?

解析 ice cube 指冰塊，本來就已經是冰凍的狀態了，前面的 frozen（冰凍的）即為多餘的形容詞。正解：第 1 句。

03 生日那天，我從家人和朋友那兒得到了許多禮物。

☐ I received many **free presents** from my family and friends on my birthday.

☐ I received many **presents** from my family and friends on my birthday.

解析 present 指禮物，禮物為餽贈之物，本就是不用花錢買的東西，因此 free 便是一個多餘的形容詞。正解：第 2 句。

04 在我們去逛街之前，先讓我在提款機領點錢。

☐ Let me withdraw some money from an **ATM machine** before we go shopping.

☐ Let me withdraw some money from an **ATM** before we go shopping.

解析 ATM 即 automatic teller machine 的縮寫，M 即代表 machine，故 ATM 後不需再加上 machine 這個字。正解：第 2 句。

05 我也許會跳槽到那間公司去。

☐ I **may possibly** job-hop to that company.

☐ I **may** job-hop to that company.

解析 may 表可能的，因此後面不需要再接同樣表示有可能地的 possibly。正解：第 2 句。

語言力 *E028*

超好聊英文
一本讓你從聊天到FB、IG、LINE隨時都能po出超人氣動態的63個潮話題

10大生活主題分類 X 63個熱門潮話題，讓你超好聊、PO文不無聊！

作　　者	Joseph
顧　　問	曾文旭
統　　籌	陳逸祺
編輯總監	耿文國
主　　編	陳蕙芳
執行編輯	翁芯俐
美術編輯	莊淑婷
封面設計	吳若瑄
音檔校對	許之芸
法律顧問	北辰著作權事務所

印　　製	世和印製企業有限公司
初　　版	2020年08月
	（本書改自《美分美秒，聽說讀寫Everyday（附贈｜「中英對話」強效學習MP3》一書）
出　　版	凱信企業集團 - 開企有限公司
電　　話	（02）2773-6566
傳　　真	（02）2778-1033
地　　址	106 台北市大安區忠孝東路四段218之4號12樓
信　　箱	kaihsinbooks@gmail.com

定　　價	新台幣320元／港幣107元
產品內容	1 書

總 經 銷	采舍國際有限公司
地　　址	235 新北市中和區中山路二段366巷10號3樓
電　　話	（02）8245-8786
傳　　真	（02）8245-8718

國家圖書館出版品預行編目資料

超好聊英文：一本讓你從聊天到 FB、IG、LINE
隨時都能 po 出超人氣動態的 63 個朝話題
/ Joseph著. -- 初版. -- 臺北市：開企, 2020.08
　面；　公分
ISBN 978-986-98556-6-2(平裝附光碟片)

1.英語 2.讀本

805.18　　　　　　　　　　　109004868

開企，

是一個開頭，它可以是一句美好的引言、
未完待續的逗點、享受美好後滿足的句點，
新鮮的體驗、大膽的冒險、嶄新的方向，
是一趟有你共同參與的奇妙旅程。

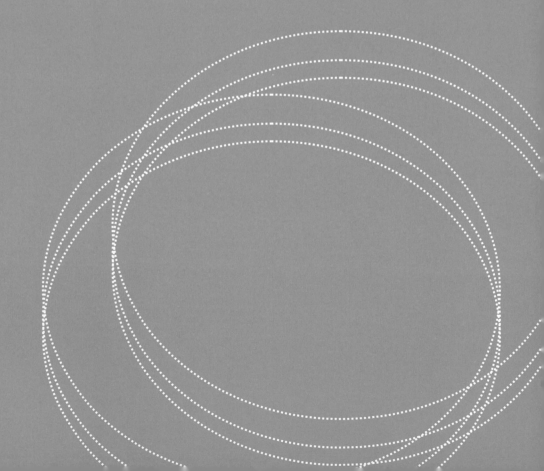